WHAT ONCE WAS PROMISED

LOUIS TRUBIANO

What Once Was Promised

Copyright © 2024 by Louis Trubiano. All rights reserved.

No part of this book may be used or reproduced in any manner whatsoever without written permission, except in the case of brief quotations embodied in critical articles and reviews. For more information, e-mail all inquiries to info@mindstirmedia.com.

Published by MindStir Media, LLC
45 Lafayette Rd | Suite 181| North Hampton, NH 03862 | USA
1.800.767.0531 | www.mindstirmedia.com

Printed in the United States of America.
ISBN-13: 978-1-963844-04-7

For Phyllis, Laura, Lisa and Sara

"... All that they say to you, all that they have promised to you it was a lie, it was an illusion, it was a cheat, it was a fraud, it was a crime. They promised you liberty. Where is the liberty? They promised you prosperity. Where is the prosperity? They have promised you elevation. Where is the elevation?

Last Statement of Bartolomeo Vanzetti, 1929

PART 1

7 PM
NOVEMBER 7, 1951
SWAMPSCOTT, MASSACHUSETTS

IT HAD BEEN nearly forty years since Domenic Bassini last held a gun of any type. That last one had been an old single-shot rifle his father would sometimes let him carry when they would go up into the mountains surrounding the village of Torre de'Passeri in his native Italy to hunt rabbits and deer. They would always take along one of their huge mastiffs to ward off the brown bears that lived in the mountains, as the old rifle would have been of little use if one decided to set upon them.

He could still feel the comforting weight of that rifle slung over his shoulder and the rocky terrain beneath his shoes with soles so thin he could feel each small pebble. He could smell the spindly pine trees that struggled up through the hard ground reaching toward the sky that in his memory was always blue. He could still taste the air so fresh it would fill his lungs with life, making it so no matter how long they walked he would never tire. Strange that he should recall all this now, so many years later, in this dank and musty basement.

Somehow that bulky old rifle, with its rusty barrel and worn wood stock, seemed far less menacing than the small .32 caliber Beretta pistol he now held in his hand. This weapon was shiny, black and sleek. To him, it seemed it could serve no other purpose than to deliver death quickly and coldly. It would be useless in the fresh air of the mountains. It was meant to rest under the heavy coats of soulless men until called upon to do its work in dark, shadowy places away from God's sunlight. Places like this.

Yet the gun feels strangely comfortable and almost weightless in his outstretched hand, leading him to think that it must possess some dark *seductive power. Or is it because his own heart has grown black and cold? How else to explain his lack of anxiety and the calmness he feels as he aims it at the head of Colin O'Riley.*

O'Riley is talking. He is animated as he speaks, his arms flailing in all directions as though trying to regain his balance while falling. His panicked eyes keep darting back and forth between the old man's face and the gun in his hand. The tone of his voice fluctuates as sharp staccato-like shrills of angry outrage interrupt the low monophonic cadence of his pleading.

But all that Domenic can hear is noise echoing off the stone walls of the basement, the sound muffled by the heavy veil of the past draped over him. The memories are suddenly so vivid they seem much more real to him than this murky present. He clings to the emotions they have resurrected as long as he can so he can remember what brought him here to this deep, dreary pit so close to hell. Then he instinctively reaches for the small wooden cross around his neck and prays. He first asks God for forgiveness. And then for the strength to shoot this bastard.

MAY 1914

SIXTEEN-YEAR-OLD DOMENIC BASSINI lies wide awake long before slivers of early morning light knife through the slits of the wood shutters covering the small, glassless window in his room to announce the arrival of the most important day of his life. Today he would leave for America. For the most part, the excitement of the young man setting out on a great adventure overshadows the sadness and fear of the small boy leaving home. But even though all the emotions that had kept him awake most the night remained churning in his stomach, he would not allow them to show.

This wasn't due just to the stoic nature he inherited from his father, who would often remind him that "calm is the virtue of the strong." It was also the strength he drew from knowing his life was unfolding exactly as it should according to L'ordine della Famiglia. La Famiglia formed a foundation for life in Domenic's small village of Torre de'Passeri that was as solid as the mountains surrounding it. It provided comfort, security, and predictability while life was being scratched out of a harsh land.

La Famiglia gave Domenic a clearly defined role to play in his family, the church, the village. He knew what was expected of him and what to expect from others. Being the eldest son brought Domenic special privileges as well as distinct responsibilities. His family needed him to go to America. So he would do so dutifully, eagerly, and without question, bolstered by both his determination and faith, sure that he would proudly return one day to be feted as a hero.

He reached beneath his bed and lifted up a small leather pouch. It contained a small broach his mother had given him the night before, which was little more than an oval of polished white Arabescato Corchia marble mounted in silver. Domenic had never seen it before.

"Your father gave this to me and told me it was for the only woman he could ever love. I was so surprised because your father spoke so little that I wasn't even sure how he felt about me." She smiled and embraced her oldest son. "When you find that woman, I want you to give it to her. You're so much like him. If you can't find the words, maybe this will help you show the lucky girl how you feel."

It was a sparkling May morning, and the familiar Abruzzo sun peaking over the mountaintops surrounding the village caressed the back of his neck like an old friend offering an affectionate goodbye as he made his way to the back house. The sweet smell from the small kitchen told him that his mother already had breakfast started, and he could make out several people plodding up the dusty road. Friends and relatives on their way to wish him well as was the tradition in the village, and he knew breakfast for all would be followed by a visit to the cemetery to ask for the blessing of his ancestors before heading to the train.

Later, as he awaited the train at the small wooden canopy that marked the Torre de'Passeri train stop, his father approached him. Domenic's father was a man of few words and not given to shows of emotion. But he embraced Domenic and spoke to him directly for the first time that day. With a crack in his voice, he whispered, "*Altre cose possono cambiare, ma noi inizio e fine con la famiglia.*" *Other things may change us, but we start and end with the family.*

He then pressed something into Domenic's hand. It was a tiny wooden cross that Domenic's grandfather, a talented woodcarver, had made out of a piece of Swiss pine from Val Gardenia in northern Italy. As small as it was, he had managed to carve the name "Bassini" into the back of the cross, meticulously filling in the tiny letters with white paint. His great aunt, a nun, had the cross blessed by the Cardinal in L'Aquila. A leather necklace went through a small hole in the top of the cross. This was, perhaps, the only family heirloom possessed by the Bassinis, and Domenic had never seen his father without it around his neck. Without saying another word, his father turned and walked away.

Domenic set out for Rome on the new Ferrovie dello Stato rail line. Despite living only some 170 kilometers from Rome, Domenic had never been to the Eternal City before. He arrived at the Central Station of Roman Railways and was in awe of its immensity. The new train station in Torre was little more than a roof on posts set up beside the train tracks. He spent the next twelve hours tucked into a corner of the station waiting for the train to Napoli. He carefully clutched his suitcase while keeping an eye out for the evil ones his mother warned him about who lurked in cities and preyed on the innocent. The stories he had so often heard about the evil La Mano Nera, *the Black Hand*, added to his anxiety.

The night in Rome passed slowly, and Domenic never really slept. The loneliness overcame any remaining sense of adventure, and he was again just a boy longing for the family whose hopes he carried to America. The grandiose station felt like a giant mausoleum to him, and each echo of footsteps during the night brought a renewed shudder of apprehension and a tighter grip on his meager belongings. It mattered little to him that his story was being played out by hundreds of thousands of other southern Italians, or Mezzagiorne, who were flocking to America to escape the uncontrollable harshness of both the land and the economy. He was alone, and he already longed for the day when he could return to his family.

Tall for his family, Domenic was a handsome boy despite the large nose with a slight bend in the middle. Beneath a mop of thick black hair, his intense brown eyes reflected the purposefulness of his nature. Molded by the strict rules of family and church, a hard land, and the weight of being the oldest child, he was not predisposed to either frivolity or idleness. There was always something to be done, a responsibility to bear. Like his father, he had little tolerance for those who wasted their time or shirked their responsibilities. Keeping busy with matters of importance, whether real or imagined, was also a way to mask his natural shyness. And while the young girls of Torre de'Passeri often mistook his demeanor as one of aloofness or, worse, arrogance, more than one were teary-eyed to see him leave.

The next morning, he took the train to Napoli and found his way to the busy port area that appeared to be a sea of transients with people of all ages jammed into every available cranny along the wharf while clutching their precious belongings. Some appeared to have been there for days. He got his first glimpse of the Steamship Cretic of the White Star line, the ship that would take him to America. She seemed immense, looming over the dock with two large gangplanks reaching down to the hordes of emigrants like welcoming hands.

Domenic became anxious when he saw passengers already making their way up those gangplanks and what appeared to be many more onboard. Should he have arrived earlier?

Clinging tightly to his suitcase as suspicious characters of all types jostled him along his way, he sought out the tent housing representatives of the Cretic as well as the Italian government. He could make no sense of the chaos surrounding the tent when a stranger placed a hand on his shoulder and spoke to him in Italian, but with a dialect he found hard to understand.

"You look lost, little sparrow."

Domenic turned and looked into the dark eyes of a man he guessed to be in his thirties. He was dressed slightly better than most of the others milling about. With him, but standing slightly behind him, was a young girl who looked to be close to Domenic's age. She was dressed in peasant's clothing, and the two makeshift bags to which she clung were in stark contrast to the stylish suitcase carried by the man.

"I am Cologero. Cologero Dragotto from Palermo. And this is Francesca, my beautiful new bride." The word "bride' was accompanied by a proud, wide grin showing a mouth full of crooked teeth.

There was then silence as Cologero looked directly at him. Domenic slowly realized he was now expected to introduce himself. Domenic hesitated, thinking of all the warnings he had received about being wary of strangers. But, not wanting to be seen a country idiot unversed in common manners, he responded with as much maturity in his voice as he could muster in hopes of matching the confidence exuded by this Sicilian.

"I am Domenic. Domenic Bassini from Torre de'Passeri." After seeing a quizzical raising of the eyebrows by Cologero he added, "Abruzzo."

"Ahh, Abruzzo. Many of my friends in America are from Abruzzo. Wonderful people. I can't wait to see them all again." He then nodded toward Francesca. "I will introduce them to my beautiful bride. I'm returning to America on the Cretic. Is she your ship as well, young Domenic?" The man had a pleasant manner but was probably one of the ugliest men Domenic had ever seen. His nose was crooked and wide as though broken numerous times and it dominated a face that also featured small sunken eyes and unusually large ears.

"Yes."

"And who waits for you in America, sparrow? Anyone?"

"Why are you calling me sparrow? I told you my name is Domenic."

"Because I can tell you are what the Americans call a "bird of passage." And what is a more common bird than a sparrow?"

"What's this bird of passage?"

"It is the bird that flies to warmer weather in the winter only to return in the spring. And you fly from Italia to help your family, no doubt? And you plan to return when the weather is warmer in Italia? When everything is better here?"

"Yes, that is my plan."

"Well, I ask you, young Domenic, why doesn't the bird simply stay in the nicer climate all year? Why go back and forth? America is such a land that you will always have a better life there. And things have not gotten better here for many generations, so I doubt they ever will. At least not in your lifetime little bird."

Domenic bristled at being called "a little bird" again. "I wish you wouldn't call me that."

"Ahh, a sensitive, proud Italian. But you'd better get used to name calling. America offers us much, but there is a price to pay. You will be called 'guinea,' 'wop,' 'dago,' and many other things much worse than 'little bird.'"

Domenic had heard none of these terms before, and they meant nothing to him. As he began to ask Cologero to explain them he saw the man's attention turned elsewhere.

"Come, Francesca. You too, little bird. They have started screening passengers."

As they walked, Cologero explained that the first and second class passengers were the ones Domenic had seen on board. Those traveling in steerage would be given a more thorough screening to weed out the sick, the criminal, or those without the proper papers or money. The steamship operators, in particular, took much interest in this process, as they were forced to provide return passage to any passengers not making it through immigration in America for any reason.

In the large tent, Domenic presented his third-class ticket, his birth certificate, and a letter from his sponsor in America, Giuseppe Rossario. He answered some questions, swore he was not a criminal or an anarchist, proved he had some money, and endured a brief physical examination. He was then given some papers and a boarding pass and sent on his way to await boarding.

He hurried along down the wharf, partly out of anxiety and partly to escape Cologero Dragatto, who made him uneasy. He now had a full view of the beautiful seascape that was the Bay of Naples. From the wharf, he could see Mount Vesuvius looming over the city behind him, and the Amalfi peninsula and even the island of Capri – all places he had heard about but never seen. But he was transfixed by the horizon. Somewhere beyond that horizon was a new land and a new life. Once again, conflicting feelings of trepidation and anticipation took hold causing a small bubble of fear in his stomach.

As he took his place in the queue of steerage passengers awaiting boarding, he made sure to avert his eyes from those around him, lest another stranger engage him in conversation. As he stood there, he noticed a young boy of maybe ten or twelve years slowly wandering throughout the roped-off boarding area. He had no bags and did not appear to be accompanied by anyone else. Domenic thought he might be a pickpocket and reflexively took a firmer grip on his bag. As he eyed the boy, he was suddenly startled by a now familiar loud voice.

"There you are, Domenic from Abruzzo. Lucky for you I found you, since we can now board together. I told the ship officer that you were a cousin so we could be assigned to the same area. This way I can watch out for you, my new friend, and we can both watch out for Francesca."

Domenic looked to Francesca and really took her in for the first time. She was no longer wearing a scarf, which was probably removed when she was checked for lice, and her midnight-black hair was pulled up atop and behind her head, held there by colorful barrettes and a ribbon in the back. She lifted her head and looked at Domenic and he was taken in by her large, dark eyes and the smoothness of her complexion. She was easily the most beautiful girl he had ever seen. But Domenic sensed strong emotions blazing behind the haunting eyes in the brief instant she held his gaze. Emotions that left him chilled and enchanted at the same time.

***

  Francesca Bernardelli had spent the entire seventeen years of her life in the small village of Montelepre in the Sicilian mountains some thirty kilometers from Palermo. Her mother passed away when she was still a child, forcing her to assume the role of looking after her two younger sisters while helping her father manage his small, ramshackle inn located on a well-traveled road that connected the towns along the western Sicilian coast to Palermo.
  Antonio Bernardelli was a well-meaning but simple man not well suited to running the business left to him by his wife's father. He drank too much of the strong Marsala wine favored by locals and guests and sat in on too many of the card games that took place at tables around the inn's public room. Francesca found herself assuming more and more of the responsibilities for running the inn, while her father assumed more and more debt.
  Oddly enough, Francesca considered herself lucky and was not at all displeased with her life. Avoiding work in the fields kept her from the sun and from becoming a wrinkled, hard woman before her time, like so many others. But it was her dreams that made her life more than bearable, because she somehow knew she would live them. On clear days as a child, she could see Monte Pellegrino beckoning her to the metropolis of Palermo, and at first her dreams would take here there where she would live behind the ancient wall that seemed to make Palermo a world apart from the rest of the Sicily she knew. Then from travelers she heard stories of America and how women there could be more than subservient slaves to their husbands, as they were in Sicily.
  The Sicilian Mafioso had its very roots not far from Montelepre, and over the years the Bonfiglio clan had emerged as the major family in the region. Antonio had grown deeply in arears to the family, and he began to fear for himself and his daughters. The clan would eat and drink whatever they pleased, but what he owed continued to grow. Then Cologero Dragatto offered him a way out and all it would cost him was one daughter. Dragotto's sister had married into the Bonfiglio family, and Dragatto, himself, had become a favorite of the clan due to his ability to think up endless schemes to help further the family's wealth and power. He was not a soldier. In fact, he feared violence

of any type. Behind his back, the Bonfiglios would ridicule him over his timid nature which he tried to keep hidden behind a constant bluster of bold words.

Cologero left for America in 1912 with the blessing of the Bonfiglios and some of their money with dreams of putting his talent for hatching profitable ventures to work in this land of immense opportunity. Three years later, he returned with tales of unbridled money-making possibilities in America and a promise to earn a fortune for the Bonfiglios in exchange for a loan to help him grow his fledging businesses. In fact, he was making his proposal to the family in the public area of Antonio Bernardinelli's inn when he first laid eyes on Francesca and was immediately entranced.

Being his oldest, marrying off Francesca to a man of significant means, as Cologero appeared to be, was best for all. He would miss her, but the money Cologero offered as a gift of respect would be very welcome, as would the favor he hoped to gain with the Bonfiglios. It was especially needed now, as the Mafiosi no longer simply expected free food and drink but also payment for "protecting" him, his inn, and his family.

For her part, Francesca accepted her fate pragmatically. She would not have her dream of falling deeply in love with a handsome young man who adored her. A young man like Enrico Pasquale, who she hardly loved but who had awakened desires in her she longed to fulfill. But she would have her dream of going to America. And after that, anything was possible.

***

As she stood on the pier now, she truly did not mind the fact that she had been married off to a man twice her age. She had already learned that beneath his confident exterior, Cologero was an insecure man who totally adored her. In time, she would control him. For now, it was important to Cologero that she remain the picture of wifely obedience, and she was happy to have him enjoy this illusion to maintain face in the eyes of the others. She wanted to be married to an important man, and she wanted to someday be important herself.

Cologero turned from Domenic as he seemed intent on introducing himself to as many fellow passengers as possible, and Francesca followed silently. Domenic became lost in lonely thought but in short order found himself following the crowd as they began boarding the

Cretic. Again, Cologero sought him out, and he followed right behind the Sicilian and his young bride up the gangplank.

He was so transfixed by Francesca that he hardly noticed as the young boy he had been observing earlier squeezed in closely behind him. As Cologero stopped to show his boarding papers and receive his berth assignment from the boarding officer at the top of the gangplank, the boy deftly darted behind him and on to the ship. Domenic started to say something but thought better of it. No need to draw any undue attention to himself.

Domenic made his way with the others down to the third class, or steerage as it was better known, decks of the *Cretic*. As he wound down the metal stairs, he caught glimpses through the small windows at each deck level of the long carpeted corridors extending through the first and second class sections. There seemed to him to be a much longer descent between the second class and steerage decks, but perhaps it was only because the stairs were now not as well-lit and the metal walls not as freshly painted. They exited the stairwell to a large corridor with bare timbered floors and large openings on either side as opposed to cabin doors.

Each opening was the entranceway to a large compartment filled with metal-framed beds stacked in sections two high and three across. As he followed Cologero down the corridor, Domenic estimated that there were around twenty of these six-bed units per compartment. He would later learn that there were ten of these compartments spread out over two deck levels, seven on the upper level and three on the lower level, which was also where much of the ship's engine and steering controls for the rudder were located. This, he would learn in fact, was how the term "steerage" came to describe the poorest accommodations on a ship.

Launched in 1902 by the Leyland Line as the "Hanoverian," the *Cretic* was originally designed to accommodate 800 third class passengers and serve the Liverpool to Boston route. When she was acquired to serve the White Star Line's Mediterranean route, third class beds were expanded to carry over 1000.

But none of this mattered to Domenic, who, upon imagining himself living among so many strangers in such a non-private manner, immediately longed for his small comfortable bed back in Torre de'Passeri. And with all the confusion and disorder around him as passengers sought out their compartments and rushed to claim rights to the best bunks, he also longed for the order and structure of his family and his village.

"We are lucky, Domenic. Our compartment is directly opposite Francesca's. We will take the bunks nearest the corridor and will almost be able to see her." Then to Francesca, he said, "Quickly, there on the top on the end, Francesca," pointing to a bunk in the women's compartment opposite the men's where he and Domenic would be. "Sleep there. That is where you will be safest and nearest to us."

Domenic found himself going along. Despite being leery of Cologero, he was still the only other person on the ship he knew – if you could call listening and nodding to someone knowing them.

For the first time in his life he was alone among strangers, and although many had a story similar to his own, he tried to remain apart, a difficult task in the crowded accommodations in steerage. Still, he quickly came to appreciate the comforting tapestry woven by the people in steerage. Despite coming from many different parts of Italy and speaking different dialects, they seemed to come together. Almost like a family in a way.

Suspicious, wary, and afraid at first, it did not take long for them to bond around what made them alike as opposed to fixating on what made them different. And as wretched as the conditions were, storytelling, Scopa card games, and lively sessions of Morra, the Italian hand game, flourished onboard, creating a sense of trust and camaraderie among the passengers. And even though he did not actively participate, Domenic watched and listened and became more at ease.

One who did participate was Cologero. As the only one in steerage who had lived in America, he had an eager audience whenever he told stories about the country where they had all cast their hopes. Describing America, he said, "She's a tough teacher who rewards the child who wants to learn and is willing to do the work but has no time to waste on those who do not.

"Look at me, a *persona ignorante* who came to America just five years ago knowing nothing. I worked, I listened and I learned the rules the teacher had to teach. Today, I am a respected businessman. I buy fresh fish every morning when the boats come in and take them to the finest restaurants in the city of Boston where I sell them at a handsome profit. Someday, I will have my own restaurant and rub elbows with the important citizens of the city."

When he was not on his pulpit preaching about the joys of living in America, Cologero could be found organizing card games or the betting on raucous games of Morra. Somehow, he also found time to give well-attended English lessons, for a price of course. Luckily, he tutored Domenic for free. Cologero was also, naturally, the "capitano" of his six-person bunk group and therefore the one who went to the galley and brought back the meals for the others in a large pot. They had each been issued a single bowl, spoon, and fork (no need for knives when meals were always a variation of stews and thick soups) that they rinsed in a common barrel of seawater and guarded with their lives – if they were lost or stolen, new ones would not be issued.

Like any large family, the steerage community had its problems. Stealing was commonplace, as were fights among the men, especially after partaking of the wine obtained through bribes of the Italian-speaking crew members. Also on occasion, the single women were harassed, sometimes resulting in vigilante justice. When a fifteen-year-old girl was groped by a drunken young man from Calabria, Domenic was among those who watched as her father and some others left him with two broken fingers on each hand. They would have broken more, but he had, after all, been drunk, so four fingers seemed adequate to make the point.

The married women were off limits in the unwritten code of steerage and were largely left alone. This did little to assuage Cologero's constant worries over Francesca. Domenic guessed that Cologero knew that the beautiful young bride with the older, ugly husband made an appealing target for the many Lotharios onboard intent on inflicting their self-perceived charms upon as many potential conquests as possible by the time they reached America.

**

Domenic slowly came to realize that he had apparently been chosen to be Francesca's guardian, as Cologero went about enjoying his busy roles as sage, bookmaker, teacher, and social director of steerage.

The second night at sea, Domenic filled his bowl from the community bucket and set out to find a quiet spot on the top deck away from his loud, cramped, smelly steerage compartment where dozens would squeeze around the one long table to take their dinner among shouts, laughter and arguments.

He settled in among some coiled ropes by a set of lifeboats and marveled at how much brighter the stars seemed at sea and wondered what this same moon looked like tonight at home. Lost in thoughts of Torre de'Passeri, he suddenly heard someone say, "Chi mangia solo crepa solo." *He who eats alone dies alone.* He looked up to see Cologero and Francesca.

"So, Sparrow, here you are." The name had stuck and Domenic had ceased protesting. "I need your help, my friend. I have organized a game of Morra with some serious players, including several from second class with deep pockets. They trust Cologero because they know I am a respected businessman and I must be there to oversee the betting. But it is no place for my Francesca. I cannot leave her alone among the rozzo, so if you have no other plans might I impose upon you to keep her company? She should not be among the single women and the older ones with families are not friendly toward her – clearly they are jealous of her beauty."

Without waiting for an answer, Cologero was quickly off, leaving Francesca and Domenic alone.

Cologero had concluded early on that the shy, quiet young man from Abruzzo could be trusted. He was clearly imbued with great discipline and a sense of responsibility. He did not drink and was not prone to joining in with the other single young men as they squeezed what little pleasures they could out of steerage. He was deeply religious and seemed strong both physically and mentally. But one thing Cologero forgot in choosing him to spend time in Francesca's company was that despite all his admirable qualities he was still a sixteen-year-old boy.

Domenic was both uncomfortable and excited when Francesca sat down next to him. For a while, neither said a word. In fact, neither looked at the other. Then Francesca, still not looking at Domenic, said, "I know what you are thinking. I know what everyone thinks. But I do not hate him. I do not hate him at all." And then she burst into tears.

"I did not think you hated Cologero!" Domenic blurted out in the hope that this would stop her crying.

"I hate what I will never have with him, but I do not hate him."

"You will have everything. Cologero is wealthy and will give you whatever you want."

"He will not give me Enrico Pasquale!" she hissed. "He will not give me what I felt with him. He will never give me the excitement, the longing I felt when Enrico touched me or even looked at me. And I will never get to feel what a young woman should feel the first time she is loved by someone she wants to love her."

Domenic just nodded and listened, unsure of what to say or do.

"I was ready to give myself to him. He was poor and lazy and stupid, but he was so handsome. Dear Jesu Christi forgive me, but he was so handsome. I could never love him, but I wanted him." She looked at Domenic. "Do you think that makes me a puttana?" she asked calmly, matter-of-factly while reaching out and touching his arm.

If a La Mano Nera henchman had jumped from the shadows, stuck a knife to his throat and demanded all his money, Domenic would have been more at ease. He was aroused by her touch in a way he had never felt before. He trembled, sputtered, and cursed himself for appearing such a child in the eyes of this beautiful creature.

"No," he finally uttered weakly, barely above a whisper.

"You are so sweet. And you are handsome yourself. I am sure you had all the girls back in Torre de, de…"

"de'Passeri."

"…de'Passeri longing for you." She squeezed his arm tighter.

She leaned forward and kissed him quickly on the lips, and as she did her hand moved from his arm to his thigh. Domenic felt himself grow aroused and was embarrassed to see Francesca looking down at the sudden bulge in his pants. She actually smiled at this. He was anxious and scared – someone could see them. There were people all around the deck escaping their small cabins and cramped accommodations in steerage to take in the night air. He was afraid of what Cologero might do if he found out he had kissed his wife. And he would deserve it.

"Will you be my Enrico, Domenic? Will you give me what I will never have with Cologero?'

"No!" his mind cried out. "Yes," his sixteen-year-old body replied.

※※※

Over the next few days, Domenic's passage to America consisted of long periods of guilt and fear interrupted by brief moments of ecstasy. He would meet Francesca late at night on deck where they would slowly, carefully explore each other's young bodies in ways neither knew much about but relished nevertheless. For Francesca, it was an ecstatic departure from the fast, aggressive approach of Cologero, which bordered on assault.

The two young lovers found they could slide beneath the bow of a lifeboat to a space between it and the deck rail that was completely obscured from sight. Every time they were together, Domenic swore to himself it would be the last.

They dared not stay away too long, since the ship had many eyes. They would pleasure each other quickly, with Francesca taking the lead and explaining to Domenic what she wanted done in ways that made him blush, but comply nevertheless. When it was over, he was always anxious to pull up his pants and hide his manliness, while Francesca seemed oblivious to having her own nakedness on display, and this often excited Domenic to a point where once again his pants were down and the passionate, albeit inexperienced, lovemaking began again.

Late one moonlit night, Domenic arrived at their usual lifeboat but saw a group of men settled in near it, passing time. He went off to find a different spot and slid under another boat out of their sight to see if it would accommodate his and Francesca's needs. His hand suddenly touched something that moved. There was a startled yelp and a foot began kicking at Domenic.

"Smettila! *Stop it.*"

The kicking stopped and Domenic heard a boy's voice ask him, "Who are you? Leave me alone!" The words were spoken in Italian, defiantly and boldly, belying the youth of the person uttering them.

"Okay, okay, I'm leaving." But as Domenic began to slide out backward, they both heard voices nearby.

"Wait!" said the boy. "Don't let them see you. Come through."

Domenic was also not anxious to explain to anyone what he was doing there, so he quietly slid all the way under the boat to the space by the railing. What he saw he could only describe as a "nido" *nest*, comprised of several blankets of the same threadbare type found on the steerage bunks. He also noticed two bowls and a small duffle-type bag that appeared empty. There must be people in steerage without blankets and bowls he thought to himself.

He looked at the boy, who was wearing a man's coat much too large for him and could see in the moonlight that it was the same boy he saw sneak on board with him, Francesca and Cologero. He looked even younger up close, maybe ten or eleven years old, but he had steely eyes that never left Domenic. When the voices subsided into the night he asked "Why are you crawling around here? What are you looking for?" Again, demanding and defiant.

"That's not your business. I'll leave you now to your little nest."

"Will you tell them about me?" Suddenly there was a slight hint of a small boy's fear in the voice.

"No, I don't need the trouble."

Domenic crawled back out to the main deck and was pulling himself out and up when he heard a voice shout out in English, "You there, stop where you are."

A uniformed crew member came up to him.

"What were you doing under there? Show me your boarding pass."

Although he could guess what the man was asking, Domenic shook his head and made the classic palms-up hand gesture to indicate he did not understand."

"Carta d'imbarco."

"Si, si." Domenic showed him his papers.

"Now what were you doing under there?"

Domenic could understand what he was asking, but how could he explain? Then there was noise from behind the lifeboat.

"Is there someone else under there? What's going on here? You had better tell me or you'll spend the rest of the trip locked up with the stowaways and then be sent right back to Italy with them too. You know *mettere dentro*." He was trying to translate "locked up."

"Si tratta di una donna," Domenic said sheepishly. "A woman. Per favore, she has a husband."

"You Italians, you're all alike. Any woman is fair game but your own. I don't need a jealous husband causing trouble. You both get out of here, and if I see you sneaking around here again, you and your putanella will both end up in lockup." And then he was on his way.

"Grazie. Grazie mille," a small voice whispered out from under the lifeboat

***

When he finally did manage to find Francesca, she was surrounded by the same men he had seen gathered near their regular rendezvous spot. When she saw him, she called out to him loudly, "Oh, Domenic, there you are, my husband." She strode over. Domenic could see the men looking at him, probably trying to decide if this boy could provide them with enough trouble to outweigh the enjoyment they might take from Francesca. But they let her go.

She took his arm, and as soon as they were out of sight she spun to him and kissed him. But he was still too shaken from his encounter with the Cretic officer and the ruffians for romance and pushed her away.

"No, no, Francesca. It's too dangerous."

"What, you no longer like me, Domenic?"

At that, she reached for his crotch and began rubbing it. He let her. Then she knelt to unbutton his trousers. He felt like he might burst through them before she was done. They were out in the open and anyone could come by at any moment. But suddenly it didn't matter. She said, "Cologero wants me to do this and I find it disgusting. But I want to have you, all of you, every way I can before we reach America." She took him in her mouth for the first time. Domenic was thrust into a new realm of ecstasy and lost all concern about being discovered.

As they walked back to the stairwell, the same *Cretic* officer who had questioned him earlier walked by and muttered something. Domenic thought he heard the word "guineas."

***

Domenic spent the next day wandering around steerage thinking about Francesca. As always, he was surrounded by others but alone. He watched and marveled at how close-knit groups, small families, had emerged from the diverse collection of immigrants of all types and from many parts of Italy, many of them speaking dialects barely understood by others. He had seen women who could barely care for their own children watching over the children of other mothers who were sickened by the rolling of the boat, some for the entire voyage. He saw others look after younger children traveling alone as if they were their own. They had become a family. He marveled at how they had come to help one another and hoped America would be like this.

Of course, there were some whose only goal seemed to be to cause problems, and Domenic now saw such a person with Cologero. They were having a very heated exchange with words and hands flying. The young man, who Domenic had noticed before, had a face that always seemed to be set in an angry frown. The huge, wooly mustache he wore only reinforced this impression.

"You are a fool!" shouted Cologero. "You know nothing about America. You know nothing about nothing!"

"You are the fool! You are the puppet of the rich who control everything."

"Anarchist!"

"Yes, and proud of it."

"Galleanist!"

"Yes, and even more proud of it. The rich everywhere get richer on the backs of ignorants like you who will do the hard work for practically nothing. America is no different. If anything, she is worse."

"You go to America because you are in trouble in Italy and you want to cause trouble in America. Stupido! You will ruin it for all of us. America holds her arms out to welcome you and give you a good life. If I were to tell the officials what you are they would never let you in the country."

"If you were to tell the officials what I am, it would be the last thing you tell anyone."

Looking at the man, no one doubted this.

After this exchange, Domenic walked with Cologero, who was still red in the face and furious. "What is an anarchist?" he asked.

"A fool who is too lazy to work and blames all his trouble on others. So his brilliant solution is to blow up everything."

"And what is a Galleanist."

"Luigi Galleani is the leader of these idiots in America. Many of our people follow his idiotic teachings"

"Do you know the name of this anarchist Galleanist?"

"Bartolomeo Vanzetti." Cologero nearly spat out the name. "I know his type. He is why some people in America look at all Italians with suspicion."

Cologero then stopped and said to Domenic, "Come with me, Sparrow. I want to show you something."

He took Domenic up to the first-class deck and spoke to the guard at the end of the corridor who smiled and allowed them down the corridor. "He won some money betting on Morra the way I told him."

They turned into a small doorway that led to a kitchen. Cologero was greeted by someone who seemed to be in charge, and he heard him say to Cologero, "OK, but be quick."

"He lost and owes me money," explained Cologero with a wink.

They pushed through a swinging door into a beautiful room with linen-covered tables set with ornate china and silverware. There were cushioned chairs, wood-paneled walls with paintings, and intricate light fixtures.

"This is what I will have next time I make the crossing. This trip I must save every lira I can to invest in my businesses. And this is what you can have if you embrace the bosom of America, young Sparrow. There will be those who will try to beat you down, to keep you from your dreams. But you cannot fight them. Not now, not yet. So you keep your smile showing and your anger hidden. And you work. There are Italians right now in Boston starting businesses, buying buildings, building churches who came to America with nothing more than the clothes on their backs. And fools like Vanzetti want to destroy it all.

Someday soon, I will be one of the *classe superiore*, living in a fine house of my own and taking Francesca to the best places in Boston. And I will say, 'Vaffanculo *(fuck you)* to those who looked down at me." Then adding almost as an aside, "I think then she will appreciate the man she married."

Domenic flushed with guilt and shame.

Later, Domenic was thinking about what Cologero said as he made his way to an open deck for some air. Did he know about him and Francesca? Domenic was disgusted with himself and vowed, as he did every day, that this thing with Francesca would end. Lost in thought, he was caught by surprise by a tug on his coat sleeve.

It was the boy.

***

The boy's name was Ermino Lentini. He was Napolitano, and like Domenic he was on a mission to America. His was to find his father.

Ermino and his parents had lived in one of the many poor neighborhoods of Naples just steps from the docks. His father worked occasionally cleaning fish but spent much more time drinking and running errands for a local Camorra clan. The Camorra pre-dated the better known, Sicilian-spawned, Mafioso by decades, giving them much more time to perfect their system of brutality and intimidation. Never a coherent whole, it was a loosely associated group of families who controlled the poorest areas of the region. Their iron grip on their respective communities made them valuable assets to the local politicians and public officials, which in turn led to their protection from local authorities. They were able to carry out their illegal activities with no fear of retribution, legal or otherwise.

As shiftless as he was, Ermino's father doted on his only son. He may have been quick to deliver a sharp slap across the face of his wife, but he was just as quick to pick up Ermino and glide him over his head in their small apartment to the boy's squeals of delight. How he came to be in trouble with the local Camorra clan was a mystery to his mother. Based on his penchant for drinking, gambling, and overall carelessness, it should not have been surprising to her that one day he was gone, rumored to have slipped aboard a ship bound for America to escape the reach of the Camorra. True or not, it was the story she told her young son Ermino. Right after that, she was visited by some local Cammorristi who wanted to know where her husband was, beating her senseless in the process in front of the six-year-old and delivering a message to others in the neighborhood at the same time. She never fully recovered, and little Ermino wound up in the care of some relatives and then the nuns at a nearby orphanage. But he spent most of his time running away, and by the time he was ten he had become adept at stealing and blending into the dirty alleyways and crowded streets of the poorest parts of Naples.

He decided he would find his father, and to do this he needed to get to America. Ermino began spending his time around the docks watching the *waves of immigrants departing almost daily. He waited for his opportunity and took it.*

Resourceful, intelligent, and determined, he had managed to survive without detection onboard the Cretic. He kept moving amongst the steerage population, not spending too much time in any compartment. There were ample opportunities to take his stolen bowl and dip into the leftovers or grab a piece of bread as groups relaxed and talked after meals.

The nights were long, lonely, and cold. Some nights, he would slip into the steerage area and sleep on the floor, leaving before others were awake. But most nights he spent wrapped in his stolen blankets somewhere on the deserted deck, listening for footsteps of the crew members charged with rounding up stowaways. After the first few days of eluding capture, the search for stowaways abated, and Ermino became confident he would make it to America.

Although he trusted no one, the man who had discovered him last night had lied to protect him. He would need help once they arrived in America, and he wondered if this man would help him again. It was this thought, and perhaps the inner loneliness and fear to which he would never admit, that caused him to keep an eye out for Domenic and wait for an opportunity to find him alone.

✳ ✳ ✳

"Hello, mister."

"What do you want, boy?" replied a startled Domenic. Seeing the boy brought back the anxiety he had felt when being questioned by the Cretic officer. The boy carried his soft bag, which was now bulging, no doubt with his blankets and other stolen wares.

"So, what is your name? Mine is Ermino Lentini."

"Why do you need to know? Why do you *want* to know?" he said suspiciously.

"Because you could have reported me and collected a bounty but you did not. You must have had a reason and I want to know what it was."

"No reason."

"Yes, there is a reason. Nobody helps me unless there is a reason. The nuns helped me so they could beat me. My cousins helped me so they would have someone to do all the work. The slime in the streets would help me so they could touch me in places I did not want to be touched. I think nobody does something for anyone else unless there is something in it for them. So why did you help me?"

Domenic looked at the boy who returned a steely, unflinching gaze that, had it come from a grown man, might have made him shudder. But it looked slightly absurd on the face of a little boy. He suspected the boy had practiced this glare to ward off those who might threaten him. It reminded him of how the small Volpino dog his mother kept as a pet, a little fluffy thing weighing less than ten kilograms, would show his teeth and growl at the huge Abruzzese Mastiffs that were employed to protect livestock from brown bears in the Abruzzo mountains. They were literally ten times the Volpino's size. Did he really believe they feared his bark, or did he know they could crush him with one bite? He suspected this boy, who was obviously intelligent, knew exactly how vulnerable he was despite his impressive Volpino bark. He smiled at the boy.

"We are Italians. We're like a big family. We should stick together. Why should I help the stuck up British owners of this ship who look down on all of us instead of a young fellow Italian like you?" Although spoken to alleviate the boy's suspicion, Domenic realized as he said these words that he truly believed them.

Ermino wanted to believe it. Despite all he had seen and been through, he wanted to believe that he could be part of a family. Any family that would have him.

"Come walk with me," said Domenic, "and tell me your story."

***

Nine days into the crossing the mood among the steerage passengers began to change. The routine and the kinship had allowed many to put the enormity of the step they were taking aside for a while. But now, with the arrival in Boston just two days away, Domenic could feel the tension taking hold. The laughter was less, the flare-ups more frequent. People began gathering their meager belongings around them and keeping a closer watch on them. No one truly knew what to expect, what their lives in their new country would be like.

Domenic's plan was to stay with Giuseppe Rossario, a good friend of Domenic's father who had left Torre de'Passeri years earlier with his wife, Maria. Giuseppe had written that he would be happy to take

Domenic in and help him find a job in Boston. He now had one son he said would welcome a big brother in his house. But now, with Francesca, things had gotten complicated. Domenic believed he was in love. He would be happy if he could enjoy the passion he felt with Francesca for the rest of his life. But he was also a religious boy and knew what he was doing was a sin. He planned to make a full confession as soon as he could get to a priest.

But what would he do when the priest absolved him and told him, "*Va e non peccare più.*" *Go and sin no more,* when he knew in his heart he would? And what of Cologero? He had every right to see both him and Francesca punished. He had seen Cologero when he was angry, and although he managed to hide it well, Domenic could tell that the man would never let any real or perceived affront go unpunished, but he was too clever to react in any way that might cause harm to himself or his ambitions. But even worse than his fear of God or Cologero was his fear of the great shame this would bring to his family. Still, he had to be with Francesca and would tell her so this night.

That evening, he took his bowl of stew from Cologero and announced he was going up on deck to eat. It was getting increasingly difficult for him to be around both Cologero and Francesca at the same time.

"Can we go up top too, Cologero?" Francesca asked.

"I have business to discuss with some people here, but you go with Domenic."

Domenic felt that Cologero was relieved to be rid of Francesca and he knew that his "business" was collecting gambling debts before the ship docked and his debtors disappeared. He had asked Domenic to go with him, but he had politely refused, not wanting to make any enemies. He needed no more complications in his life. He also did not want to be seen as Cologero's lackey. Ironically, Cologero then recruited the intimidating Vanzetti to assume this role, no doubt for a share of the collections. This was typical Cologero, who hated the man but would not hesitate to use him to suit his needs.

On deck with Francesca he had no appetite and just watched as Francesca devoured her dinner. Finally, he spoke, "What are we going to do, Francesca?"

"How do you mean, Domenic?"

"I mean. How do we tell Cologero? Where are we going to go? I cannot ask Rossario to allow us to live in his home together. I must find work right away and..."

"Stop, Domenic," she spoke firmly. Then her voice softened. "My dear, sweet, beautiful Domenic. You have given me great joy. You have made me feel like the bride I wanted to feel like and you gave me the passion I have never had with anyone else and never will. I will not remember this as the journey that brought me to America but the journey that brought me to you. But Cologero is my husband and he will always be my husband. When I step off this ship, I begin my life as an American wife. And I will never betray him again."

Domenic was stunned. "But I love you!"

"No, Domenic," with a coy smile, "you love *making* love *fare l'amore*. And you are very, very good at it."

"No, it is you I love," he protested. "Here, I will prove it."

He reached under his coat and untucked his shirt from his trousers to reveal the pouch he always kept strapped around his midsection. Francesca had seen this before, but she had never seen him open it as he did now. From it he slowly took the small marble broach his mother had given him.

"My father gave this to my mother to show he would love her forever and now I give it to you to show I will love you forever." He attempted to place it in her hand but she recoiled in horror as if he were handing her a dead rat.

"No, Domenic, you cannot give that to me."

"Take it. You must take it, Francesca," he said loudly, tears were welling in his eyes.

"Shh, Domenic. People are watching. Okay, okay, I will take it, but someday you will regret it. Find me that day and I will give it back to you." With that she stood up and kissed him on the top of head. "This is the last time we will be together." With that she walked away.

Domenic sat alone, stunned and unable to think or move. He sat there a long time. When he finally returned to his bunk, he could see Francesca asleep in her bed near the corridor. He could swear she was crying, and somehow this made him feel better.

***

The next evening, the *Cretic* docked at Commonwealth Pier in South Boston. Since it was late in the day, anyone who was not an American citizen was not allowed to leave the ship as immigration inspectors would not be available until the next morning. Domenic stood on the deck and looked out on the city and pondered what his new life in America would be like. From his vantage point at the end of Commonwealth Pier, he could see the entire panorama of Boston's circular inner harbor, from the downtown area to the North End to East Boston directly across the harbor. It seemed immense to him, with lighted buildings silhouetted against the evening sky as far as he could see.

He had spent the day reflecting on his situation and had come to the conclusion that God in His infinite wisdom had saved him from himself and delivered him exactly where he was supposed to be. He had prayed for forgiveness and the strength to be an honorable man. He was calm and once again confident in his purpose.

Seeing Boston was like being awakened with a splash of cold water. His head was cleared of crazy thoughts of stealing away with Francesca, and he thanked God that he had been saved from bringing shame upon himself. When he finally drifted off to sleep that night, he dreamt he was standing at the head of a huge classroom and the teacher, a matronly old woman, was pinning on him a broach made of gold. At the same time, she turned to tell the rows and rows of faceless classmates that seemed to go on forever, that if they worked as hard as Domenic they too could have a golden broach. But when she looked back at Domenic, she was no longer an old woman—she was Francesca.

***

The next day was total bedlam. There was no centralized immigration facility in Boston, and all entering immigrants were processed into rooms on the various steamship docks set aside for this purpose. At Commonwealth Pier there were two such rooms, or sheds, on the second level of the three-story building set out on the pier. One was for first and second-class passengers, the other much larger one for third-class or steerage passengers.

Confusion reigned in the crowded waiting area as families fought to stay together while clinging to their belongings as everyone pushed forward toward the bottleneck leading into the examination room. Even though awaiting friends and family members were not allowed in the waiting area, favored "agents" of immigration officials were. This group was comprised primarily of individuals who preyed on the ignorance of the new arrivals. They were employees of carriage companies who overcharged for their assistance in providing travel to local destinations or to train stations, representatives of immigrant banks who collected large commissions to convert Italian lire to American dollars, transfer agents who collected exorbitant fees to convert prepaid travel vouchers into valid stateside tickets, and the "padrones."

The padrones were the most dangerous as they were Italians who sought to lure the many young, healthy men into their stables of cheap labor. They enticed them with offers of a place to live, usually a cheap, overcrowded boarding or tenement house, and the offer of work. They neglected to mention that over half their wages would go to themselves. The padrones would have them sign a "contract" before they had access to any friends, family, or the immigrant aid workers who waited just beyond the examination room. Sometimes they would take the unsuspecting immigrants directly to trains where they would be shipped off to areas around the country to toil in mines, farms, and factories in need of willing, cheap labor.

Domenic had been forewarned to avoid such people by Rossario. He warded off their advances, spoke to no one and stood in the queue awaiting his turn to proceed through immigration. He could not see Cologero or Francesca; apparently the Sicilian who was adept at finding him whenever he needed him no longer had such a need.

Although Domenic knew all his papers were in order, he was nonetheless anxious. He had heard stories of people being turned away for all kinds of reasons. Suddenly, one of those reasons was standing beside him along with a padrone.

"You must help me," said Ermino.

"Ermino! What do you want? I can't help you." He looked quizzically at the padrone and his heart began to race. "They will not allow you through. You are not on the passenger list. You are a small boy alone who cannot take care of himself."

"Everything you say is correct, my friend," said the padrone. "But you will soon learn that in America everything is for sale. I am selling your young friend's entry into America."

He then took out what he called a "customs pass."

"I paid much to have this. It allows me to come and go as I please. And if I tell that guard by the door I am leaving and that this boy is a family friend, he will not question me. Particularly when I tell him this while handing him twenty American dollars. Now, this boy tells me you have forty dollars."

"Forty? I thought you said twenty."

"I do not work for free, my friend. This is America, and business is business." He sounded like Cologero, thought Domenic.

Domenic carried in his waist pouch the equivalent of thirty-two dollars. This he had guarded with his life since leaving Torre de'Passeri.

"I can't help you, Ermino. That will not leave me any money to go through immigration. I need to show I have some money or they will not let me in."

"But you must. You must, Domenic. I need to find my father. You said we were fellow Italians and should take care of each other. Like a family. You said that!" He was starting to cry.

"Maybe I can help here," the padrone spoke up. "You look like a strong boy, Domenic. Are you a hard worker? If so, I can find you all the work you want. Good work. And you pay me nothing unless I find you this work. If you agree to this, I will help your young friend into this great country for free. A gesture of my good intentions for your future in America."

"Please Domenic, please."

"For how long do I have to work for you, signor…"

"Fratelli. One year."

"You were willing to help us for forty dollars. I will work for you until I pay you forty dollars."

"That we will be forty dollars above and beyond my normal commission which is forty cents on every dollar you make. Sixty cents if you require a place to live. Do we have a deal?"

Domenic looked at Ermino.

"Yes." He shook hands with signor Fratelli.

"Now do you have a place to stay in Boston?"

"Yes."

"Good for you. What about our young friend here?"

Domenic hesitated. "Yes," he finally said. Ermino cast a quizzical look toward Domenic upon hearing this. But Domenic knew he did not want to see Emilio thrust into the same type of life he had in Napoli. And he did not want him around Fratelli.

"Okay, I trust you, young Domenic. Once you leave immigration, meet me by the viaduct that goes across to the freight yards from this level of the Pier. You can collect your friend there."

***

Everyone entering the examination room was first checked off on the ship's manifest of passengers. His documents in order, he was not recorded "without papers" or "wop" but would soon learn that did not matter in the eyes of many in America. He was then asked a number of questions designed to weed out any arrivals who might present a danger to, or a drain upon, the public. Domenic showed them his letter from Rossario offering a place to live and proved he had some money. His bag was then searched, as was he. He wrote his signature beside his name on the long list of passengers and then got into the men's line for his physical examination. His lasted about a minute.

Fifteen minutes after entering the examination room, Domenic stepped out into the hazy sunlight of a hot June day in Boston and stood amidst a mass of bewildered immigrants. Since leaving home he had fucked another man's wife, lied to authorities, helped to smuggle a stowaway into America, and given away his mother's treasured brooch to a woman he would probably never see again. But he was now standing on American soil and ready for a fresh start.

He found Ermino and Fratelli waiting for him along with about a dozen other young men, several of whom Domenic recognized from the crossing.

"So, Domenic, where is this place you are staying?"

Domenic showed him Rossario's address and Fratelli slowly nodded.

"Good. I know this address and now I know where to find you should you forget to show up for work. Here is where I expect to see you tomorrow morning at six." He handed Domenic a business card in both English and Italian and then offered to transport him to the North End with the others and pointed to a large horse-drawn wagon with wooden seats running along each side to carry its human cargo.

Just then he thought he heard his named called. Then he was sure he heard it.

"Domenic Bassini. Domenic Bassini," someone was shouting.

He looked and recognized Giuseppe Rossario from his father's photos. With him was, he guessed, his son, who looked to be around nine or ten years old. They, like many others, were wandering about the recently arrived passengers trying to find family and friends.

"Giuseppe Rossario! Here, here," shouted Domenic.

Giuseppe came over and gave Domenic a bear hug of an embrace. "You look just like your father did at your age. It is like I am looking into his face, only it looks better on you," he declared with a laugh. "Did he tell you we were the best of friends? Here, this is my boy. Everybody calls him "il piccolo Giuseppe." *Little Giuseppe*. But he prefers Joseph. He was born in America and has decided he is American."

Joseph offered his hand to Domenic, who instead of taking it lifted the boy up and gave him a hug. This delighted both he and his father. "It looks like you have a new uncle, Joseph," proclaimed Giuseppe. But his mood changed when he noticed Fratelli lurking about.

"What are you doing with this man?" he asked. "I hope you have not let him get his hooks into you."

Fratelli seemed to take no offense. "You wound me, Rossario. Your young friend here is no fool. We made a deal but he will be free of me soon enough if he keeps up his end of the bargain."

"Come, Domenic, you can explain all this to me on the way to my home."

He put his arm around Domenic to turn him away but Dominic hesitated. "There is one other thing, Giuseppe." He nodded toward Ermino.

"You are full of surprises, young Domenic."

***

The Rossario family lived in a wood-frame house on North Street near North Square. It had once been a single family home built in the early 1800s by a wealthy merchant with family roots in colonial Boston, but it now housed four apartments. Surrounded by larger tenement buildings, the entrance to the two rear apartments was off a narrow alleyway called Salutation Alley that meandered through a maze of overcrowded tenements from Hanover Street to Commercial Street and the waterfront. It earned its name from the Salutation Tavern at its foot near the docks, and was one of dozens of such alleys that began appearing in the North End in the mid-1800s as tenements and apartments sprung up to accommodate waves of Irish immigrants in areas that were once courts or the interior yards and gardens of homes built by some of Boston's earliest and wealthiest citizens.

The house had two common kitchens, each shared by two families. Rossario's apartment had two bedrooms, its own bathroom, a living area, and the kitchen it shared with the smaller front apartment. When Giuseppe first showed it to Domenic, he asked him, "Do you know why this is the most beautiful house in all of Boston?" Domenic shook his head. Beaming with pride, Giuseppe answered his own question. "Because I own it."

He had taken every penny he had saved after ten years in America to procure a loan from the Banca Italiana located in North Square in what was once the home of Paul Revere. When the building was purchased by the Paul Revere House Memorial Association in 1911 to be restored and preserved, Giuseppe had no idea who Paul Revere was, nor did he care.

The other three apartments were rented to fellow Abruzzese. In fact, the entire immediate neighborhood was comprised mostly of immigrants from Abruzzo, and it was surrounded by other small neighborhoods made up of Italians from the provinces of Molise, Sicily and Campania.

The North End was Boston's oldest neighborhood, and it always seemed to serve as the home to the city's newest citizens. It was where John Winthrop first settled Boston in 1630, and its proximity to the commerce of the waterfront encouraged wealthy traders, merchants, and shipping magnates to build their homes there. The beginning of the great Irish immigration into the city in the mid 1800s changed the face of the North End forever as the old Brahmin families moved their affluence to the Back Bay, Beacon Hill, and Cambridge. When the New North Congregational meetinghouse on Hanover Street with roots going back to 1714 was sold to the Catholic Archdiocese of Boston in 1862 and renamed Saint Stephan's, it served as a symbolic exclamation point on the neighborhood's transformation from its Puritan roots to the Irish ascension. Old mansions and unused warehouses were subdivided into shabby tenements as the North End evolved into the city's poorest neighborhood and its first slum. Lacking basic sanitation in the hastily built tenements, it was often overrun with disease.

As the Irish began to acquire some wealth and power, they gradually ceded the poorest sections of the North End to the growing Italian population. The migration of the Irish to other areas of the city, primarily South Boston, took place quickly. In 1880, there were close to fifteen thousand Irish living in the one square mile that defined the North End. By 1890 the number had shrunk to under five thousand. The Italian population, meanwhile, exploded even more rapidly. The dedication of New England's first Italian American Church, St. Leonard of Port Maurice, in 1876 to serve 800 Italians living in the North End signaled the start of an astonishing ethnic change. By 1900, there were fifteen thousand Italians, and by 1905 over twenty thousand. When Domenic first set foot in the neighborhood, the North End population of thirty-four thousand people included over twenty-eight thousand Italians.

Domenic's first impression of the North End was one of dirty streets, congestion, and poverty. He was used to seeing the open expanse of the Abruzzo mountains beyond the vegetable garden and fields behind his small home, so he could not appreciate that what he now saw as squalor actually represented conditions that were greatly improved from just a decade earlier. But he would soon come to appreciate the spirit of generosity and mutual support that formed the cornerstone of life in his new neighborhood, and the pride and industrious nature that permeated throughout it. A strength of family had emerged that allowed the residents of this tight-knit, insular enclave to endure all the hardships and challenges they faced.

The Boston that had greeted young Domenic was a city of contradictions. And it was rapidly changing. The iron grip the old Yankees once had on every aspect of the city had slowly been pried lose by the relentless influx of the Irish, who outnumbered the native-born Yankees in Boston in 1914. John "Honey Fitz" Fitzgerald, who once lived in the North End in a house not far from Rossario's, was mayor, and although the Yankees maintained their social and economic dominance, they had gradually ceded political power to the Irish. The election of Ireland-born Hugh O'Brien as mayor in 1887 had signaled the official arrival of the Irish as a force in the city and commenced a virtually unbroken string of Irish mayors and political dominance that would last nearly one hundred years.

While the tight-knit Italian community of the North End fought for basic city services, the city was in the midst of great growth and prosperity, living up to John Winthrop's glowing vision of "The City on the Hill." It had long been a city recognized for academics, publishing, and the arts but was now experiencing unprecedented economic growth.

In the year leading up to Domenic's arrival, Boston had increased its land mass by some three thousand acres with the annexation of Hyde Park; began operation of its first subway line; opened its first zoo at Franklin Park; completed construction of the Boston Fish Pier, the largest of its kind in the world; and poured millions of dollars into developments all around the city. A brand new ballpark called Fenway Park opened, and the hometown team, the Boston Red Sox, responded with a World Series title. President Taft himself laid the cornerstone for a new YMCA building, the luxurious Fairmount Copley Plaza Hotel opened and a major new hospital, the Peter Bent Brigham, was nearing completion.

At the same time the Irish of Boston were busy cementing their dominance in city politics, law enforcement, labor and the Catholic Church. This power spawned the inevitable cottage industries of graft, corruption, and organized crime. The Irish accomplishments had not been achieved easily; the discrimination they faced from the native born Bostonians had been immense. And they were not about to cede anything they had fought so hard to gain to the Italians. The Italians might be useful as voters, laborers, victims, and contributors to the coffers of the Archdiocese, but they were also a threat.

***

By the time the group of Domenic, Giuseppe, Ermino, and Joseph completed their walk from Commonwealth Pier around Boston Harbor to the North End, the two youngsters were best friends, and Domenic felt as though he had found a second father. Joseph said he was more than willing to share his room with two new roommates instead of one. "Now we just have to convince the real boss," said Giuseppe. But the initial look of consternation on Maria Rossario's face quickly became one of resignation, albeit with a sideways look at Giuseppe that said "you'll pay for this" in Italian, English, or any other language.

***

Domenic's assimilation into his new surroundings was made much easier by the fact that Rossario was well known and well liked throughout the North End. For some reason, he was one of those people always referred to by his last name, with only Maria and a few others using his given name of Giuseppe. Shortly after his arrival in Boston, he found a job working for Pietro Pastene, whose business of importing and selling Italian packaged goods was flourishing. Started by his father, Luigi Pastene, who began by selling produce from a pushcart, the business was expanding, and the industrious Rossario was now in charge of all the truck deliveries throughout New England from the Pastene packing facility in a North End waterfront warehouse.

The original Pastene shop and offices were located on Hanover Street next door to the home of George Scigliano, the most respected and influential Italian in Boston. Scigliano was born in the North End in 1874 and had gone on to become a lawyer and the first Italian American to serve in the Massachusetts state legislature. He was also a champion of immigrant causes, preaching and practicing the need to help the newest arrivals adjust to their new world.

It was he who helped Rossario get a job with his friend Pastene. Rossario would never forget this kindness. When Scigliano died at the young age of thirty-two, the entire North End mourned, and Rossario made a promise to himself to offer the same kindness to others that Scigliano had shown to him.

Rossario wanted to help Domenic procure a job at Pastene, but Domenic felt he had to first honor the deal he had made with Fratelli.

This meant working the worst of the day-labor jobs offered up by the Irish labor bosses with whom the padrones partnered. Italian day laborers had come to be called "day-o's" by the Irish, and that had evolved to "dago," a term Domenic would hear often in the two months it took to earn the money to pay Fratelli. Toward the end of one hot September day spent shoveling muck along the waterfront so pipes could be laid by the higher-paid Irish laborers, a man with a thick Irish brogue approached Domenic.

"I been watching ya for a couple days now, boy. You're a hard worker, smart too, according to Fratelli." The Irishman was huge, and it appeared that he would burst from the wool suit he wore at any moment. He was sweating and kept removing his straw hat and wiping his brow with the back of his forearm.

"I got a good deal going with the Navy over at the shipyard," he said, referring to the Boston Navy Yard in Charlestown, just across the Mystic River from the North End. "They be crankin' up over there 'cause of the war started in Europe and need more workers. Plus they been getting pressure from the neighborhood to hire more dagos, sorry boy, I mean *Italians*, seeing as the shipyard is pretty much surrounded by your type. But only good, reliable ones. I hear ya be comin' off Fratelli's books soon, and I can get ya in over there and you'll make some good money. Three times what you're making now even before Fratelli's take. But if you make me look bad I'll have your dago ass kicked. So what say you?"

His thick accent, along with Domenic's limited understanding of the English language, made it tough for Domenic to grasp everything he was saying. But he understood he was being offered a coveted shipyard job.

"I have to pay you like Fratelli?"

"One time. I won't be taking from your pay every day like that guinea bastard. I get paid legitimate from the Navy to find them good workers. You paying me is like a bonus. Like I said, the locals been complaining about no Italians getting jobs so I need to throw a few good ones at them. Everybody wins here, son. It's the American way."

"I'll tell you tomorrow, OK?" Domenic wanted to discuss this offer with Rossario.

"I'll give you the one day. But I know a thousand guineas who would leap at this so that's all you're gunna get."

***

After Domenic started at the Ropewalk in the shipyard and paid the Irishman, whose name he never learned, his $50 (most of it borrowed from Rossario who thought the shipyard was a great opportunity) he sent money home to his family in Torre de'Passeri for the first time. The feeling of satisfaction was immense. This was why he was here, and he imagined the feeling of pride his father and mother would have when they opened his letter. This was why he worked harder than anyone else in the Ropewalk, burning through a pair of gloves a week as he guided the stretched strands of yarn on to the machines and stacked heavy coils of rope that would find their way on to all types of Navy ships.

Just seventeen years old now, he couldn't believe his luck in not only finding a job so soon after arriving in Boston but finding one that opened up such possibilities for his future in America. The Boston Navy Yard was being modernized and expanded. A second huge dry dock was set to open as the Navy planned to make the country's oldest shipyard into a major supplier of Navy vessels. Even the old ropewalk that covered nearly a quarter mile had had its old steam boilers replaced by electricity and new equipment installed. There would be a need for skilled riggers, pipefitters, shipfitters, electricians, welders, carpenters, and there was talk of apprentice programs being established to meet the demand. Sure, the Irish would control access to the jobs, just as they seemed to control pretty much everything based on what Domenic had seen so far in Boston, but they would need men like Domenic willing to work long hours and do a good job at little pay so that the ward bosses would look good in the eyes of the Navy. This was why the Irish often worked with the Italian "padrones" to keep a pipeline filled with willing Italian workers.

Life in the Rossario home had taken on a comfortable routine. Domenic would leave for the shipyard each day at sunrise for the twenty-minute walk across the North End and over the Charlestown Bridge to the Navy Yard, returning at dusk to one of Maria's meals, usually pasta with an added ingredient culled from whatever she could buy cheaply at market that day. Although Rossario and the boys would arrive home much earlier, they always waited for Domenic before beginning their supper.

While Joseph attended the Saint John's Catholic School a block away, the Rossarios enrolled young Ermino at the public Eliot School as they could not afford to pay another tuition fee, small as it was. Saint John's was affiliated with the Sacred Heart Catholic Church across North Square, which was established in 1888 in what was once a Methodist bethel. It was founded by Italians who wanted to celebrate mass in their native Italian language, a practice prohibited at Saint Leonard's by the Archdiocese. It was where the Rossarios, and now Domenic and Ermino, worshipped, although Ermino was usually dragged along reluctantly.

Domenic came to love Sundays, the only day he did not work. These days consisted of a long high mass at Sacred Heart, after which he and Rossario would retire to the basement home of the Torre de'Passeri Society, one of some thirty such mutual aid societies in the North End formed by immigrants from different villages and towns in Italy. These societies were like second families where small dues were collected to be used to help members in times of special need. If a husband died, the society paid funeral expenses and provided the widow with a small amount of money. If a job was lost, money was used to purchase food. Some societies even had doctors on retainer for their members.

The societies were also where members celebrated special times together. Wedding showers, anniversaries, First Communions, Confirmations… The happy interludes in lives that for the most part consisted of long days spent simply trying to make it to the next long day. They were also where the men would meet for wine, card games, conversation, and bocce in a few of the larger clubs that had the space. After Sunday mass, the club was always packed, as the men gathered while the women went home to start the big Sunday meal. Domenic loved the camaraderie and the many stories and friendly arguments. He also loved the relative quiet of the Sunday streets thick with the smell of simmering tomato sauce as he walked home afterward.

Life in America was hard, but it was a life shared with others. And he was proud to now be able to pay his own dues to the society, provide some rent to the Rossarios, and send money home. He needed very little for himself, as he seldom went out with others his age, preferring to spend time being a big brother to Ermino and Joseph.

He felt he was where he was supposed to be.

1915

DOMENIC HEARD THE crack of the wooden bobbin snapping at the same instant he felt it hit his eye. The strand of fiber being stretched tight to make rope launched the piece of bobbin still attached to it with such speed that it knocked Domenic to the ground, and in the stunned instant before the pain set in a thousand thoughts ran through his mind. He could hear shouting and footsteps and workers speaking English too fast for him to comprehend, but he wasn't really trying. The panic that was setting in was not from the physical damage he knew he had suffered but rather from the effect this would have on his new job in the Ropewalk at the Boston Navy Yard. The fear of losing it was far more frightening than that of losing an eye. He refused to believe that God would bring him across an ocean and away from his family to have him fail. Someone pried his hands away from his eye and a piece of cloth was placed over it. His freed hands instinctively reached for the cross around his neck. He clutched it and prayed. Domenic continued to cling to it tightly as he felt himself being lifted and then carried.

"I will be fine! I will be back to work," he kept repeating as he held a wet towel pressed to his bloody eye on the way to Massachusetts General Hospital. He was first taken to the dispensary on the base, but the nurse there quickly had him put in a Navy vehicle and taken to the hospital. It was the first time Domenic had ever been in a car.

He could only think about keeping his job and keeping his promise to his family. The people he loved were counting on him. That was why he was here. He could not, would not become a burden to them instead. He asked God why he was being punished, and the thought that it might be because of Francesca entered his head. Then they were at the hospital.

He had been lucky. He left the hospital in two days with an ugly dead eye that would never see again. The doctor who treated him had recommended an enucleation and ocular prosthesis – removal of his old eye and insertion of a glass eye. But this was just cosmetic and Domenic had neither the time nor money to waste on his appearance. A patch would serve the purpose for now of protecting others from the sight of the black slit of an eye that always stared straight ahead, never working in conjunction with the good one.

Domenic was back at work at the Navy Yard in a week. It seemed inevitable that the United States would soon be entering the war that was raging in Europe, and the Navy was ramping up production of ships, needing every able worker. It was now all business at the Yard, and Domenic was a proven, reliable hard worker. His foreman welcomed him back to help the Ropewalk meet the increased production demands placed upon it. In a few months, Domenic was supervising three other workers, each of whom resented taking orders from a seventeen-year-old, one-eyed Italian immigrant who spoke broken English. Domenic's attitude did not help in his relations with his co-workers, none of whom were Italian. He was all business and never joined in any of the banter during the twenty-minute lunch. And he never stopped in the Blue Mermaid outside the gates after work for a drink. But they had to grudgingly respect his work ethic and attention to detail. He would do his own work and correct theirs without comment or criticism, And he never reported problems. It was hot, often dangerous work under steamy, tough conditions…and they knew they could depend on him.

As Domenic and so many of his fellow North Enders went about their business of building lives in their new country in 1915, they were oblivious to the powerful spheres of influence in Boston that were colliding in a battle to shape the future of the city – a future that would have a profound effect on their neighborhood and their ultimate assimilation into mainstream Boston.

The business, professional, and philanthropic leaders of the city were in a long-standing pitched battle with the Irish Democratic ward leaders and their heavy influence on government. City affairs were being directed from Irish Democratic clubhouses where the art of patronage ruled. The soaring costs of municipal contracts due to graft and kickbacks had resulted in increased taxes levied on business property.

In response, the Good Government Association was created by the social progressive Justice Louis Brandeis. It was comprised of the Associated Board of Trade, the Chamber of Commerce, the Merchants Association and the Boston Bar Association. In 1909, a member of this group, investment banker and philanthropist James W. Storrow, ran against John "Honey Fitz" Fitzgerald for mayor of Boston. Fitzgerald, the Irish ward boss for the North End, had lost the mayoral race in 1905 due to a major investigation authorized by the Republican-controlled state legislature into illegal city construction contracts. A result of that investigation was the formation of an independent Finance Commission to review city expenditures.

The Finance Commission, or FinCom as it came to be known, determined that ward-based city government resulted in inflated spending to create municipal jobs and capital projects made even more expensive due to graft and corruption. The solution was to recommend a strong mayor charter to dilute locally based, Irish-controlled city government. Ironically, in the hotly contested race between businessman Storrow and ward boss Fitzgerald, Fitzgerald prevailed. Fitzgerald, however, with his new four-year term and increased mayoral powers, showed a willingness to work with the reformers and build a spirit of cooperation between the public and private sectors for the good of the city.

That was why the 1914 mayoral race was pivotal. Fitzgerald's opponent was James Michael Curley, who had already served a term in prison for fraud and thrived on conflict and divisiveness. When he won the race for Mayor in 1914, he cast a heavy shadow of antagonistic politics over Boston that would last for forty years. He flaunted his power and acceptance of graft immediately by having city contractors build him a grand mansion his first year in office, an action that elicited a recall election he barely survived. He made it obvious that nothing would progress in Boston without the approval of, and profit to, the Irish political elite. And he had no intention of cooperating with those who would reform Boston.

Almost in concert with the rise of Curley was that of William Henry O'Connell, Archbishop and later Cardinal of the Archdiocese of Boston. Like Curley, he was the son of Irish immigrants, and like Curley he held the old Yankees, who he liked to refer to as "Puritans," in complete disdain. "The Puritan has passed. The Catholic remains," he once proclaimed publicly. "The child of the immigrant is called to fill the place that the Puritan has left." He too had no appetite for cooperation. He would take care of his flock, and anyone outside it be damned.

After a century of discrimination, the Irish now held the power in Boston, and it was in the hands of two men who made no bones about their intent to keep it and use it to their own ends. While the rift between the Irish and the Yankee would grow, so would that between the Irish and any other group that might come to challenge their power. Curley and his cronies passed a resolution that all city councilors would be elected "at large," meaning the voice of individual neighborhoods would be muted in city government by the Irish majority. This gave birth to a greater isolation of the newer immigrant groups in Boston. While all around Boston the Irish, Italians, Jews and Eastern Europeans were living side-by-side and assimilating into their communities, the city itself was doomed to tribal warfare under the iron grip of the Irish for decades to come.

What this served to do was make Domenic's North End community an isolated world unto itself, where Italians could be comfortable living their traditions, taking care of one another, and improving their own neighborhood. By 1930, there would be 44,000 people living in the North End, making it one of the densest communities in the world. Ninety-nine percent of this population was Italian. Ironically, it would also have the lowest crime rate in the city. It was a family, and every day he was there Domenic came to appreciate it more and more.

AUGUST 1915

FOR ERMINO, THE transition to life in America was not going well. He did not belong with the Rossarios, where he saw himself as an extra burden. He knew, although he was not supposed to, that Domenic paid Rossario additional room and board on his behalf. Little escaped Ermino.

No one seemed to understand that he was here to find his father, not to go to school or to church or to help out with all the projects in which Rossario tried to involve him. As much as he might want to be a part of this family, he knew he was not. Even though, at Joseph's suggestion, everyone now called him "Ernie," the Americanization of Ermino was going poorly. The Rossarios already had Joseph, who like his father seemed to effortlessly blend into the colorful fabric of the North End community. He hated belonging to nobody, but he hated people feeling sorry for him even more.

No one in the North End had ever heard of his father, Enzo Lentini. That meant he must be someplace else in America, and so he had to go someplace else to look for him. He would have to figure out how and where, but he would. In the meantime, there was no point in wasting time going to school. He needed to instead make some money for his travels. No one at the Eliot School seemed to care if he showed up or not. The school that had once educated Paul Revere as well as future governors, senators, and college presidents, was now a conduit from one world to another for many Italian immigrant children who lived in poverty and spoke little or no English.

There were many other children like Ermino who saw no point in wasting time in school. They felt trapped by their neighborhood and their language in a tiny world, while endless adventures and opportunities, or so it seemed, loomed beyond it. So they would skip school together often to try and take a little of the American dream for their own. Their petty thefts of produce from the carts around Quincy Market escalated into stealing crates of goods off the docks. Intelligent and fearless, Ermino was a natural leader in this world.

One day, while wandering through the bustling Quincy Market area with his friends, he noticed a basement window off an alley that was open but barred beneath a tobacco shop.

"Look at that," he said, pointing it out to his crew. "We'll come back after dark and I'll slip down there and hand out whatever I can."

"You can't fit between those bars! They're way too narrow."

"I can fit. We meet under T Wharf at midnight."

That night, they met as agreed and made their way to the shop. The window was still open. Then, to the surprise of everyone else, Ermino removed all his clothes, leaving only his underpants, and doused himself in olive oil. It was a cool September evening, but Ermino did not seem to mind. Then he slipped feet first between the bars and into the basement, barely squeezing through his head and shoulders.

At almost the same instant, two police officers turned into the alley and shouted at the boys, who ran off leaving Ermino stranded with no way out. The cops shined their lanterns into the basement, saw Ernie, and burst out laughing.

"Looks like we got ourselves a drowned, naked rat down there."

"Aye. Looks to be one of those little Eye-talian breeds."

"C'mon out, kid. You've got no place else to go," he called, reaching his hand down through the bars.

The cops took the now-shivering Ermino back to the Rossarios where they pounded on the door. The look on the sleepy face of Rossario quickly went from surprise to concern upon seeing the nearly naked Ermino to anger upon hearing the story from the officers.

"We suggest you keep a better eye on your lad."

"And try washing him in soap and water instead of oil from now on," the officer said with a huge guffaw.

His slippery escapade that night earned Ermino the nickname "l'anguilla." *The Eel*. It would stay with him the rest of his life.

***

Although others thought the story funny, to a proud Rossario who would rather die than see his good name shamed in any way, this was close to the last straw. It was important to him to protect his own reputation, the reputation of the neighborhood and that of all Italians. It was humiliating to him to be made fun of by the Irish cops. He was at his wits' end with Ermino. What kept Ermino from being kicked out of his home was the friendship that had emerged between him and Joseph, although Rossario sensed it was more adoration than friendship on Joseph's part.

Rossario had big dreams for Joseph. Inspired by George Scigliano, Rossario saw what a Boston Italian could accomplish despite an abundance of prejudice and a lack of influence. He might be uneducated and weak at English, but Joseph would be neither. And although he dreamt of becoming an American citizen, Joseph was born one. One day, Joseph would make his family, his neighborhood, and his nationality proud. The Italians of Boston would need a leader to fight for them in the halls of power, and he wanted Joseph to be that person.

Part of his education, his preparation, of Joseph was to have him work for someone he considered to be a leader of the North End community. James Donnaruma founded and published *La Gazetta del Massachusetts,* the only Italian language newspaper in Boston. He was a staunch advocate for the rights and treatment of Italian immigrants, and his newspaper was read by everyone. Joseph would deliver copies of the newspaper all over the North End each week.

His original intent in volunteering Joseph for this job was to expose him to the words and thoughts of Donnaruma. And in dropping off bundles of papers in the stores, societies and businesses of the North End, Joseph was getting to meet the community's *prominente*. But lately he saw the fact that this job pried him away from Ermino for a time as its most valuable benefit.

Rossario practiced what he preached about compassion and support for all who settled in the North End, and for this he was greatly admired and respected. Taking in Ermino was further proof of this. But family came first. If Ermino became a threat to Joseph's future, he would not hesitate to send him on his way.

***

Joseph watched the clock in the classroom tick ever so slowly toward three o'clock, hoping that Sister Claire would for once notice the time and release them promptly. It was not that Joseph did not like school, or Sister Claire for that matter, but he was an eleven-year-old boy filled with energy, daring thoughts, and a newfound sense of mischief that transcended the limitations of a parochial school classroom. He was, in the eyes of the nuns, an ideal student with excellent grades who was also respectful and religious. But after three o'clock, his adventurous spirit, neatly tucked away all day beneath his starched shirt, would be released and allowed to soar.

He would run from the school, shedding the moral shackles fostered by the Sisters of Saint Joseph along the way. Awaiting him was the marvelously unpredictable and exhilarating world of Ernie and his band. Where his world was one of rules – at home, in school, in church – the world of the streets had no rules. Although only slightly older than himself, Ernie was rapidly becoming a master of that world, and Joseph felt honored to be allowed to be part of it. While Joseph did his best to help Ernie navigate through the societal structure of *la famiglia*, on the streets Ernie was in charge and looked after Joseph as he would a little brother.

Occasionally the two would sneak out their bedroom window late at night, oftentimes just to walk the streets of the North End with no particular direction or plans for any type of mischief. The streets that were so alive and teeming with people during the day were now refreshingly quiet, and the two boys would simply walk and talk about the very different lives they lived under the same roof. The night exposed secrets that were hidden by the bustle of the day. They sometimes explored alleyways they had no idea existed. There was refuse around the warehouses and businesses that offered up treasures to two curious and adventurous boys. And some of the sights they witnessed around the taverns of the waterfront frequented by merchant sailors and a growing number of uniformed servicemen were an education unto themselves.

During their evening excursions, they would discuss things they dared not talk about even in the refuge of their room. Although they both liked and trusted Domenic, he was not sworn to the same unspoken *omerta* the two boys shared. Although he could be trusted to keep some things in confidence, if he knew of the worst of their escapades, particularly Ernie's, he would have to tell Rossario. Joseph lived with one foot in each of two separate and very different worlds, both of which he relished.

***

"Ermino, why do you keep doing these things?" Domenic asked pleadingly. After the "eel" incident, Rossario had asked him to speak with Ermino. Domenic felt responsible having brought Ermino into the house and wanted nothing more than for the boy to stop creating problems.

"My name is Ernie. You should know that, Dom. I am the little American Ernie that no one can claim. I do not have papers, I do not have a family, I do not have a past. I just magically appeared."

Domenic gave Ermino a stern look and said nothing. Like Rossario, he was growing weary of the burden of constantly worrying about what Ermino might do next. Ermino, for his part, took note. Domenic was not prone to speaking without purpose. Nor was he prone to showing his emotions, a rarity among Italians as far as Ermino could tell. So an angry look and a lecture from Domenic, a person to whom he owed much, would be borne with as much respect as he could muster for anyone or anything.

"Sorry, Dom."

"Sorry Dom, sorry Dom. It's always sorry Dom with you, Ermino. If you were so sorry you would stop so I could relax for once and not worry that one day I will come home from work to learn you're in jail or dead."

Ermino almost said "Sorry, Dom" again but thought better of it. Instead he remained silent. Had this been anyone else lecturing him, his natural reaction would be to give the *"Ma chi se ne frega"* *(I don't care)* gesture by flicking his chin in an outward motion with his fingertips and walking away. But he respected Domenic more than he had ever respected anyone.

"If you don't like the school, you can go to the North Bennett School and learn a good trade. Rossario will get you a spot there… You listening to me?"

"No. I mean, yes, I'm listening to you, but I don't need a school."

"You stupido! I wish I had a school. I wish I had a chance like you to learn good English and a trade and be somebody. I work and work and work, and I will always work, but I do it for others. You do nothing for nobody but yourself. When people help you, instead of saying *grazie*, you say *vaffanculo*. What is wrong with you?"

"I don't know!" screeched Ermino, startling Domenic. Tears began to appear in the corners of his eyes. "I don't know what is wrong with me! I don't fit here. I didn't fit in Napoli. I don't fit anywhere. And I don't know why. You tell me, Domenic. You tell me what's wrong with me, and I'll fix it."

With that he walked away. He did not like anyone to see him cry.

***

Gaspare Messina arrived in the North End from New York in 1913 and opened a bakery on Prince Street similar to the one he had run in Brooklyn. He did not come to Boston, however, to bake bread. He came to serve as the *capo* of the fledging Sicilian Mafia in New England. Prior to his arrival, criminal activity among the Italian population was unorganized and perpetrated by unassociated gangsters of all types. They preyed on their innocent countrymen with rackets and intimidation, still practicing the crude craft of Black Hand extortion. Killings from feuds and vendettas among the criminal element were not uncommon.

Messina quickly brought order, structure, and, in a perverse way, honor to Italian criminal enterprise in Boston and beyond. When a prominent North Ender, Gaspare DiCola was murdered at the front door of his home in the North End after he did not respond to a Black Hand extortion letter, the two perpetrators were later found with their throats slit under an abandoned pier. Notice had been served by Messina that it would not be business as usual anymore.

From his bakery, and later from the G. Messina and Company wholesale grocery business on Prince Street, Messina oversaw a burgeoning crime empire. It involved many old and disparate tentacles – extortion, protection rackets, gambling, heists, bribes, prostitution – but it became an organized business. And Messina became its president and CEO. At the same time, he became a benefactor and protector of the community. If you did business with Messina and the Boston

Mafia, it was on his terms and by his rules. If you chose not to, you had nothing to fear.

The short, stocky Messina, who sported thick glasses and looked more like an unassuming accountant than a Mafia *capo*, was often seen around the neighborhood with his wife and four children. After his arrival, random violence and crime gradually abated in the North End. The Irish gangs began to focus elsewhere, and elements of the Boston Police Department realized a new revenue stream by agreeing to look the other way for a price.

***

Cologero Dragatto sat nervously in the office of the president of the Banca Etorre Forte. He was leveraged to the maximum and was asking for more. He now owned three trucks that were delivering fresh fish all over Boston and beyond every day. He also had a fish market in a storefront he rented right by the Fish Pier in South Boston, steps from where he stepped off the *Cretic* with his new bride just over a year ago. He had built upon his relationships with the Italian fishermen by guaranteeing he would meet or beat the going rate for every catch. He would pay a little more and sell it for a little less and make it up in volume. His fishermen were happy, and his customers were happy, but to do the volume his plan required he needed more trucks, and soon. The Bonfiglio family back in Sicily was growing weary of waiting for the return on their investment he had promised.

He had not anticipated all the expenses his clever business plan would incur. The money was flowing in, but too much was also flowing right out. Besides the loan payments, there was the huge cost of ice every day, the gasoline and maintenance of the trucks, the wages for his drivers, the rent on his store – it all added up. Then there were the "unofficial" costs. He provided financial backing to help form the Del Soccorso Di Sciacca Society in the North End to ingratiate himself with the Sicilian fishermen. Although not a religious man, he saw the advantage of helping to honor their patron saint, the Madonna del Soccorso, and each year he was recognized at the huge feast honoring the Madonna. Soon after opening his store, he was visited by some Irish thugs demanding regular payments to operate his store in their neighborhood. Then he had to pay the Irish police to protect him from the Irish thugs. He had been threatened numerous times by fellow Italians claiming to be members of La Mano Nera. He despised them even more than the Irish for turning on their own countrymen – lowlifes who preyed upon hardworking Italians who had made something of themselves. Now it appeared he might have to pay Gaspar Messina to end those threats.

But it was all part of doing business. In the end, he would have the money to control these nuisances and have the type of life he had promised Francesca in America. For her part, she had been everything he had hoped for and more, the beautiful wife who everybody adored. In the neighborhood, she was involved in everything, befitting the wife of a prominent businessman like himself. She turned out to be a wonderful cook and kept a spotless home in the new four-family apartment building where they lived. Most astoundingly though was her business acumen. She had proven to be a valuable and trusted advisor. She ran the store efficiently, and all the customers loved her. The only thing missing in their relationship was love…and passion. But he was a businessman, and all-in-all the marriage could be labeled a successful transaction.

Alfredo "Al" Bonnasaro, the president of the bank sitting across from Cologero was also nervous. His was one of several immigrant banks in the North End begun in the back of another business, in this case a grocery store. Notoriously unregulated, oftentimes these banks would go out of business along with the hard-earned deposits of their customers. George Scigliano had made regulation of these banks a priority during his brief time in the Massachusetts legislature. Bonnasaro was basically an honest albeit greedy man, but he was a grocer, not a banker, and for the amount of money Dragotto wanted to borrow he would have to go to one of the Yankee private banks on State Street and split the interest income with them. But he would be responsible should Dragotto default on the loan.

"Cologero, you already owe this bank over three thousand dollars."

"Yes. And have I ever missed a payment, Al?"

"No, but another two thousand is a great risk for my small bank. I would have to ask for more interest than you are now paying."

"On the new loan?"

"On the entire balance of all your loans."

"Ma cosa dici! *I don't believe it*," responded Cologero, pressing his hands together as if in prayer and rocking them up and down. "We are friends. Don't I have my man drop off the thickest cod of the catch every week right to your doorstep? You arrive home, and your beautiful wife, who is friends with my own lovely Francesca, has your favorite meal of fresh fish cooked in oil with tomatoes and green peppers waiting for you."

Bonnasaro could taste the delicious cod. "Okay, Cologero. I will charge you the higher interest only on the new money."

"Ahh, my friend Al. You're making so much money off me now. Why do you need to make more? I tell you what. At this year's feast for the Madonna del Soccorso, we are honoring the most outstanding members of the community. As the most respected banker in the North End, you should be so deservedly honored. And I will personally see it done."

Bonnasaro could see right through the bribe aimed at his ego but still liked the idea. He didn't know that Cologero had made the same offer to many others from whom he sought favors. There would be a long line of honorees at this year's feast.

"Okay, okay, Cologero. The interest stays the same."

"Then let us make it four thousand dollars."

"Four thousand!"

"Yes, I have my eye on the perfect spot for a restaurant."

***

Domenic walked into the Rossario apartment near midnight after working a double shift and was surprised to see all the lights on and Maria in her nightgown pacing the living room.

"Oh, Domenic, thank God you're home." She rushed to him and gave him a hug.

"What's wrong?"

"Joseph and Ernie are missing."

"Missing?"

"Giuseppe went into your room long after they went to bed, and they weren't there. He is out looking for them now."

Domenic felt a rush of guilt. He knew Joseph and Ermino would sometimes sneak out. He had heard them coming and going and had asked them several times to stop, threatening to tell Rossario. But they were in a way both his little brothers and his closest friends. And friends did not tell on friends.

"I'm sure they're fine," he said. "I'll go out and look around the neighborhood."

He set out in the direction of the waterfront, which he thought would offer the greatest allure for two young boys bent on mischief. Domenic did not frequent the taverns favored by the seamen and the more unsavory elements of the community, preferring instead the familial comfort of the Society clubhouse.

Walking south along the waterfront minutes later, Domenic heard some voices through the darkness coming from under the pilings of an abandoned creaky pier near the Long Wharf. As he approached, he recognized little Joseph's voice but its tone sent a shudder through Domenic, and he broke into a run. He leapt down from the dock and saw Joe and Ermino with three older boys. One was holding Joseph while the other two were beating Ermino.

"I'll be teaching you a lesson, you little guinea bastard," a high-pitched squeak of a voice screamed out. As one held Ermino, the owner of the voice swung what looked like a piece of wood directly at Ermino's head. The object shattered as it glanced off Ermino's shoulder before striking his head and dropping him to the ground.

"Stop it, you. Stop!" yelled Domenic in English. The three turned and looked at Domenic. Joseph turned toward Domenic with panic in his eyes. Ermino was on the wet rocky ground groaning, and all three of the assailants glared at Domenic. "Get out of here, wop," said one with a hint of an Irish accent. "This ain't none of your business. We're having some business with this one." He pointed to Ermino.

"Help us, Dom. They're going to kill him," screamed Joseph. "They said they're going to kill him."

"Get lost wop, or you're dead too."

"Leave them alone." As frightened as he was, Domenic's voice was calm.

"You can have this one," said the ringleader, pointing to Joseph, but that one's a dead wop. He stole from us and he's got to pay."

Domenic had never been in a fight in his life. In the increasing darkness under the pier, he found it difficult to see with his one good eye. His work boots were slipping on the wet rocks, and he was petrified with a putrid feeling of fear that had his whole body shaking. But he never hesitated. He kept coming, his fists reflexively clenched. The two boys who had been beating Ermino and who looked to be about fourteen or fifteen years old started toward Domenic.

They all stopped and glared at one another with the two boys circling Domenic like wolves surrounding their prey. Then the one who had wielded the stick rushed at Domenic and tried to tackle him. At the same instant, Domenic swung an arm muscled from pulling rope ten hours a day and delivered his fist to the side of the ringleader's head. There was a loud crack, and the boy yelped. At the same time, the second boy leapt at Domenic and brought him to the ground. All three grappled on the wet, rocky sand. Domenic had the advantage of being stronger and bigger, but there were two of them. Finally, with all three near exhaustion, they had Domenic pinned to the ground. Then the ringleader reached for a rock and held it above Domenic.

"I warned ya, wop." Suddenly he was struck from behind by a piece of wood. He fell to the ground clutching his head. Ermino was up and wanted blood.

Seeing the numbers now turned against them, the two other boys ran off as Ermino got ready to deliver a second blow to his tormentor. But Domenic screamed, "Arresto, Ermino!" He kicked at him from the ground, knocking him down. He then kneeled over the boy, who was clutching the side of his face where Ermino had struck him. Blood was pouring from between his fingers.

"Let me kill the dirty mick bastard, Domenic," screamed Ermino.

"No, get away!" Domenic took off his shirt and wrapped it around the boy's head.

"Ernie, listen to Domenic," pleaded Joe, his voice and body both shaking. "We have to get away from here. Let's go home." He put an arm around Ernie and took the piece of wood he held away from him.

Ernie's face was swollen and bruised where he had been struck by the boy, who was now crying and moaning on the ground. Luckily the driftwood was rotten and porous or Ermino would likely be dead.

"Joseph, you two go home. I have to get this one to a doctor."

Minutes later, Domenic was half carrying the Irish boy toward Quincy Market when he spied a policeman. "Help," he shouted, "my friend has been hurt." The cop came running over and looked down at the boy, who Domenic had sat down on the sidewalk, still clutching his head.

The cop knelt down, unwrapped the shirt, and looked at the ugly wound. "Saints alive, ain't you Brendan O'Riley's boy?" He looked up to ask Domenic what had happened, but he was gone.

* * *

The fight was the last straw for Rossario. Ermino had to go. There was an organization called the New England Home for Little Wanderers that had its roots in the North End going back to 1865 when it was formed to help children left orphaned and homeless by the Civil War. The Home had just opened a new building across Boston, and Rossario felt this was the ideal spot for Ermino – away from his cohorts in the North End. Now thirteen years old, Ermino would be one of the older children at the home, which worked aggressively to find real homes for their orphans, sometime sending them by orphan train as far away as the Midwest. Rossario hoped that Ermino would find his way onto one of those trains.

For his part, Domenic knew this was the best thing for Ermino. While Rossario remained shaken over what might have happened to Joseph that night, Domenic was haunted by the image of Ermino crumbling under the blow to his head. He thought then that Ermino was dead, and he was sure now that he soon would be if he kept down the path he was following. In his heart, though, he knew that no orphanage would be able to contain "The Eel."

Joseph was also shaken that night. He felt like the moth who had been dazzled by the flame and was lucky not to have flown into it. He had enjoyed the taste of danger with Ernie, but he lost his appetite for it that night under the pier. Thank God for Domenic. He still loved Ernie like a brother and always would. Thanks to Ernie, he now knew that he had it in him to go outside the rules if needed, but he would be more careful in the future about how he did it. So gaining revenge against those dirty Irish pigs who were ready to kill over a few stolen pieces of copper might take a while.

Domenic went with Rossario across town to Huntington Avenue to deliver Ermino to the orphanage. Little was said on the streetcar. When they arrived, he was amazed at how large and spotless the recently opened building was. Its huge four-story brick façade was impressive, and he had never seen floors so shiny. The building epitomized a history in Boston of wealthy Yankee Protestant efforts to support the downtrodden of the city. There was no shortage of agencies with the noble effort of improving the lot of the unfortunate, particularly the poor, ignorant immigrants who washed up on Boston's shores. These immigrants might not be welcomed into their homes, neighborhoods, clubs, offices, or banks, but the Christian thing to do was to save them from themselves. This assistance often came with lessons in Protestant religion and morals.

After Ermino was delivered into the hands of an efficient, stern-faced woman at the orphanage, he turned to walk away down a long corridor leading to the dormitories without saying a word. He then suddenly stopped, turned, and ran back to Domenic and threw his arms around him in a strong embrace.

"I'm sorry I let you down, Domenic. I'll never forget what you did for me. Never."

***

6:30 PM
NOVEMBER 7, 1951

THE TWO MEN sat in silence in the overstuffed leather chairs in Ernie Lentini's study. Not a word had passed between them for nearly an hour. Domenic had turned his chair to face out one of the two windows overlooking the long driveway that split the expansive front lawn and ended in a circle at the house. Ernie would occasionally get up, stretch, and walk about the room. But Domenic simply sat and stared out the window, barely moving and seemingly oblivious to Ernie's presence. The light from the lampposts nearest the house illuminated a portion of Domenic's face as he watched and waited. To Ernie, it seemed like a death mask set in hard resolve with only the sadness of the eyes offering any sign of life behind it. Dominic barely blinked as he looked off trancelike into the growing darkness.

Ernie decided to stand once again, placing both hands on his knees and rising slowly with a soft grunt. He had hoped the sound would at least elicit a glance from Domenic, but apparently it was not strong enough to penetrate the heavy barrier of history Domenic had dragged into the house and planted firmly between them. It signified there would be no discussion, no compromise.

After stretching his back, Ernie walked to the second window of the study, pulled back the drapes, and looked out. He cast a quick sideways glance at Domenic, as though even looking at his old friend would violate the unspoken rules that had been set. While still gazing into the night and without turning, he said, "It's not too late, Domenic. I can take care of this. You don't have to be involved. I swear to you the result, in the end, will be the same."

Domenic said nothing, not that Ernie expected him to. They had covered this ground before. "Please, Dom, I beg you…"

Domenic replied without looking at Ernie, "This is about family, Ermino. You should understand."

To Domenic, he would always be Ermino, never Ernie and definitely never The Eel, a nickname Domenic had always despised. In a way, it was comforting. It had been so long since he had been simply Ermino, and it reminded him of a very different time. An all-too-fleeting time, it seemed to Ernie, when the future was still a hopeful, mysterious place waiting to be explored.

"Why should I understand?" he replied. "Where is my family? You think these pagliacci around me are family? They are soldiers, mercenaries—they're not family. You, you have family, which is exactly why you should leave this to me."

"You understand family, Ermino, or we wouldn't be here now."

"Bah, you're just a crazy old man," muttered Ernie, even as he accepted the truth of Domenic's words without acknowledging them. Then he made one last attempt at changing his mind. "So you think this will be an easy thing to do? An easy thing to live with?"

"I don't know. Why don't you tell me?" Spoken calmly but laden with the same steely anger that Ermino had come to know so well over the years. Ernie had faced the uncontrolled wrath of furious, vicious men, but somehow he always found the quiet, controlled anger of this peaceful man to be more chilling.

"Oh, so you think this is something I do all the time?"

"Having others do it for you is the same thing."

Ernie felt his own rush of anger but quickly forced it aside and shook his head in surrender. No sense pushing any further. Things might be said that best remain unsaid. There was no need, and now was certainly not the time to enter the caverns of the past. Besides, he had never won an argument with Domenic and knew he never could. Maybe no one could. Domenic saw things in black and white with no acknowledgement of shades of gray. So being right was always easy for him.

Then Domenic spoke again slowly and quietly, almost as though talking to himself, "I can live with it. I could never live with doing nothing."

Accepting the inevitable, Ernie walked over to the desk, opened a drawer, and took out the small handgun he kept there. As he was handing *it to Domenic, lights appeared in the driveway. "That would be O'Riley," he said with resignation. Then, businesslike, "Here, the safety is off. You just point and squeeze the trigger."*

Domenic took the weapon without a word.

***

SEPTEMBER 1917

THE FEAST OF Madonna del Soccorso, or the Fisherman's Feast as it had come to be called, was held in September. In the four years since it began, it had grown to become the largest celebration of the year in the North End. Streets were decorated for blocks extending in every direction from the Fisherman's Club at the corner of North and Fleet Streets. Vendors and stores from all over the North End set up stands along the streets, selling all manner of food and goods. The societies were all represented with their colors, and bands played almost continuously for two days. It was as close as the neighborhood came to a day of thanksgiving when everyone came out to greet neighbors and enjoy the familial spirit of their cramped but vibrant neighborhood.

Maria Rossario walked with her arm locked in Domenic's. Joseph and Rossario walked in front of them side by side, constantly stopping to seemingly greet everyone in the crowd. If Domenic had been like a son to the Rossarios before, since saving Joseph from the "Irish monsters" he was more like a saint. Every time Joseph told the story, Domenic's heroics increased. "They were about to bash both our heads in when Domenic came running up and knocked down all three of them…" was the latest version being told.

"Domenic, come here," called Rossario. "I want you to meet James Donnaruma."

Domenic, of course, knew who Donnaruma was. Everyone knew the popular newspaper publisher. "Rossario tells me you work at the Navy Yard and are doing well there. I wish we could have more from our neighborhood get some of the good jobs they have to offer, and I thank you for representing our family there so well."

He had said *"our family,"* and Domenic knew he truly meant it. "Grazie, Signor Donnaruma."

"Please, call me James. And speak English. Not speaking their language is the greatest obstacle to overcome if we are ever to gain the respect of this city." Then he immediately went on bantering in Italian with Rossario.

A short, meticulously dressed man approached the group. His suit fit his stocky build perfectly, and an expensive-looking pin held his tie in place. Rossario placed a hand on Joseph's back, directing him toward Maria. "Go keep your mother company."

"Rossario, James, good to see you both. What an inspiring day this is. This celebration of the Madonna is finer than any we had in Brooklyn." He then offered his hand to Domenic by way of introduction. "I do not believe we have met. I am Gaspare Messina."

"Domenic Bassini."

"Ahh, you are the famous savior of children. I understand you rescued Rossario's son and another boy from a gang of thugs."

"I think the story has become much greater than the truth," replied Domenic, who was always uncomfortable talking about the incident... or himself. He of course knew who Gaspare Messina was. Everyone knew who he was. He also knew neither Rossario nor Donnaruma cared much for him.

"We are grateful to Domenic, and I think my boy Joseph learned a valuable lesson about the type of people he should associate with," interjected Rossario in a tone that added more meaning to his words.

Gaspare looked straight at Rossario. "Of course. And perhaps he also learned that sometimes it is not always a fair fight. When the odds are against you, it is good to have the, uh, how should I say it, *muscle* of someone like Domenic to protect you. Unfortunately, there are those in this world who will not stop nibbling at you until you show them you can bite back."

"Let us hope that today there will be no nibbling or biting, unless it is of one of Regina Molinaro's cannolis," interrupted Donnaruma, steering the conversation in another direction. "I know she has them for sale outside her building. Today is a day to celebrate all we have here in our neighborhood. We can discuss all that we do not have another day –

although I am afraid we might need more than one day to go through that list."

Messina smiled. "You are right as always, James. This is why *La Gazetta dei Massachusetts* is the respected voice of our neighborhood. Its publisher is a wise man. I leave you all to Mrs. Molinaro's cannolis." With that he gave a polite nod to the group while his fingers brushed the rim of his hat and took his leave.

"Figlio di puttana." *Son of a bitch.* Rossario nearly spat out the words under his breath as Messina walked away.

"He may be," responded James. "But to me he is not as bad as some of our other countrymen who prey only on their own kind, the padroni, *La Mano Nera, or* the Galleanists who cause everyone to distrust Italians. At least Messina builds his dark empire only on the backs of anyone foolish enough to do business with him."

"How can you say that, my friend? He lends money at exorbitant rates to those who are desperate, and when they cannot pay he takes all they have or forces them to commit crimes for him. And when they get caught, he is protected and they go to jail. We have seen the wives and daughters of people we know working in his whorehouse along the waterfront. He controls the lottery with every society forced to pay him a percentage. Not to mention that anyone who defies Messina's *Mafioso* ends up dead or missing."

"Mostly true, but in many ways he has made our neighborhood safer. Gangs from outside the North End do not come around anymore to prey on innocents. The police do not harass us as much, and even the anarchists fear him. I think that, maybe, it's not so bad for now to have an Italian who commands…" James searches for the right word. "…*consideration* by others who would make their own plans for us."

"You yourself refused to sell him an interest in your newspaper."

"Yes, I did. And he accepted that and leaves me alone, although the new printing press he offered to buy was a beauty. He advertises his business with us and that is appreciated. All the churches and the causes to which he gives money appreciate it too."

As usual, Domenic listened, adding little. To him, anyone stupid enough to go to Messina for anything – whether for a loan, a job, protection, a bet, a woman – deserved what might follow. If you did not take the enticing bait, you avoided the hook.

Domenic and Rossario took leave of Donnaruma to rejoin Maria and Joseph, and the four slowly continued meandering down the crowded street, greeting friends, sampling foods, and stopping to listen to bands and musicians. Soon the statue of the Madonna, which was making its way around the streets festooned with ribbons to which money could be pinned, would return to the center of activities outside the Fisherman's Society. There everyone would gather to hear from a series of speakers.

***

When he first saw Francesca walking toward him arm-in-arm with a beaming Cologero, he barely recognized her. The simple clothing she had worn during the crossing was replaced by a beautiful, bright stylish dress. She wore makeup that made her appear even more attractive than he remembered. Cologero for his part, despite the handsome suit, was still an ugly bastard, thought Domenic. He was hugging everyone he encountered as though they were a long lost relative, reminding Domenic of the first time he met Cologero on the dock in Napoli.

Amico di tutti e di nessuno e tutt'uno, thought Domenic. *A friend to all and a friend to none is one and the same.* He tried to avoid the couple, but Francesca caught his gaze, smiled, and came toward him, half-dragging the preoccupied Cologero by the arm.

"My dear, dear Domenic, how are you?" The Rossarios seemed surprised to see the two knew each other. Francesca hugged Domenic then stepped backed and put a hand on the side of his head next to his eyes patch. "I heard about your accident. I am so sorry." She held his glance for a long moment and then turned to Cologero. "Look who it is, our friend Domenic."

Domenic could see that Cologero had no idea who he was. He was a man practiced at remembering the names of anyone who could help him, as well as their children's names, but Domenic was someone of no significance to him, and so he had been eliminated from his memory. Francesca, seeing this too, added, "From the crossing."

Cologero slowly smiled and said, "Of course, I called you… Sparrow! Tell me, are you still a sparrow, or have you been seduced by the wonders of America?" He glanced toward the Rossarios and smiled.

Domenic then introduced them all, avoiding the question. Rossario knew of Dragotto by reputation but had never met him.

"Domenic was a great comfort to me during the crossing," explained Francesca. "I shall never forget the kindness he showed the both of us." She cast a glance at Cologero, which commanded him to confirm this.

"Yes, yes. Young Sparrow here was a good friend. Helpful in all ways."

It appeared to Domenic that Francesca's plan had come to fruition. She clearly had the mighty Cologero Dragotto wrapped tightly around her lovely little finger.

"Sparrow, I like that," chimed in Joseph. "I think I'll call you that from now on."

Everybody laughed at that, and after a few pleasantries Cologero indicated that he and Francesca must get to the Fisherman's Society for the festivities, reminding everyone that he was expected to say a few words.

As they left, Francesca again reached out to touch Domenic's cheek. "I am so sorry."

Maria gave Rossario a sideways look at this, but he was oblivious. *Stupid men*, she thought. Any woman could see that Francesca was talking about more than Domenic's injured eye.

***

"So, Domenic, what would your answer have been?" asked Rossario as they walked toward the makeshift stage set up outside the Fisherman's Society.

Domenic gave him a quizzical look.

"Have you fallen in love with America, or do you still plan to return to Torre de'Passeri someday?"

"I don't know," he answered honestly.

"As much as I find your friend Dragotto a bit of a stronzo *asshole*, I agree with him. There is so much more we can have here than back in Torre, I think. If not us, then our children for sure."

When they arrived at the stage, there was already a group of the North End's *prominente* gathered on it. The statue of the Madonna was on the stage too, as was a band whose members all wore red, white, and green sashes.

Dragotto was speaking, introducing the men standing on the stage who had so generously contributed to the feast to support all the good work undertaken by the society. Among them stood the banker Bonnasaro and Gaspare Messina. When he introduced Messina, the Sicilian from Brooklyn made a grand gesture of waving a hundred dollar bill in the air, which he then pinned onto the statue. Many in the crowd applauded.

"Penso che sto per vomitare," said Rossario. *I think I am going to throw up.*

***

Later that evening, Domenic walked home alone after enjoying some wine and cards at the Torre de'Passeri Society. The club was one big room in the basement of a building with a butcher shop on the first floor and apartments above. There was a makeshift bar and mismatched tables and chairs set about. But the warmth and comfort Domenic felt there belied the spartan nature of the club. This was like being among family.

While he walked, he thought of Francesca and their meeting that day. He had long wondered what he might say, what she might say, the first time they spoke. He had seen her on occasion and had avoided her, but he could not avoid the surge of burning emotions it always brought.

Although he might go for days and even months without thinking of her, the simplest of reminders – a foghorn from a ship, a glimpse of raven hair, one of Dragotto's trucks – would bring it all back. And when she did enter his thoughts, he no longer felt only the bad emotions – the guilt, the shame, the pain – but the pleasurable ones as well. When other young men would boast of their conquests, he would think to himself that if he were to ever describe what went on behind a lifeboat between him and the beautiful young wife of Cologero Dragotto, he would be the envy of them all. But the important thing was that he force himself to accept that their lives would never intertwine again.

When he arrived home, Maria greeted him warmly. Joseph was in bed, and Rossario was still at the club.

"So, my surprising Domenic, tell me abut you and Francesca Dragotto."

"I don't know what you mean." But the blush gave him away. "We were friends on the crossing. That's all. How could you think such a thing?"

"Friends, huh? Is she the one who spoiled you for other women? I wondered why you resist all the girls who shamelessly flirt with you. So many mothers asking about you for their daughters." She was teasing him now. "It is good to know that you are not one of those men who is only fond of other men."

"I'm tired. I'm going to bed."

***

A few days later, Domenic was walking home from the shipyard oblivious to the police car following behind him. But as he walked along Commercial Street, it slowly pulled up beside him, and the passenger window rolled down, causing his heart to skip a beat and anxiety to take hold. But he kept walking until he heard, "Dago, get in we want to talk to you."

The cop on the front passenger side got out and opened the door to the backseat. Domenic was scared and confused. He wanted to ask "Why, what did I do?" but the glare on the policeman's face and the hand on the nightstick told him that there was no room for discussion. He got it in. Sitting in the back seat was a big, ruddy-faced cop who stared straight ahead and did not even cast a glance at Domenic. The door closed behind him, the first cop got back in, and the car drove off without anyone saying another word. Domenic was totally petrified. He tried to think of a reason why he was there and could think of only one.

***

Police Lieutenant Brendan O'Riley was tired. He felt as though he had been fighting someone or something all fifty-six years of his life and he was tired. Born in Ireland, he fought for food handed out by the bosses after coming to America at the age of six with his parents and then liter-

ally fought for money in any prizefighting match he could find, earning a reputation for toughness and perseverance. You might beat him, but you could never get him to quit.

He fought the Yankees and their prejudices. He saw the way they looked at him evolve from disgust to fear, and he preferred the fear. And now they needed the Italians to fear them.

He fought to get a job on the force by doing the jobs for the ward bosses that others didn't have the stomach for, like scaring poor families from their dump of an apartment so the building owner would have no rental income and no choice but to sell to the "right" buyer at a rock-bottom price. He fought for his share of the take as a cop. Of course he did. But he could have taken much more, like a lot of the other greedy sons of bitches who didn't give a shit about the police force. Now he was fighting the younger cops who wanted to form a union. They didn't want to pay their dues, like he had. Like all of the others had. They wanted to upset the applecart that the older cops had built and stocked.

And he was fighting his youngest son, Colin. He had three daughters before the Lord saw fit to reward him with his first son, Kevin. He sometimes would think he should have quit then but would immediately regret having such a thought and beg the Lord for forgiveness. Colin reminded him of himself, always angry, always ready to fight. But he didn't have to. His older son Kevin had taken what Brendan had earned for his family from a life of fighting and flourished. But maybe because of Kevin, who displayed the great gift of promise, or maybe because of himself who was respected and feared in equal measure throughout South Boston, Colin felt the need to make his own name. It didn't help that Colin inherited both his own coarse looks and his temper, while Kevin had the handsome delicate features of their mother as well as her quick mind and even temperament. What he inherited from neither was their acceptance of hard work. So the only way for Colin to stand out was by breaking rules, because playing by them would get him nowhere.

* * *

O'Riley sized up the poor one-eyed guinea kid sitting petrified in the backseat of the cruiser next to him. He was a good judge of character, and this kid was no punk. Poor bastard probably just wanted what most wanted, what he wanted fifty years ago when he arrived here with his family. A chance. But they needed to keep the heavy yoke of fear around the Italians' necks to keep them from standing up. So far they had been successful. Despite their smaller numbers. The Irish still controlled the politics and policing of the North End, and hence the power. The Italians couldn't have what the Irish had earned. That was part of his job. He would take it easy on this kid, but the poor kid would never know that.

Without a word and without even turning, Brendan Riley swung a backhanded clenched fist that caught Domenic squarely under his chin. Domenic gasped and choked. He felt blood in his mouth. Then he heard the big cop speak slowly, calmly.

"My name is Brendan O'Riley. Lieutenant Brendan O'Riley. You remember that. That was my boy Colin you beat on the other night. I'm only letting you live because I'm a cop, not a killer. Besides, if I kill you, it only makes more work for the detectives who don't like to waste their time investigating dead guineas. But you'll never lay a hand on my son or any other Irishman in this city again, or I will kill ya. And no one but your stinkin' whore of a guinea mother will care."

Now he turned toward Domenic for the first time. "Do you understand me, you stupid fuckin' wop?" he asked with as much anger in his voice and fury in his eyes as he could muster. It had the desired effect on Domenic, who feared for his life despite the cop's claim that he wasn't going to kill him. But before Domenic could answer, O'Riley drove a practiced left hand into Domenic's stomach below his chest as hard as he could. Domenic felt the air rush out of his body and couldn't breathe.

"I said, do you understand me?" A right hand hit Domenic's mouth before he could answer, carefully avoiding his patch-covered eye.

Domenic brought his hands up over his head and pulled up his knees to protect himself. But he didn't cry out and didn't beg. To O'Riley, it was as though he accepted the need for punishment and would bear it the best he could. Brave kid. He held his hand out to the officer in the front seat, who handed him his billy club without a word. He swung the club across Domenic's forearms as they protected his face. *That'll leave a nice little bruise but do no real harm,* he thought.

Then he stopped and nodded to the cop in the front to get out and open the door. The cop gave a surprised look that said *"that's it?"* but complied. O'Riley then swung up his legs, braced his back against his door and literally kicked Domenic to the curb. He leaned out the door and his last words to Domenic were laced with venom, "If I ever have to come lookin' for ya again for any reason, I'll kill ya, and no one will ever find ya worthless body." Then he slammed the door shut.

As they drove off, the driver remarked to O'Riley, "Getting a little soft in your old age ain't you, Brendan?"

***

On the sidewalk, his face, his forearms, and his stomach all throbbing, Domenic was at first relieved. It was over, and he knew he would be okay. Then he was angry. He was angry at Ermino, angry at the Irish cops, and angry at himself for being stupid. He cursed the day he met Ermino and cursed himself for bringing him into America and the Rossario home. He cursed America for being so unfair that he could be beaten by a police officer with no choice but to accept it. This was supposed to be the land of promise and opportunity. But the promises were lies. Then he made himself his own promise. He promised he would never again do anything to jeopardize himself and his obligation to his family. And he prayed to God while clutching the cross around his neck to give him the wisdom and the strength to keep that promise.

DECEMBER 1917

MUCH TO ROSSARIO'S constant consternation, Domenic kept to the promise he made to himself to focus on only the essential things in his life and avoid anything that might keep him from them. This consisted of work, saving money, family, and more work. It left little time for fun beyond the few hours a week he spent at the society, and no time to get involved with Rossario, Donnaruma, and others in battling all the injustices they saw heaped upon North End Italians.

He was now twenty years old and, if Maria was to be believed, a handsome man who could have his choice of any number of young women in the North End. His hard work in the Ropewalk had been rewarded with a cherished apprenticeship in the electrical department of the shipyard. He would have settled for a sheet metal or pipefitting apprenticeship but instead was recommended for the highly coveted electrical apprenticeship where he absorbed his instruction with ravenous delight. He now earned enough money to help Rossario with the mortgage on his new building and send money home every month while still putting something away.

He missed his family in Italy, but the Rossarios had become just as much of a family to him. He laughed with them in good times and cried with them in sad ones, as families did, and the past few years had seen much of both. He would infuriate Rossario with his steadfast reluctance to consider the world beyond his own sphere of work and family. "You wear the blinders like the race horses," Rossario would often say when trying to enlist Domenic in a political or community cause.

But at the same time Rossario knew he could depend upon Domenic as he would a brother or a son. And Domenic was thrilled that he was able to give back in so many ways to the man who had taken him into his cherished family.

The neighborhood too had changed, mostly for the better in Domenic's mind. But to many others who saw more of the city and the world beyond the confines of the North End Italian ghetto, things were not improving at all.

When Rossario received an offer to sell his old rundown wooden house to a North End businessman who wanted to put up a new four-story brick building, the amount he offered was too good to refuse. The proceeds from the sale of the house were enough for the down payment on an old building on the corner of North and Lewis Streets with a storefront on the first floor and three apartments above.

Domenic worked every free moment with Rossario and other friends from the Torre de'Passeri Society to improve the building. While this was going on, Maria announced that after eleven years of trying, she was pregnant with their second child. Rossario was ecstatic, and the excitement of the new arrival and the pace of work being done on the new building rose to a feverish level. But it was now a labor of love for both Rossario and Domenic.

In early 1917, the Rossarios moved into their new apartment on the second floor of their very own building. The first floor space was rented to a purveyor of imported foods and wines from Italy, a Pastene customer who Rossario knew well. Domenic and Rossario had managed to add a small studio apartment on the top floor, which became Domenic's, although he spent most his time with the Rossarios. The middle two apartments were rented to families from Abruzzo, providing a healthy rental income and a building teeming with life and family. When little Andrina was born that February, the Rossarios asked Domenic to be her godfather. From the myopic perspective of Domenic's neat little universe, everything seemed perfect.

***

The Rossarios were not very different from many other North End Italians who managed to improve their lot in Boston. Rather than flee to a better part of the city or the growing suburbs, they elected to stay in their neighborhood as opposed to abandoning it as others before them had done. Even as the population swelled to over 70,000, they remained and opened businesses, built new buildings, supported the churches, and worked to make a better neighborhood for all. To Domenic, it seemed that the heart of the neighborhood beat louder each day, drawing its strength from the common will of a people determined to build their American dream within this dirty, worn-down square mile of city that no one else wanted. They were a family building a home together piece by piece, a small garden emerging where once there was trash, a new barber shop replacing a boarded-up storefront, a playground appearing on a vacant lot.

But there were other forces at work within and beyond Domenic's neighborhood that would both challenge it and change it. As the North End became more and more exclusively Italian, the meager opportunities their new city begrudgingly offered became more and more inadequate in the eyes of many of its residents. Spurred on by community activists, Italians for the first time were beginning to harness the influence their growing numbers afforded them. This inevitably led to confrontations with those unwilling to relinquish any power of their own. Capitalizing on this conflict were what Rossario called the "bottom feeders" of the neighborhood, the anarchists and the Mafioso.

***

A chilling wind blew off the water and through the North End on the evening of December sixth of 1917, but the crowd gathering in North Square seemed to hardly notice. The fiery words from the speakers representing the International Workers of the World provided all the warmth they needed. Their words and the mood of the crowd were in sharp contrast to the spirit of the season offered up by the Christmas decorations around the storefronts and in the windows of the tenements. Closely monitoring the situation were about twenty police officers from the station on Hanover Street with billy clubs at the ready. The IWW was known to be populated by many North End Galleanists who had galvanized since their leader Luigi Galleani had taken up residence in nearby Lynn, Massachusetts, where he published his *Cronaca Sovversiva* advocating the use of violence to eliminate the "tyrants and oppressors" of government. There was a tense standoff as the speakers ignored the demands of the police to move their meeting off the square and indoors as originally planned. There was shouting from the crowd and some shoving from the police as they awaited mounted officers to help disperse the crowd.

Domenic was oblivious to all this as he made his way into the square on his way to the offices of *La Gazetta del Massachusetts* under orders from Maria to pick up Joseph and march him home. Joseph had taken to spending long hours at *La Gazetta* soaking up the news of the day and bringing it home to Rossario, which evoked long discussions during and after dinner. Domenic listened but remained silent during most of them, relieved whenever the talk turned to more familiar topics, freeing him from Rossario's demands to offer an opinion.

Domenic heard the commotion from the crowd as he walked up North Street. As he entered the square, he suddenly heard shouting and screams. Some people came running in his direction from the square, and there appeared to be a human mass of confusion behind them. He stayed away and made a wide swath around the mayhem. As he did, he saw Bartomolo Vanzetti running from the square. He stopped and looked directly at Domenic for a brief moment and then kept on running.

Then Domenic saw something much more chilling. Standing on the running board of a police car and pointing in his direction was the big cop who had beaten him. Domenic turned away in panic to make his way back out of the square, but as he did he felt someone grab his arm. It was a policeman.

"I think the captain wants a word with you."

Moments later he was once again face to face with now Captain Brendan O'Riley. O'Riley looked at Domenic for a few moments, slowly shaking his head back and forth as if saying, "You again."

"I remember you," he said, "and I'm sure you remember me." The words were void of emotion. "You really should get rid of that eye patch, my eye-talian friend. Makes you easy to spot."

"What do you want with me? I have done nothing," Domenic asked with a hint of defiance while telling himself, *Calm is the virtue of the strong*. He was determined that this time he would not submit so timidly to the cop.

O'Riley seemed to sense this. "Oh, don't get all prickly on me, ya little bastard. I just want some information and you can go about your business. I know you seen that troublemaking coward wop bastard who might have stuck one of my men not ten feet away from where I stood. He ran off, and I seen him look at you, and you at him. Like you were old friends. I want to know who he is and where I can find him."

"I don't know his name. I've seen him around. But I don't know his name."

"My boy, that ain't the answer I'm lookin' for." The way the words were spoken, so coldly and firmly, sent a shiver down Domenic's spine. "One of my own's been stabbed. If I have to beat every wop in the North End to find out who done it, I will. Beginning with you."

Domenic ran the possibilities of what could happen through his head and none of them were good. If he gave up that bastard Vanzetti, the anarchists would surely learn of it and come after him. If he didn't, the Lord only knew what this crazy Irish cop would do to him.

There was a sudden rap on the window beside O'Riley. He slowly lowered it, and Domenic was surprised to see Gaspare Messina peering in.

"Brendan, why do you have a good boy like Domenic Bassini in the back of your car when there are so many evil ones out here running around ruining our neighborhood?"

"Hello, Gaspare. This boy a friend of yours?"

"This boy is a friend of the neighborhood. He works hard, keeps his nose clean. He's no troublemaker."

"Maybe not, but I thinks he knows someone who is. Someone who stabbed one of my officers."

Gaspare shot a quick glance at Domenic. His raised eyebrows asked, "Is this so?"

"I told him I don't know the man he saw running away. I have seen him around, but I do not know him. I don't associate with the *istigatori*," he said, using the word some Italians used to describe the anarchists.

Messina turned back to O'Riley. "If Domenic says this is so, this is so. He's not a liar, and he holds no sympathy for the troublemakers."

O'Riley never took his eyes off of Domenic as he spoke to Messina. "If you're tellin' me I should let this boy go, I'd be tellin' you I'd be doing you a big favor in the interest of…community relations to do so. This boy is smart. I see it in his eyes. And smart boys watch things and know things. As sure as my name is Brendan O'Riley, he knows who that mustachioed motherfucker is who stabbed my man. But it don't matter. We'll find him. Go ahead, boy, be on your way. If you're the standup guy Mr. Messina says you are, you'd never rat out anyone anyway."

***

In the offices of *La Gazetta*, Domenic still shook from fear and cold as he sipped a glass of wine and told his story to a rapt audience of Joseph and James Donnaruma.

"Why would the Irish cop listen to Messina?" asked the ever inquisitive Joseph. "Isn't he a cop and Messina a criminal? At least my father says he's a criminal. I know a lot of other people who say he's a good guy."

"Sometimes things aren't simply black and white, my young friend," replied Donnaruma. "Messina and the police have many common interests. The most important one being they both like money. Messina makes his from his many "enterprises," shall we say, and the cops make it from Messina by looking the other way so he can run these enterprises without interference. I call it the unholy alliance."

"So the cops are criminals, too?"

"From the mouths of babes!" laughs Donnaruma. "But there are benefits in this relationship for us. The anarchists are the greatest threat to our neighborhood, and both the cops and Messina's people hate them for different reasons. Messina hates them because he cannot control them and they rile up the people. The cops hate them because they are dangerous and threaten the stability of a system that works out quite nicely for those who hold all the power. They also hate them because they are Italian. Maybe even more so because they are Italian. I hate them because their actions only serve to provide everyone who is not Italian a reason, or a better word is rationale, to fear and hate us all." Turning to Domenic he added, "What do you say, Domenic? Have I summed it up?"

"I think we would all be better to just take care of ourselves, look after our families, and avoid the police, and Messina, and the *istigatori* altogether."

"Perhaps someday we will be left alone to do that, Domenic. Perhaps someday." Then he turned to Joseph. "And how about you, young Mr. Rossario? Do you want to go through life with your head in the sand like Domenic?"

"I think that all real Italians need to stick together. We need to stick together and stand up to all the sons of bitches who want to control us."

"I feel like this is your father talking," says Domenic. "And watch your language."

***

The fuse that had been lit that cold December day soon exploded. Two weeks later, the police arrested Alfonso Fagotti, a well-known Galleanist, for stabbing a policeman during the North Square riot. The very next day, a bomb ripped through the Salutation Street Police Station in the North End. Some in the neighborhood cheered, some feared what would come next, and others plotted.

***

The building of the Dragotto empire was going well. He now owned three fishing boats he leased to Italian fishermen and over a dozen trucks that delivered fresh fish to restaurants and stores all around Boston and beyond. His retail shop was flourishing, as was the small restaurant he had added on to it. His considerable skills in the areas of persuasion, cajoling, and when necessary bribery, were now focused on the construction of his dream restaurant on the Boston waterfront.

The one thing not going smoothly was his effort at conceiving an heir to his burgeoning fortune. Francesca had proven to be a tremendous asset to him as he elbowed his way to success. She now spoke nearly perfect English and supervised the day-to-day operation of his businesses while Cologero immersed himself in his new project, but in private she was aloof. An unspoken understanding had evolved between them that she would submit to his needs, but on her terms. Sex was strictly a business arrangement. It would be quick, and it would be over. She would fulfill her wifely obligation to bear his children, but she would not allow passion or affection to enter the act, or their lives.

Cologero, for his part, would have been fine with this, except he had become convinced that her failure to give him a son was because her heart was not in it.

For Francesca, running the businesses kept her from thinking about what she did not have in America and in her life. Her days were a flurry of activity as she tended to the important details of running a business that Cologero found so boring. Much of her time was spent cleaning up messes Cologero created. She often warned him, "Chi cammina con la testa sempre fra le nuvole spesso un passo nella merda." *He who always walks with his head in the clouds will surely step in shit.* She knew that Cologero, and that meant her as well, was mortgaged to the hilt. If any of the banks, or worse the "friends," called in their loans with the interest owed, they would be in trouble. So Francesca took precautions that even Cologero knew nothing about by hiding money in places known only to her.

So her life was lived with much to keep her occupied and satisfied. She was admired for both her beauty and her brains by everyone around her. She was loved for her generosity in supporting all manner of causes in the North End. She was seen as one of the few Italian women who was truly a leader in their community.

But often, and without warning, she would feel the need to cry. And she would ask herself if she would have been happier if she had walked off the *Cretic* that day with Domenic Bassini. She had taken to keeping his mother's broach with her. And when she lay beneath Cologero as he grunted over her, she would look up at the face of Domenic framed by a star-speckled ocean sky.

JUNE 1918

JOE WALKED DOWN the steps of Boston Latin High School lost in thought. The end of a very successful freshman year was fast approaching, and he thought back on how hard he had originally fought not to attend the school at all. But his father had insisted he attend Boston Latin, the oldest public school in America, to learn alongside the sons of many of Boston's most prominent citizens. Entrance into the school required a strong recommendation from one's elementary school, and although the Sisters of Saint John's outdid themselves as they wrote glowingly about Joe's character and accomplishments, the Latin School administrators frowned upon accepting applicants from Catholic elementary schools. But when James Donnaruma called in favors from a few of the city councilors and state representatives he had endorsed in his newspaper, Joe was quickly accepted.

The first time he entered Boston Latin, however, he felt an immediate affinity for the feel of the school and the culture it embodied. He reveled in the freedom of thought that had been so restricted at Saint John's. Although the building was only forty years old, it carried the spirit of enlightenment, curiosity, and intellectuality instilled in its original 1635 bones. The theme of "dissent with responsibility" led to spirited debates with his instructors that delighted Joe and put the knowledge he gained from reading the newspapers each day under the tutelage of Donnaruma and Rosario to great use. Those around him felt a future in politics would suit him well.

His first year as an eighth grader, his outgoing personality and quick wit made him popular among his all-male classmates. They also admired how he unabashedly approached any of the girls at the neighboring Girls Latin Academy he pleased. He had been elected president of the freshmen class, and now as other students looked forward to the upcoming summer vacation, Joe looked forward to the following fall semester when he would run for president of the entire student body.

His campaign planning came to an abrupt halt, however, when he saw a familiar figure directly outside the gate on Warren Street, leaning against a car parked along the curb, his ear-to-ear grin punctuated by a cigarette. It had been over two years since Joe last saw Ernie, and although he recognized him instantly, he marveled at how much he had changed. Now fifteen years old, Ernie looked and dressed like a grown man. He wore a suit with a brightly patterned shirt open at the collar. Joe hastened over to him, and the two embraced.

"I didn't know if I'd ever see you again," blurted Joe. "You could of at least let us know you were alive you asshole."

"I'm alive and well, Joe."

"So where have you been? The first time Dom and I came to visit, they said you were gone, and that was all we got. I wasn't surprised you ran off, and neither was Dom. But we've been worried ever since."

"I've been around. It's a long story."

***

Ernie spent his first few weeks at the orphanage getting the lay of the land and planning his inevitable escape. In the meantime, the food was good and the chores and lessons bearable. His English improved, and he even took on reading Moby Dick. He loved the story as it was discussed in his class but found the book too hard to understand on his own. There were far too many words in the English language he had yet to learn. But he decided he would one day finish this and other books that took him away from a life being lived in never-ending uncertainty.

The Home for Wanderers was nothing like the orphanage in Naples where the days had been filled with hard work, religious instruction, and regular beatings. But there were some similarities as well. The chores, though much less burdensome, were still chores. And the punishments, though much less severe, were still punishments. But the natural rebelliousness that burned within Ernie's soul could not be cooled, and he would find himself lashing out at authority even as he knew he had little reason to do so. He would lay in his bed at night in the large dormitory and ques-

tion what burned inside him that made him so damn contrary. And restless. He had thrown away the opportunities Domenic and the Rossarios offered him. He knew he would throw away this opportunity to maybe be adopted into a real home. He wanted this yet abhorred the thought of it at the same time.

He had to admit he didn't know what he wanted. But he knew he couldn't bear being confined and being told what to do. So he planned his escape while constantly coming up with reasons to delay it.

Then the decision of when to leave the orphanage was made for him. There was a boy even older than himself who had been at the Home for Little Wanderers for several years and would soon be aging out of the orphanage. He believed his age and seniority allowed him special privileges. He would bully the younger children, helping himself to whatever he wanted of their meager belongings. He would often force them to make his bed, do his laundry, or do his chores. Anyone who didn't comply was met with a sharp blow to the head or kick to the ass, with a future beating promised if they complained to the staff. He stayed away from Ernie, and Ernie saw no upside to interfering with the bully's reign of terror.

Near the start of his fifth week at the orphanage, a young Italian boy around eight years old was brought to the dormitory in the early evening and given a bed not far from Ernie's. He carried a small sack of belongings and an old wooden cigar box. After the matron left, he just remained sitting on the bed, his belongings beside him, holding the box and staring at nothing as tears rolled down his cheeks. He remained like that for a while, seemingly oblivious to the few other children who approached him. When the lights flickered, announcing that it was nearing time for everyone to get to their beds, Ernie watched the bully get up and walk toward the child.

"What you got in that box there?" he asked the boy with a threatening tone.

When the boy didn't respond, he spoke even sharper and louder, "Hey, are you deaf or just stupid? I'm talking to you."

At this the boy looked up at him, teary eyed and expressionless. He began to tremble.

"I said, what you got in the box? I want to see." He reached for the cigar box.

The boy pulled away, clutching the box to his chest, speaking to the bully in Italian.

"Lasciami in pace. Lasciami in pace." No one but Ernie knew he was saying, "Leave me alone. Leave me alone."

"Stop your damn Italian jabbering, kid." Then he spoke very slowly, pointing to the box, "I want to see what's in the box. The box, give me the box." He reached for it again.

"Laasciami in pace! Lasciami in pace!" screamed the boy.

Ernie pushed himself off his bed and walked to the bathroom entrance off the dormitory. He grabbed the empty mop bucket the children used to swab the floors and walked quickly but deliberately to the boy's bed, where the bully had pulled the cigar box away, while fending off the wailing boy with one hand. "Restitulio! Restitulio!" cried the boy.

"Don't know what you're saying, dummy," said the bully.

Walking up behind him, Ernie said "He's saying to give it back, you asshole."

As the bully turned, Ernie swung the bucket as hard as he could at his head. The boy screamed and grabbed the side of his head where blood immediately began gushing from a gash along his temple. He went running from the dorm seeking help, leaving a trail of blood.

They'll probably make me clean that up, thought Ernie.

Ernie picked up the box that the bully had dropped to the floor, its contents spilling out. There were photographs, a pocket watch, and some papers with Italian writing on them.

He handed everything back to the quivering boy and said in Italian, "Here, you have a lot more than I had when I got here. Be strong. Don't let anyone push you around even if it means taking a beating now and then. You'll be okay." Then he went back to his bed and calmly awaited the consequences.

The consequences were swift. He'd be put on a train headed to New York City where he would be put on another "orphan train" headed west. At each stop, he would have the opportunity to be "adopted." Of course, he knew, and most people knew, that was basically the same as being sold into slave labor to work on a farm or provide some other form of manual labor for a family. But the thought of seeing New York City was enticing, so he went. And maybe someone there knew of his father. No one in Boston seemed to. When he packed up his things, he made sure to include his stolen copy of Moby Dick.

Minutes after the train arrived in New York, he was off on his own wandering the streets of New York, marveling at how much larger it seemed than Boston.

***

"New York wasn't for me, Joe," said Ernie as they walked toward the North End. "So I made my way back to Boston where I hooked up with a buddy I used to run with, Frankie Costa, whose father is a bookie in East Boston. I've been living in their basement and running numbers for him."

"So you've been living in Eastie and never thought to get in touch?"

Ernie hesitated. "I thought it would be best for everyone if I stayed away. Your father hates me. Dom, I think, is done with me…and I'm nothing but a bad influence on you."

Joe stopped walking. Ernie took a few more steps and looked back. "A bad influence?" said Joe. "Hell no. You're not a bad influence. You're a terrible fucking influence." And they both laughed.

"So what are you, like a bookie in training?" asked Joe.

"Funny way of putting it, but yes. Thing is I'm ready to graduate."

"Uh oh, what's that mean?" Joe rolled his eyes.

"Well, I'd been picking up bets and dropping off winnings for a lot of the really small-time bettors. What I noticed is that very few actually ever won. So saving what Big Frank paid me plus tips, I had enough to cover some of these small bets so I began keeping a few to myself."

"And Big Frank never noticed?" asked Joe.

"Hell no, this was small potatoes to him. Him and Little Frankie dealt with the really big regular gamblers. But it was pretty big potatoes to me. Those three, four, five dollar bets added up. Joe, I got over five hundred dollars stashed away."

"Ya, five hundred belongs to Big Frank if he ever finds out…"

"I know, I know," said Ernie, "which is why I'm ready to move on to bigger and better things."

"I don't like the sound of that, Ernie. Are you going to do something stupid? Remember how you got the nickname The Eel."

"No. The way to make money is to work for Messina. Jesus, every bookie in the city pays him a cut, including Big Frank. Plus he gets a cut of practically any job pulled around here. Not to mention a cut from anyone running hookers or fencing shit. Then there's the protection money. He controls everything. No, I want to work for him."

"So what do you do? Fill out a job application?"

"No, I take my money and invest it in my own crew and my own jobs. And I pay Messina a cut. You know what these guys like to say? *A rubar poco si va in galera, a rubar tanto si fa cariera.* Steal a little, go to jail. Steal a lot, make a career of it."

"That's quite a business plan, Ernie. What about maybe finding a real job and going to work? The worst that can happen is you get fired. With your plan you could end up in prison or at the bottom of the harbor."

"I just ain't cut out for that, Joe. Don't have the patience for it."

"That's such bullshit."

Ernie stopped walking. Joe looked over at him and saw the confident façade Ernie always wore sag and sadden. "Truth is, Joe, I don't deserve that life. I'm not good enough for it."

OCTOBER 1918

AN UNSEASONABLY COLD wind sent snow flurries swirling around Domenic as he made his way back to his apartment from an evening at the Society. He smiled to himself as he thought of how Maria Rossario called it "The Penthouse" as it sat atop what should have been the roof of the Rossario's new three-story walkup. Domenic loved it for the view of Boston Harbor and the growing Boston skyline. He could walk outside onto the roof and look down onto busy North Street and watch the colorful tapestry of the North End be rewoven every day.

But he especially liked the solitude and privacy it afforded him. Although he spent most of his time in the Rossario's apartment on the first floor, it was pleasant having his own space where he could escape. Sometimes young Joe would come up and give Domenic his news of the day and share with him things he felt he couldn't discuss with his parents, especially when it came to his bourgeoning awareness of the allure of the opposite sex. When Joe had received his confirmation, Domenic had been his sponsor, and as such Domenic felt obligated to offer what little advice he could. But the discussions always brought back thoughts of Francesca. And even though Domenic had no shortage of young girls from the neighborhood who made their interest in him known in no uncertain terms, when he was around them they elicited none of the feelings he had experienced with Francesca.

It was late, so he decided he wouldn't stop, as he usually did at the Rossario's first floor door but rather make his way straight up the stairs to the third-floor landing where a new set of stairs had been added that led to the door that opened directly into the penthouse. He looked forward to the quiet of the apartment and going through the new electrical manual he had as he studied to become a journeyman electrician. His apprenticeship at the Navy Yard was going well, and he wanted to be prepared to move on to a promotion and higher pay when it was completed. One day he would become a master electrician and maybe even start his own business.

His thoughts about his promising future were interrupted when a figure slowly emerged from the shadows of the stoop and took a few halting steps toward him. Although all he could really see was the outline of a trembling figure clutching an overcoat tightly about itself, he somehow knew immediately that it was Francesca.

***

Francesca sat at Domenic's kitchen table staring at the Caffè Lungo with a shot of sambuca he had prepared. She had not asked for this but looked to him as though she needed something to either warm or calm her or both. But now he had no idea about what else he could do for her. She was still trembling despite the warm blanket he had placed over her shoulders and had not spoken since she whispered to him, "Please can I come in?"

He suspected the trembling was not entirely from the cold but did not know how to ask. So he stood quietly leaning against his kitchen sink while she sat there, slightly slumped over and not looking up. Her black hair was wet from the snow and sparkled from the light bulb above the table. He could see black lines running down from the corners of her eyes, which he guessed were from some type of eye makeup. Was it the snow or tears that caused it to run? Despite this and the cheeks flushed a pinkish red, her face seemed even more beautiful to him than he remembered.

Gradually, he could see Francesca begin to compose herself. The trembling lessened, and she managed a fleeting half smile as she briefly glanced up at Domenic. It was as though she were summoning all her inner strength to regain control of her emotions before speaking. She slowly straightened up, and her shoulders stiffened. She looked at Domenic again, and this time held her gaze as she said, "I must look a mess."

"No, no," blurted Domenic, "You look, you look…"

"Don't you dare say beautiful, Dom."

"But you do, to me." He was instantly embarrassed by his words. Too bold, too honest.

Francesca smiled. "I've missed you. I think about you often."

Domenic wanted to tell her how much he thought about her. He wanted to tell her to stay with him and never leave, but he couldn't bring himself to say anything. He felt like the young boy again who became enraptured and tongue tied around this beautiful creature who owned his dreams and his desires as he fought the urge to take her in his arms right now and hold her, comfort her, love her as he did on those nights during the crossing.

Francesca sensed his unease and said, "I'm sorry I surprised you. I was upset and had no place to go. No one I could turn to. No one to trust. It was selfish and foolish of me to come here, to come to you after all this time knowing that it was wrong and would make you uncomfortable. I should go."

But the words were spoken without conviction. They were not spoken from the heart, nor were they meant to be believed. The warmth of her eyes belied the words and spoke the truth. Domenic felt those dark and knowing eyes, beautiful and glowing through their sadness, reach into his heart. And he knew.

He walked over to her, lifted her chin, and looked into her eyes, into her soul, and raised her from the chair. She rose willingly, and they kissed, locked in an embrace that somehow grew more and more intense until they seemed as one. Domenic's desire was overwhelming, and he felt Francesca succumbing to it completely. There were no words spoken. There were none needed.

✸✸✸

Domenic rose in the heavy midnight darkness and without turning on any lights found his pants and pulled them on while sitting on the edge of his bed. He walked over to his small kitchen and fumbled for a candle in a drawer and lit it, not wanting to turn on any lights for fear of disturbing Francesca. He looked back over his shoulder at her and was surprised to see the light of the candle dancing in the wide-open eyes looking back at him. Then he saw a slight smile appear as she spoke.

"I see you are still the modest Domenic I remember from the crossing. So eager to cover up what makes me your willing slave."

Although embarrassed by that, Domenic was happy to see her smile. It was as though the shaken, vulnerable woman he took to his bed was gone, replaced by the confident, vivacious woman he knew her to be.

"I didn't mean to wake you," he said. Then as usual he was unable to put words to either the thoughts in his head or the feelings in his heart.

Francesca sat up in the bed, uninhibited as the sheet slipped down, exposing her breasts. Domenic felt an immediate awakening beneath his pants and was glad he had been quick to put them on.

"I suppose I owe you an explanation, Dom," she said, "or an apology or both."

"No, you don't owe me anything. I should probably apologize for…" Words failed him.

"For taking advantage of a poor, distraught and partially drunk innocent woman," she finished the thought for him with a sly grin. Then turning serious, she said, "You saved me, Dom. God knows where I would have gone, what I might have done if you hadn't been here for me. You didn't ask me one question about why I was here. You still haven't. And that was what I needed."

Then the smile returned as she said, "The lovemaking was a bonus."

Domenic blushed. "I didn't know what to do when I found you outside. I just knew I was happy to see you and felt guilty and selfish that I should feel that way since you were so clearly upset. I was afraid of saying or doing something that would make you want to leave."

"I don't want to leave. I have to leave. But you should know what brought me to your door. It was a horrible night. Another of Cologero's dinners with some so-called important people I cannot bear to be around. He was drunk, and as we left he began suddenly to scream at me asking why I couldn't act more friendly like the other wives. And that they probably would go home and happily fuck their husbands who gave them nice homes and easy lives while I was as cold as the fish he sells. Then he grabbed my arm and told me that when we got home he was going to show me what a man can do to a wife whether she liked it or not. I told him he was not a man, that he was a beast, and slapped him as hard as I could and ran off not knowing where I was going at first. But suddenly I wanted to see you. To be with you."

"Why do you stay with such a man, Francesca? You are beautiful, smart, respected. You don't need him."

"I have no choice, Dom. My family back in Sicily would surely suffer at the hands of his evil partners there if I ever left him. He is a proud man, and if I embarrassed him he would be sure to seek retribution.

"But most of the time it isn't so bad. In the morning, he will come to me and apologize for his behavior. He will ask for forgiveness and promise never to treat me like that again. And I think he means it when he says this. And I get to live my life very much apart from his. I can help people and do so much using the Dragotto name and money."

Francesca paused. "He wants a son, Domenic, and I would gladly give him one if it would keep him away from me, but it seems I cannot get pregnant. Or he cannot get me pregnant. I would love a child but also dread the thought of what Cologero might turn him into."

Now there were tears in her eyes again, and Domenic's heart broke over the life she was being forced to live. She got up and began to get dressed as Domenic turned away to give her privacy.

Then he heard the other Francesca, the Francesca she was born to be, say, "Oh, Dom, you've seen all I have to show."

Later, he quietly walked her down the stairs, hoping no one in the building heard them. As they stepped outside into what was left of the cold night, she turned to him, kissed him, and said, "I know this is wrong, Dom, but can I see you again? Can we…"

"Yes. Yes, we can."

***

Along with sailors returning from the war to the ships and camps along the Boston waterfront came a deadly new strain of virulent influenza that soon found fertile ground in the crowded and unsanitary North End. The first cases among sailors were reported in early September, and by the end of the month more than one hundred Bostonians a day were dying from the outbreak. But as it seemed with every crisis, every catastrophe falling upon a population, the most vulnerable suffered the greatest yet persevered the most valiantly. The heartbeat of the North End slowed, but the day-to-day effort to carve out lives amongst the horror went on. Neighbors helped neighbors care for their sick and bury their dead. As thousands died, orphans were taken in, food was shared, the bereaved were consoled. And life went on.

Francesca spent her days volunteering at Massachusetts General Hospital where she had also donated as much money as Cologero would permit and even more he didn't know about. She also assisted Father Antonio Sousa from Saint Leonard's in mobilizing the Italian community to help the many orphaned children of the North End and raising money to establish an Italian Home for Children. Despite the grief all around her, Francesca's days were full and rewarding. And there was always the possibility each day of seeing Domenic. As Cologero scrambled to appease his investors and keep all his enterprises afloat while cursing the flu for crushing the business at his new restaurant and costing him workers, she was able to sneak away more often to be with Domenic.

For his part, Domenic would arrive home each day and try to scrub away any remnants of the invisible killer he imagined could be clinging to his skin before joining the Rossarios for dinner. Then he would spend the rest of his evening hoping that Francesca would come to him. And with more and more frequency, she did.

One night, with the warmth of the sex still radiating throughout his entire body from where Francesca lay her head on his chest, Domenic whispered quietly, "I love you."

He did not plan to say it, nor did he mean to say it, but the words flowed easily and naturally, as though they had grown in his mind and were ready to finally blossom. But saying them now, he realized, would pierce the protective bubble of the make-believe world they shared. One that kept the real world away when they were together.

Francesca's slow, sleepy breathing stopped. "I know, Dom. And I love you. And that's the problem, isn't it?"

They both knew that what they had could not last, could not breathe if brought outside of their private womb. So they never spoke of the world beyond the penthouse or of the future. They immersed the entirety of their selves into the time they spent together.

In their hearts, they wished it would never end, but both knew it would. And it did on a frigid night in December two months later.

NOVEMBER 1918

KEVIN O'RILEY SAT on the old couch in the small room off the parlor that had long served as his father's sanctuary. It could not be called an office or a study, as it had no desk, no bookshelves, or nothing much of anything for that matter. There was a large overstuffed chair with an ottoman squeezed into one corner with a small table next to it that always seemed to have a newspaper, a full ashtray and an empty glass or two on it whenever Kevin had ventured into the room as a child. In the corner opposite his father's chair was another small table with some photographs and a telephone. His father not being a sentimental man, Kevin was sure it was his mother who put the photographs there to add some touch of warmth to the room.

The couch Kevin sat in ran along the windows that faced through the glass-paneled sliding doors into the parlor. Years of cigar smoke had darkened the glass in the doors, and the husky smell of cigars clung heavily to everything in the room. Seated next to him fingering one of his father's cigars was his younger brother Colin, who still wore his new policeman's uniform. They awaited their father, who had asked to speak to them both after dinner. The two brothers found it hard to engage in even the lightest of conversations, separated as they were by years of traveling starkly divergent paths to manhood. Kevin, the recent graduate of Boston College, had brought nothing but pride to his parents. Colin, the new policeman, had brought nothing but worry. That their father was able to get him on the force at all with his record of trouble was testament to Brendan O'Riley's stature in the department. Try as he might, Kevin was never able to break through the wall of resentment Colin had built toward him, and it troubled him that he and his only brother were not closer.

Brendan entered the room with a glass in hand, sat in his chair, and lit a cigar. O'Riley family etiquette now allowed Colin to light his own. Kevin got up and pulled the doors closed, enforcing his mother's rule that if a cigar was being smoked, the doors were to be closed to spare her parlor furniture and curtains its odorous effects.

"Well, the idiots have gone and done it," began Brendan. "Peters is going to be mayor, and that is nothing but a piece of spoiled meat for us no matter which way we slice it." Kevin wasn't sure who his father meant by "us," but he knew all about Andrew James Peters, the darling of the old Brahmins held in low regard by the Irish who controlled the police force. When the ward bosses backed James Gallivan against the popular but increasingly independent James Michael Curley in the 1918 election, it split the Irish vote, allowing Peters to win.

"But there is opportunity here for the both of you." Kevin's curiosity was aroused. Colin appeared bored. "James Michael needs to keep his eyes and ears inside city hall, and that is why you'll be working for Mayor Peters, Kevin."

"What?"

"Thought you'd be surprised at that," Brendan responded casually but with a hint of a grin as he took a sip of his whiskey. "It's done. James Michael suggested I convince Peters that he needed a way to know what was really going on inside the department with all this union and strike bullshit being thrown about. He knows Commissioner Curtis is out of touch with what is going on in the department. I'll tell you what we want Peters to know, and you'll be sitting at the right hand of the Brahmin soaking up everything you can. See how they get things done, how they think, and it will serve you well when James Michael is mayor again."

Colin listened as best he could, but the conversation seemed like more of the same noise he had been hearing all his life, his father's plans for Kevin. It was always about Kevin.

"And you," Brendan spoke loudly to get Colin's attention. "You'll be my eyes and ears at these damn meetings of the troublemakers. In fact, I want you to be a troublemaker, because if there's going to really be a strike, which I can't truly believe, we want it over and done with on Peters' watch.

For the both of you, there will be rewards aplenty when this is all over. James Michael don't forget his friends." This was spoken with an air of certainty that made both sons know it would be so.

DECEMBER 1918

DESPITE THE MANY people sitting and standing about the Rossario apartment, the silence and stillness was suffocating. Most wore masks to guard against the flu that had laid its hand so heavily upon the family. The only sound above a whisper was the raspy sobbing of Maria Rossario as she lay propped up in her in bed holding the lifeless form of baby Andrina. Rossario sat at her side, his face frozen in grief, with even the tears streaking his cheek seemingly sculpted in place. He slowly looked up to the crucifix hanging above the bed and prayed, *Please, God, I can't lose them both. I can't.* But as he turned and looked into the grim face of the doctor standing across the bed from him, he knew his prayer would go unanswered.

✳ ✳ ✳

Three weeks later, on New Year's Eve, Domenic sat in the same apartment where the foul scent of death still hung heavy. All attempts at conversation with Rossario had long since been abandoned, and Domenic could only watch as his old friend slowly emptied glass after glass of wine to put himself to sleep in his chair. Young Joseph was already asleep, curled up on the couch. Domenic rose and quietly made his way to the stairs to return to the penthouse, the heavy sadness he bore weighing down each step. As he entered his apartment though, his spirits were immediately lifted as he saw Francesca sitting at his kitchen table. But as she looked up at him, he knew instantly from her expression, the sadness in her eyes and the lips squeezed tight while her whole face seemed to tremble, that something was wrong. She had not removed her heavy coat that sparkled from the melting flakes of snow that had been falling all day. This would be a short visit, and Domenic suddenly felt as though he had swallowed a heavy weight that settled in the pit of his stomach.

Francesca started to speak but could not seem to force out any words except, "Oh, Domenic…"

"What's wrong, Francesca?" he asked as he stepped up to her and put his hands on her shoulders while she sat. She wrapped her own arms around his waist and buried her face into him.

"I'm pregnant, Dom," she said softly. "I'm pregnant, and I'm so sorry."

Domenic let the weight of her words sink in for a moment. Then he asked the question they both knew was coming, "Is it mine or Cologero's?"

"I don't know, Dom. I honestly don't know. But I do know that for all of us it has to be his. It must be his. It will be his."

"But why?"

"Think about it, Dom. Both our lives would be destroyed if he knew he was not the father of this child. He could never let me live with the shame that would bring him, and his vengeance would be ruthless. He would come after you as well. He knows the people and has the money and power to do whatever he wants. My family in Italy would be shamed and punished as well. Your own family in Italy could also suffer consequences."

Domenic said nothing as his mind raced. Everything Francesca said he knew to be true, but how could he ever watch another man, a horrible man at that, raise his child?

"I know what you're thinking, Dom. But put it out of your head. There is no way you can be part of this. And it likely is Cologero's child anyway."

"But we may never know that."

"I'll know, but it will make no difference to me."

"So what now, Francesca?"

"Now, my love, we say goodbye. Again and forever."

JANUARY 15, 1919

JUST AFTER NOON on January fifteenth, a fifty-foot tall steel tank containing over two million gallons of molasses ruptured and sent a fifteen-foot wave of molasses racing at fifty feet per second through the congested North End, destroying anything in its path. The sound of the tank collapse was heard across the harbor in Charlestown, and word quickly spread throughout the Navy Yard about what had happened, causing workers with families in the North End, including Domenic, to rush to the scene.

Even before he crossed the Charlestown Bridge, Domenic was astonished by the devastation he could see along Commercial Street. Buildings were destroyed, and pools of molasses were everywhere, with people, horses and cars stuck in them. As he sloshed through the site, he saw a lifeless man being dragged from the molasses by some rescuers. His entire head covered with the gummy molasses filling his eyes, ears, nose, and mouth.

A block further down he saw a young girl holding a child up above the waist-deep molasses that pinned her against a car that had itself been pushed up against a warehouse building by the force of the wave. She was crying and pleading in Italian for help. People were trying to get to her through the molasses but were having little luck.

Domenic was able to make his way to the back of the building, where he broke through a window and then found his way to the opposite side and another window above the car. He climbed out on to the roof of the vehicle and was able to reach the girl. She handed the little boy up to him, and he took him back into the building where he set him down. He then went back out for the girl. She turned as much as she could in the hardening molasses, and he took her hand but could not extricate her. He then settled flat on his stomach, and their faces were inches apart as he took both her arms and slowly began to lift her out. They locked eyes as he lifted her up, saying in English and then in Italian, "It's okay. You're going to be okay." He was struck by the innocence of her gaze and how pretty she was as she gritted her teeth and placed her faith in him uttering, "Grazie, grazie, grazie…" When he got her up on the roof of the car, she flung her arms around his neck and buried her head in his chest and asked through her sobs in Italian, "Is my nephew okay?"

"Yes, he's okay," Domenic answered softly as others began making their way through the building to the window. Then they looked into each other's eyes for the longest brief moment. He was humbled by the veneration her look exuded while fighting an urge to kiss her at the same time. "What is your name?" asked Domenic.

"Pasqualena. Pasqualena Pica."

***

Twenty-five people were killed and dozens more seriously injured in the Great Molasses Flood, almost all of them Italians who lived or worked in the North End. The tank had been hurriedly constructed and shoehorned into the densely populated North End because the population there held little power to stop it. The monstrous tank had been constructed hastily in 1915, since molasses could be easily converted to industrial alcohol needed in the manufacture of munitions. When dark, shiny streaks of molasses began running down the sides of the tank almost immediately, the owners painted it brown to disguise the leaks. And after the disaster, the owners, the United States Industrial Alcohol Company, tried to blame the explosion on Italian anarchists. In the end, however, USIAC was ordered to pay over $630,000 in settlements.

***

Two weeks after the disaster, there was a knock on Domenic's door. He opened it to see three women. Two he did not know, but the other was Pasqualena Pica. She smiled shyly as one of the women said, "Mr.

Bassini, we are here to thank you for saving our little sister Pasqualena the day of the explosion. If you had not acted so quickly, she might not have been able to hold my little son above the molasses much longer. She cannot stop talking about you and your bravery." Then she added with a smile, "Mostly about you. Do you think you could join us for Sunday dinner this week so we can show our appreciation?"

"Yes. Yes, I can do that," he said, looking from the woman to a beaming Pasqualena.

After providing the address and exchanging pleasantries, the small group left. As he was closing the door, he heard one of the women say to Pasqualena, "You were right. He is very handsome."

***

It turned out that Pasqualena Pica was sixteen years old and from Avellino near Naples. Sickly as a child, she was cared for by her two older sisters after their parents passed away. When the sisters moved to America with their husbands, Lena, as her sisters called her, was still weak from a bout of scarlet fever and stayed with her father's sister. The sisters promised to send for her when she was a little older and, hopefully, stronger. That time finally arrived, and Lena joined her sisters where they all lived together in the North End with their husbands and three small children. Lena loved being a nanny to her little niece and nephews, helping with meals, laundry, and cleaning. She suffered lingering effects of scarlet fever in the form of chronic ear and sinus infections and sore throats but learned to soldier through as best she could. Often described as "cute" by those around her, her large eyes, small sharp nose, and light complexion (some would call it pale) contrasted with her coarser, darker-skinned, and much heavier sisters.

As much as they loved her, her sisters and their husbands, in particular, weren't overly thrilled with the extra mouth to feed in their overcrowded apartment. When they saw the way she gazed adoringly at Domenic during Sunday dinner, they hoped for the best.

For his part, Domenic carried a heavy heart as he went about his life. The loss of Maria and Andrina sucked the life out of Rossario, and the entire building felt like a mausoleum. He was eager to be away from it any chance he could. Accepting Francesca's decision was painful, and he often wondered about her and the child she would bear. As he got to know Lena, he came to see her less as a child and more of a companion with whom to share his thoughts. His natural reticence would leave him when they were together, as she seemed to hang on his every word while speaking very little herself.

They would occasionally kiss, and the more they did the more comfortable it became for him. There was none of the passion that kissing Francesca had sparked within him, but he enjoyed the warm feeling it brought him. Thinking about his future practically, Domenic was lonely and knew he needed someone. He also knew he wanted a family. Lena would soon be seventeen, more than old enough to marry. She clearly adored him, and he enjoyed being with her.

He asked her to marry him in March, and they were married in May at Saint Stephens Church, where Lena's family worshipped. After the small but loud reception at the society clubhouse, they walked back to the penthouse and had sex for the first time. It was awkward and uncomfortable for them both, but both tried their best to make it better for the other.

***

Shortly after his marriage, Domenic received a letter from Massachusetts General Hospital. To his surprise, an eye surgeon there was offering to provide enucleation surgery to insert a glass eye for him at no charge. His ugly, scarred dead eye would no longer need to be covered by a patch. The doctor assured him that after the surgery and insertion, few would notice the eye was not real. The letter added that a benefactor wishing to remain anonymous was funding the surgery.

Domenic was surprised and skeptical, but the postscript beneath the doctor's signature was telling. It read, "The anonymous benefactor wished me to convey to you sincere congratulations on your recent marriage." This was a wedding gift from Francesca.

In July of 1919, Domenic left the hospital with a glass eye that matched his good eye perfectly. Not long after, Francesca was rushed to the same hospital, where she delivered a stillborn baby boy.

SEPTEMBER 1919

KEVEN O'RILEY TOOK his time making the short walk from city hall across School Street to the Parker House for a few reasons. First and foremost, he needed a little time to digest what he had heard in the meeting he was leaving and decide what warranted reporting to his father.

But he also loved this time of the year, particularly as the evenings gave the first hint of summer turning to fall with the sun setting earlier and the heat of the day vanishing more quickly. He stopped at the wrought iron fence in front of city hall that ran along School Street to take in the air and watch the sun descending behind the steeple of King's Chapel. In the chapel's burial ground next to city hall lay some of Boston's most prominent past citizens, including John Winthrop, Massachusetts's first governor, who famously proclaimed how Boston would become a biblical "city on a hill."

Kevin had no doubt that the two other men in the meeting, Police Commissioner Edwin Upton Curtis, and Mayor Andrew James Peters, had ancestors buried there. They also probably still believed in Boston's own manifest destiny to ascend to be that city on a hill. He mused how his own grandparents, who he had never met, were in graves somewhere in County Cork. And how Boston now seemed to have become more of a city on a tightrope, ready to topple at any time on the selfish whims of all those who would control it.

Kevin despised Curtis, who he saw as embodying the smugness of the Yankee Republican Brahmins who firmly believed their God-given superiority entitled them to either control or rehabilitate all those they viewed as beneath them. The fact that Curtis was the commissioner of the Boston Police Department at all was an affront to Boston and the Irish. In 1908, the Brahmins who still controlled the Massachusetts State House, shifted control of the Boston Police Department from the city to a single commissioner appointed by the governor in response to the growing fear of an Irish takeover of the force and the city. Curtis was named commissioner by Republican Governor Calvin Coolidge, whose hardline anti-immigrant stance was a cornerstone of his campaign platform. In the meeting that just ended, Curtis made clear he had no intention of giving into any of the patrolmen's demands, and if they actually dared to strike, which he still believed they would not, he was determined to crush what he said would be "a rebellion fueled by immigrant anarchists."

Kevin saw Mayor Peters, on the other hand, as merely a pawn in the hierarchy of the Yankee Republicans. The year before, he was complicit in working with the state legislature in passing a ridiculous law prohibiting mayors of Boston from serving consecutive terms – an obvious effort to keep James Michael Curley from controlling the city. By doing so, Peters was acting as the good soldier and sacrificing his own potential second term. Peters would even sometimes express sympathy over the dreadful working conditions and pay for Boston policemen to Kevin and others but never to Curtis or the Governor.

Based on what Kevin heard from his brother Colin, not only could there be a police strike, but one was imminent. That Curtis, Peters, and the others could not see this amazed him. He was equally as sure of the outcome. There would be chaos and violence, and the estimable Mayor Peters would be the one made to be at fault.

He carried these thoughts through the School Street entrance of the Parker House as he headed to meet his father in Parker's Bar as they usually did. But he saw his father standing in the lobby, and when their eyes met, his father signaled him to follow him to a stairwell off the lobby. He did, and they climbed up one flight and went to a small private meeting room where he was surprised to see both his brother and James Michael Curley himself waiting.

They sat at a large conference table that filled the small room, each with a drink in hand, clearly poured from the single bottle of Irish whiskey that was the table's only adornment. A joke or a story had just been shared, as the arrival of the two new O'Rileys interrupted their laughter.

"Well, well, if it isn't the great KO O'Riley himself," said Curley, using the nickname Kevin had earned as an amateur boxer in college. When he knocked out a boxer from Harvard in the first round of an unofficial grudge bout between Boston College and Harvard's best fighters, the Irish of the city rejoiced.

Colin, on the other hand, did not seem so happy to see his brother. It was as though he was intruding on his time with Boston's most famous and powerful Irishman.

After some pleasantries, and with Brendan and Kevin now having their own drinks in hand, it was time for each to give their assessment of the police situation. There was no doubt that Curley would be mayor again in two years' time, just as Brendan had predicted a year earlier, and he was eager to hear the reports of the three O'Rileys.

"There's going to be a strike any day now," Colin immediately blurted, drawing James Michael's attention first. "The fools think they can actually walk off the job and get away with it. You should hear some of the baloney thrown about at their meetings. Nothin' but a bunch a crybabies. But they're ready to go. Once Curtis rejected every single one of their stupid demands, the final nail was hammered into their own coffin." He then sat back smugly with a look that said, "Top that, Kevin."

"Thank you, Colin," responded Curley, adding with a wry smile, "I see attending their meetings hasn't exactly fostered any sympathy for your fellow patrolmen."

"What's there to be sympathetic about?" snapped Colin. "They made their bed and now they have to sleep in it."

"There's a lot to be sympathetic about!" shouted Brendan suddenly, startling the other three in the room. "Damn it, Colin, you got the benefit of a roof, my roof, over your head, and you're responsible for no one but yourself. A lot of your brothers, yes brothers they are, aren't so lucky. They have families and work seven days and some eighty hours a week and barely make enough to live on. This city depends on them, but they make less than any unskilled laborer. They sleep in rat-infested station houses and are made to run errands for those of us lucky enough to be higher in rank. Now, don't get me wrong, I'm dead set against this union bullshit, but by God they got a right to earn a decent living."

The outburst stopped as quickly as it started. Brendan turned to Curley and said quietly, "Sorry, James, guess I'm getting a bit cranky in my old age."

Curley smiled. "No, you're not getting cranky, my friend. You've always been cranky!" He burst out laughing, as did they all. Curley then turned his attention to Kevin.

"And what about you, KO, what say you about all this nasty business? What is going on in the closed minds of those Republican bastards running our city and state…at least for now?"

Kevin spoke matter-of-factly and without emotion, "I believe that Curtis and the governor would welcome a strike. They know that public opinion would be on their side, and they would emerge as heroes when they fire all the strikers and bring in the State Guard to patrol the city, as they surely will have to do. Peters has some sympathy for the patrolmen and would negotiate with them, but he has no real say here. If things go off the rails and the city ends up lawless for a period, which is inevitable in my opinion, Peters will be blamed for not acting quickly enough and being seemingly too sympathetic toward the patrolmen."

"Very insightful, my young friend," replied Curley, "and probably correct. Curtis is a bastard and always has been. And Peters is a wimp. But if there's to be a strike, and it seems all are in agreement on that, let's get it over with. When I'm elected mayor again, we'll make things better for our police and our own. And it will be a very good day for the O'Rileys as well. I promise you that."

1921

DOMENIC GIUSEPPE BASSINI was born in March of 1921. The arrival of a healthy nine-pound baby boy after two earlier miscarriages should have been a source of boundless joy for Lena and Domenic Senior, but the difficult delivery and heavy bleeding Lena endured resulted in a hysterectomy, ensuring that young Dommy, as they called him, would be the only baby she would ever bring into the world. If the baby had been delivered at home, as most in the North End were, Lena would have surely died. But because of her earlier miscarriages and fragile overall health, she was taken to a hospital to deliver the baby, where the doctors were able save her.

Domenic's heart was lifted and broken at the same time. He had a son but felt for his wife, who had struggled with an iron determination to bring the baby full term and deliver his boy to him. As she held her son in the hospital bed for the first time, it was difficult for him to tell if the tears she shed were of joy or sadness or both. But he knew she would be a wonderful mother.

Although Rossario was honored to have given Dommy his middle name, it was young Joe who was asked to be the godfather, a responsibility Domenic knew he would cherish, and draw their informal family into an even closer one.

That June, Joe graduated from Boston Latin High School. He gave a rousing speech as the class president and then went to work the following Monday selling insurance for the New England Life Insurance Company. Although urged to go to college, young Joe was eager to begin earning money to help his father, who worked only sporadically since the death of his wife and baby daughter during the flu epidemic. He was also a young man in a hurry to make his mark in the community. With an eye on political office, he never missed an opportunity to forge relationships with those who could help him. Selling policies throughout the North End and to Italian families all around Boston, he was soon a top sales agent for the company, with the dual goal in mind of opening his own independent insurance agency and running for office, hopefully by the time he would have been graduating from college. He had no qualms about taking the financial support being offered by Ernie to accomplish both.

***

Ernie "The Eel" Lentini was also making progress in his chosen field. He took what he had learned about bookmaking from "Big Frank" to the poorer neighborhoods of the city and then to surrounding towns where he could steer clear of the major operators and the Messina family's growing reach. In between, he would plan and execute small burglaries with his small and trusted group of accomplices, always careful to avoid taking unnecessary risks and confrontations. He insisted that anyone working with him have a real job, as did he as a dockworker, to avoid suspicion.

Although he was making money, he spent little on himself and saved as much as he could to finance larger jobs in the future. When Prohibition took effect in January of 1920, Ernie was ready. Reading through the entire Volstead Act, he took advantage of a loophole that allowed "the head of a family to make up to 200 gallons of wine exclusively for family use." He organized families throughout the North End to produce and bottle wine up to their annual limit so they ran no risk of running into trouble with the Feds. He would then sell the homemade wine at a handsome profit. He also used the money he saved to buy a rundown building on the waterfront, which he converted into a still that could put out fifty gallons of alcohol a day. He knew that this enterprise needed protection from the authorities, and his inquiries into the process led him to his old nemesis Colin O'Riley, who was now a police department sergeant.

It was an awkward meeting that took place on a windy wharf not far from Cologero's restaurant on the South Boston waterfront. The chill in the air was mild compared to the frost between the two men.

"Wasn't far from here you gave me this scar, Eel," was the first thing Colin said as he approached Ernie, pointing to his head.

"Sorry, Colin, that was a long time ago when I was young and stupid."

"Oh, so now you're old and smart?"

"Smart enough to offer you a chance to make a lot of money for doing nothing."

"And why should I trust you, you guinea bastard? Last time we did business you fucked me over pretty good."

"Like I said, a long time ago." Ernie went on to explain his plan for a still and his need for protection from the police and the Feds. Then he added, "This is business, Colin. We don't have to be friends. You can hate me all you want while you take my money. A lot of my money."

"You know, your guinea bosses might not look too fondly upon you setting up such an enterprise in their backyard."

"I plan to inform them and pay them their share too. In fact, I can make some introductions that might be helpful to you. I know Messina's right-hand man Joseph Lombardo would be happy to have his own reliable contact on the force. He's the one I run all my stuff through. I don't want any trouble or hard feelings. I just want to make money for everyone."

Colin was silent for a minute while he looked hard at Ernie. "My man Billy Flynn will be your contact. He'll be counting bottles to make sure you pay me what I got coming. But by Jesus, you fuck me over or cheat me, you'll end up buried under that friggin' still."

The meeting ended with Colin saying nothing more and turning away. There was no handshake.

✱✱✱

Following the loss of her child, Francesca plunged herself into her charity work and keeping all of Cologero's varied business ventures organized. Cologero seemed to have an aversion to keeping proper books and paying taxes. He was too busy making deals and keeping his various business partners happy and his backers paid to focus on details. Protection did not come cheap, and the Bonfiglio clan had stopped underwriting his various enterprises and expected regular payments from their initial investments. Francesca marveled at how the man was able to navigate the elaborate labyrinth he had built of lenders, investors, protectors and partners – many of whom knew nothing of the others.

Prohibition was a boon to the restaurant. In addition to a fine dinner, patrons, including many of Boston's most prominent citizens, knew they could enjoy a drink in what had been made into an elaborate bar in the basement level. Obtaining the illegal wine and alcohol was expensive, but his supplier was the Messina Family, and their deal came with protection from the Boston police. The family also used Cologero's fish trucks as cover to transport their booze all over New England, an arrangement that paid Cologero well. Payments to a few politicians who enjoyed Cologero's gracious hospitality also kept the federal revenue agents away.

Managing the cash and payments fell upon Francesca, and she actually enjoyed the challenge. What to bank, who to pay legally, and who to pay clandestinely became an activity in which to immerse herself, a game with many moving pieces, which kept her mind on the task at hand and not the child she lost or the husband she detested. Or on Domenic Bassini.

FEBRUARY 6, 1922

COLIN O'RILEY STOOD with his back to the bar at Amrhein's in South Boston, one elbow resting on the bar as he lifted a mug of beer to his lips and looked out into the crowded room. Prohibition was in full swing, but that did not pertain to a privileged establishment like Amrhein's that was a favorite gathering spot of Boston policemen, as well as many of the movers and shakers of Boston's Democratic Party. And especially not today as South Boston celebrated the inauguration of James Michael Curley for his second term as mayor of the city.

James Michael himself was expected to drop by Amrhein's soon, and thoughts of the past and future mayor brought Colin back to the promises he had made to the O'Rileys three years earlier that he would no doubt keep. His father Brendan, who was already a well-respected deputy superintendent on the force, would be named superintendent-in-chief tomorrow, Curley's first day in office. His brother, Kevin, would be joining Curley at city hall as the mayor's chief of staff. And he, himself, expected to be promoted to lieutenant. At twenty-two, he was already the youngest sergeant on the force, a rank he was given when over three-quarters of his fellow patrolmen were fired following the police strike. Colin smiled to himself as he thought of his good fortune. Many said that Calvin Coolidge, who was now the vice president of the United States based primarily on his hawkish handling of the strikers, was the greatest beneficiary of the strike. But Colin believed that he, himself, benefitted more than anyone. Even while spying on his fellow patrolmen, he was able to convince a select few not to strike with promises of better pay and promotions if they stayed on the job with him. He claimed his connections to city hall, James Michael Curley, and his own father would ensure this.

After the strike, when Curtis refused to rehire any of the strikers, the new hires and patrolmen who stayed on the job received higher salaries, more time off, and city-provided uniforms, the very things requested by the original strikers. And with his promotion to sergeant, Colin was able to pick and choose some of the new recruits, several of whom were friends from his days spent breaking the law rather than enforcing it.

He now controlled a loyal group of officers within the department he could trust to follow him outside the lines of pure policing and into more lucrative enterprises with impunity. Higher-ranking officers would look the other way for fear of alienating his father or Mayor Curley. He had plans, big plans, for the days ahead. He would work with anyone willing to pay for the protection and support of the Boston police, even the Italians.

He knew his father disapproved but would ultimately turn a blind eye. He thought of their conversation just days ago, his father practically pleading with him to become what he called a "smart cop."

"Listen to me closely, Colin," he had said. "You've been given a great opportunity here. Don't fuck it up. Be smart. You need to think more about doing the job and less about using it to get rich. Sooner or later, it's going to come back and bite you in the arse."

But to Colin, the words of his father meant nothing. He knew he would always protect him, as he had been doing all his life, as he promised his mother he would. And he knew he wanted to be rich, needed to be rich. Because as far as he could tell, money made all the difference in this world. It made you matter. His father could have had a lot more and given them a better life, but he didn't. He chose to live humbly, adequately. Colin wanted more. He wanted a summer house on the ocean in Nantasket and a boat to take him there whenever he wished. He wanted to travel around Ireland in style and dine in the finest restaurants in Paris.

But most of all he wanted the power that money seemed to give to those who had it. The power to control people and events. The power to punish your enemies and reward your loyal friends. The power to be somebody.

As he looked out on his fellow police officers celebrating into the evening, the door opened, and along with a cold blast of winter air in came Mayor James Michael Curley with his father, the new superintendent in chief of the Boston Police Force, close behind him. Colin took a long swig of beer, slammed the empty mug on to the bar, and walked over to greet them.

MARCH 1927

ERNIE STOOD ANXIOUSLY outside the office of Gaspare Messina holding a satchel. He did not know what would happen in the next few minutes, but he knew it would change his life and fortunes one way or another. A steely eyed Messina associate everyone called "Big Quiet" eyed him relentlessly, and Ernie simply stared back, refusing to be intimidated. It was rumored that Big Quiet served in the Italian army along the Austrian border in the war, where he fought fearlessly against the Germans and Austro-Hungarians. But his skill at killing didn't stop with the enemy, and he wound up murdering an Italian officer from Il Nord with his bare hands following what he perceived as an insult to his Sicilian roots. As Ernie stared back at him, he thought he could saw the slightest of grins pick at the edges of his mouth. Somehow, that was much more unsettling than the cold, motionless eyes.

Ernie's plan had led him to this point. It was, to Ernie, a perfect plan because only he knew of it. There were no others to contradict the story he was about to tell Messina, not even the four members of his crew who had unwittingly helped him put it all into play.

Ernie was tired of being seen as a small time, outside crew operator by Messina's people, particularly the ill-tempered underboss Joseph Lombardo. Because he was not Sicilian and had no pedigree, as well as no mentors or influential friends in the organization, he was limited in how far he could ever hope to rise in the Boston mob. He might never even be made a soldier, never mind a Caporegime with his own crew of soldiers.

He kept pulling jobs and paying tribute, but they were always his jobs, his plans. He was never asked to be in on anything important. It particularly galled him that Lombardo acted as though Ernie worked for him, taking credit for Ernie's successful heists and keeping him away from the insulated Messina.

But now Ernie had a plan to break free or literally die trying. For months, he had meticulously watched the coming and going of trucks in and out of the South Boston piers he guessed were carrying liquor. He believed since these trucks were running out of warehouses in South Boston that they were probably controlled by the Irish, but one night he was close enough to see a driver and his guard and recognized them as Messina's men. He had heard rumors of a rum-running and distribution alliance called "The Combine" involving the New York Mob, the Boston Mob, and Boston Irish gangs, but he had dismissed them as just that, rumors. But here was evidence that there were dealings afoot at a higher level than he would ever reach. Unless he found a way to force his way in.

Ernie decided that he was going to get Messina's attention. His small crew didn't flinch when he told them they were knocking off a liquor truck run by a small time Irish operator. But this had to go perfectly. No one could get hurt, his men couldn't see who the drivers were, and the drivers couldn't recognize any of them.

Ernie followed trucks leaving the warehouse for weeks until he could anticipate schedules and routes. One route ran south through Quincy, where the truck would make a delivery at a speakeasy near the busy Quincy Shipyard. The speakeasy was a single building that rose in the field opposite the shipyard's main gate that was ostensibly a restaurant. While everyone knew it served liquor, the authorities would look the other way, while the clientele was primarily thirsty shipyard workers ending their shifts. So deliveries were done through the small back door that was quite a ways from where the truck could park. The driver would stay with the truck and inevitably have a cigarette while the guard took one case at a time to the door.

On a moonless night a week earlier, Ernie had stood alone behind a tree next to where the truck would soon be parked. Ernie's man Renzo hid further back in the field awaiting the truck and Ernie's signal. Ernie had timed the delivery, and it took the second man in the truck less than three minutes to walk from the truck, make his delivery, and return. A lot had to happen in those three minutes, and it had to go perfectly. If not, people would have to die. Ernie puffed on his cigarette and watched a group of workers cross Howard Street from the shipyard and head toward the front door of the restaurant. He thought about what their lives must be like. Go to work, have a drink, go home. What was the frigging point? Raise some kids and work yourself to death, some life. He told himself they were all suckers. But then his thoughts took him to when he had lived with the Rossarios and those times when he wanted to really be part of the family in a way he never truly believed he could.

"Maybe I'm the sucker," he said softly to himself. But the sound of an approaching truck brought his thoughts back to the task at hand, and he felt the familiar rush of adrenaline that came with every job he planned and executed. It was the same feeling he would get years ago on the streets of Naples when deftly stealing items from street merchants. And he knew he could not live without it.

The truck pulled off of Howard Street and backed up as far as it could on to the dirt that passed as a parking area off to the side of the speakeasy. Ernie snuffed out his cigarette as he watched it roll to a squeaky stop. The guard got out, went to the back of the truck, and pulled out one case of liquor that he hoisted on to his shoulder. The driver got out too, as he always did, and lit a cigarette. As soon as the guard turned the corner headed to the back of the dive, Ernie surprised the driver from behind, put a gun to the back of his head, and forced him to the ground. As he pulled a hood over the driver's head, Renzo ran from the bushes and jumped into the truck. The truck was already moving as Ernie leapt into the passenger seat. They were on their way in less than a minute.

It didn't take long for word to reach the street that two of Messina's men had lost a truckload of liquor. Now it was time for Ernie's ploy.

Standing outside Messina's office, Ernie was having second thoughts as he looked into the face of Big Quiet. He might not leave here alive. Finally, the door to Messina's office was opened by Joseph Lombardo, and he was beckoned in with Big Quiet following right behind him.

Messina sat behind a desk, but he rose and greeted Ernie warmly when he entered. Lombardo watched Ernie with suspicion. He knew the kid was smart and had been a good earner, but he also knew he was ambitious.

"So, Ernie, or should I call you The Eel," Gaspare said with a slight grin. "What is so important that you insisted to Joseph that you had to see me?"

"I come to beg your forgiveness and to promise you that I will make everything right if you'll let me."

"And what exactly do you need forgiveness for? I'm not a priest, you know."

"For hijacking your truck last week in Quincy and selling the load to the Morelli family in Rhode Island."

There was a stunned silence in the room. Messina simply looked at Ernie with a look of mild astonishment. Then Lombardo screamed, "You stupid bastard sonofabitch!" He started toward Ernie. But Messina held up his hand and said firmly, "Wait, I want to hear what he has to say."

Now came the moment of truth, Messina would either buy his story or he would be leaving with Big Quiet. It didn't help that the fearsome bodyguard now had his pistol in his hand.

"Please, Mr. Messina, I have always been a good and faithful worker. I swear I didn't know that this truck belonged to you. It came from the South Boston warehouses so I thought it belonged to the Gustins or some other Irish." Messina cast Lombardo a sideways glance.

"I had planned to pay Joseph a percentage as I always do. But when I found out it was your truck I came to you immediately with this." He opened the satchel to reveal the money inside. "This is every penny we got from Morelli. If it's not enough, I'll earn more."

Ernie could almost hear the gears spinning in Messina's head. Then he spoke. "How did you know where to hit my truck?" Ernie recounted how he had studied the routes to determine the best opportunities.

"So these trucks run the same routes, the same days, the same times? Not very smart on our part," said Messina, again glancing at Lombardo, who was still fuming. Then he seemed to think some more.

"I understand it was well planned, and I know nobody was hurt. But I want to know who was with you. I want to talk to them."

"I know who runs with The Eel," piped up Lombardo. "I'll see what they have to say about all this. We'll get the truth."

"Please, Mr. Messina, they know nothing more than I've told you. They are good, loyal friends who trust me and follow my plans without question."

Messina proceeded to look Ernie up and down. "So you are a leader of men, Mr. Eel?"

"No, Mr. Messina. I mean, well yes as far as my crew, but I, I…" He knew he was babbling.

Messina held up his hand to stop him and smiled. He then turned to Lombardo and said, "Joseph, I think you should find ways to keep Mr. Eel busy. Maybe you can put him in charge of some more significant projects than he has done on his own in the past. I want him to earn enough to pay us back plus another fifty percent above what he gave us today as reparations. A third of that will go to you as his Caporegime."

Ernie couldn't believe what he heard. Messina had just officially put him into the organization.

"Thank you, Mr. Messina. I won't let you down."

"It is Joseph you had better not let down, Mr. Eel. And from now on you will not even think about stealing a stick of gum without Joseph's permission. Now get out of here."

Ernie turned to go and was halfway to the door when Messina shouted, "Wait!"

Ernie turned back to face Messina.

"So where the hell is my truck?"

AUGUST 23, 1927

IT WAS NEARLY one in the morning when Domenic was awakened by a loud knock on his first-floor apartment door. Pasqualena stirred but did not awaken as Domenic grabbed his bathrobe and hurried to the door. He looked quickly into little Dommy's room to see if he was awake and saw him sitting up looking toward the door.

"Daddy?" he muttered in a muffled, sleepy voice.

"Go back to sleep, Dommy. Everything's OK."

He got up against the door and asked in a sharp voice, "Who's there?"

"Dom, it's me, Joe, and my father."

Domenic quickly opened the door and was surprised to see Ernie Lentini also standing there with the two Rossarios. He appeared to be supporting Giuseppe Rossario, who had one arm around Ernie's neck, while his other was around young Joe. They were all soaking wet from the rain and looked exhausted.

Dommy motioned them to come in while eyeing Ernie suspiciously. Joe and Ernie deposited Giuseppe into Domenic's easy chair.

"Is he hurt?" asked Domenic, kneeling in front of the chair.

"He's drunk," said Joe. "He would be hurt if it wasn't for Ernie."

"What happened?"

"We were outside the prison when they executed Sacco and Vanzetti tonight. So were a lot of other people. You know how fixated my dad has been on this whole damn debacle. He'd been at the prison for hours and drinking most the time. When word came that Sacco and Vanzetti were dead, he went crazy and wound up throwing a bottle that hit one of the mounted cops controlling the crowd. The cop actually pulled his gun and pointed it at dad, who just stood there staring at him. He didn't say anything, didn't try to run away. Just stood there staring…" Joe hesitated as he gathered himself. "And then he started crying and shouted, 'Shoot me! Shoot me! Kill us all! That's what you want!' I tried to drag him away, but he wouldn't budge. The cop got off his horse, still pointing the gun. Then he pulled out his billy club with the other hand and was about to clock dad when Ernie shows up out of nowhere and drops the cop with one punch. Then we both grabbed dad and took off. Didn't want to go home because a lot of people know my father, and the cops might go to our place. So we came here, running and half dragging my father."

Domenic sighed as he looked at his old friend sitting half-conscious in the chair. The life went out of Rossario when the flu pandemic took his wife Maria and his baby girl eight years ago. He began drinking and lost his job as well as his interest in everything he was once so passionate about. If not for financial help from Domenic, Ernie, and the Torre de'Passeri Society, he would have lost his building and home as well. When he became obsessed with the arrest and six-year legal odyssey of Sacco and Vanzetti that followed, Domenic knew it was driven by the grief and sadness that festered inside him. He was angry at the world.

Domenic stood up and turned to Ernie. "So you just happened to be there?"

"I was worried about Rossario. I saw him today when he was headed to Charlestown and the prison. He was already pretty drunk. He didn't want me to go with him, didn't want me near him. So I called Joe and then headed over to the prison to keep an eye on him."

Domenic nodded in a way to let Ernie know that what he did was appreciated. "This whole Sacco and Vanzetti business, it should never have dragged on like this. It should have been over and done with years ago."

"But you don't mean they should have been executed sooner, do you, Dom?" asked Joe.

"When you spread seeds of hatred, you should not be surprised that they grow. Those two both knew that by preaching their poison they were courting trouble. And it came to them."

"But what if they're innocent of these charges of murder, as they certainly seem to be?"

"They are guilty of other crimes. And of being stupid."

"That's bullshit, Dom!" They were all startled by the sudden, loud interruption by Rossario, who seemed awake and alert. "All they were guilty of was being Italian. That was their crime."

There was a knock at the door. They all had the same thought, *The police are here*. Domenic went to the door as Ernie and Joe began helping Rossario out of the chair to head to the back door.

"Domenic Bassini, it's me James Donnaruma. I saw your lights on and thought Rossario might be here."

Domenic let James in and he surveyed the scene. His eyes settled on Rossario, and the others could see the sympathy his look conveyed. His old friend who once joined him in their ongoing crusade to better lives in the North End looked disheveled and drunk, the constant cheery face once known to all now a frozen contortion of anger.

"Here's another who has forgotten how to be Italian," said Rossario, his words dripping with spite. "Why are you here?"

"I'm here for the same reason everyone in this room is. We care deeply about you."

"I don't need your concern. I need your voice, the voice of La Gazetta, which has been so silent while our brothers have been persecuted."

Donnaruma sighed. This was an old debate he and Rossario had over the last several years. Since the initial arrest of Sacco and Vanzetti in 1920, through two trials and multiple appeals, which garnered national and international attention due to the dubious evidence against the men and the clear prejudices of the presiding trial judge and law enforcement officials, *La Gazetta del Massachusetts* had remained silent. While Rossario was active in helping to form The Sacco-Vanzetti Defense Committee, Donnaruma's influential newspaper kept to short, neutral reports on the case while assiduously avoiding any editorial commentary.

"You know my reasons, Rossario. We've been down this road many times."

"I know that nothing has changed for us in this country. I arrived in America in 1891, the same year eleven of our countrymen were lynched in New Orleans. Tonight, America lynched two more. Those who run this city, this state, this country will always do what they can to remind us we will never be their equals, only their pawns," Rossario shouted through his tears.

Joe went to calm his father, but he wasn't done.

"Domenic, I love you like a son, but you bury your head in the sand. You take care of your family, you help others, you are well respected, but you wear blinders. You think by ignoring all the shit around us you can avoid its stink."

Domenic said nothing. He stayed calm and let Rossario have his rant. But the hurt in his eyes was unmistakable.

Rossario turned to Ernie. "Ahh, the Eel. I remember so vividly the night you earned that name. But you, my friend, were right after all. Their laws don't apply to us, so why follow them? You live by your own rules, and now I respect that. You take what you want without asking permission from the Brahmins or the Irish. Maybe we should all be like you."

Like Domenic, Ernie said nothing, his expression giving no clue to what he was thinking or feeling.

"And you, my son. My precious American Joe, who I love with all my heart. You sell insurance for a company that makes the rich richer. You were going to help usher in the glorious future of Italian Americans in Boston. But perhaps there is no such thing, and I feel sorry for putting such thoughts in your head."

"No, Dad," protested Joe, "you were right, and I will squeeze the pricks who run this city until they respect us. But I won't do it with bombs and threats. I'll do it from the inside. I'm running for city council in November, as we always talked about. And I will win. I promise you I will win. James and Ernie will help me."

Both Ernie and Donnaruma nodded. Domenic realized that this had long been planned.

"He's right," says James. "He will have the full endorsement and support of *La Gazetta*. As for Ernie's contribution to the campaign, I really don't want to know what that might entail."

Everyone was quiet for a moment. Then Donnaruma spoke again, "Rossario, you need to know that tonight the police asked everyone they could outside the prison who threw that bottle and who struck the officer. I know, I was there. Not as a journalist but as an Italian. And not one of the others would say a word. They protected you, and you too," pointing to Ernie. "That is solidarity. We may not agree on how to get there, but I know we are making progress, and I know that anarchists delay that progress. Now I have to go."

Donnaruma left the four others who once shared the same roof. There was silence until Ernie spoke. "I should go, and Rossario should stay here and sleep it off. Is that okay with you, Domenic?"

"Of course. I owe much to Rossario."

After Ernie left, Joe said "You should cut Ernie some slack, Dom. I know you disapprove of what he does, but he is a loyal friend, and he loves you."

"I have a young son and a family, Joe. I can't have anything to do with Ernie and what he does. You need to be careful as well if it's a career in politics you want."

Joe laughed. "Dom, what Ernie does in the dark and what the Irish politicians and their cronies do in broad daylight aren't much different." He leaned in and gave Dom a hug. "Sorry we all barged in on you tonight."

"You don't have to thank me. This is what family is for."

DECEMBER 22, 1931

ERNIE STOOD CALMLY off to the side in Joseph Lombardo's office at C & F Importers on Hanover Street, his right arm down at his side with the pistol in his hand pointed at the floor as ordered by Joseph Lombardo. On the other side of the door, young Frankie Cucchiara nervously held a shotgun at his side that Lombardo had shoved into his hands moments earlier. For his part, Lombardo sat calmly behind his desk facing the door, gun on his lap. To Ernie, Lombardo's face seemed unnaturally calm with a frozen half smile that reminded Ernie of an embalmed corpse. But his eyes gave away the anger boiling below the placid surface, and Ernie noticed a single bead of sweat start to trickle down by his ear from the perfect haircut to the collar of his custom-tailored shirt.

In Ernie's mind, Lombardo had been a poor choice to be named a co-boss of the Boston mafia by Gaspare Messina, at least in name, while Messina assumed the role of *capa dei capi* – boss of bosses – or the supreme leader of the Sicilian criminal society in the United States. Although from New York City, Messina was the first capo dei capi whose base was in Boston and not the city where the Mafia was established and nurtured. He never sought the position, but it was agreed by all the major bosses that as one of the oldest and most respected among them he should assume the role to broker an end to the war between then boss of bosses Joe Messeria and Salvatore Maranzano, who had challenged Messeria's authority with the support of some other crime families from around the country. It came as no surprise to Ernie that Messina was chosen for this honor. The man had all the qualities necessary to lead, most importantly his ability to stay calm, think things through, and only then take action.

In his wisdom, and some believe under some pressure, he had allowed the Angiulo Family to operate independently in Boston as their own family on equal footing with Lombardo and his family. He knew that the mercurial Lombardo was prone to overreact to the slightest provocation. And what the Gustin Gang had done was more than a slight provocation. Even Ernie had to admit that they had to have large balls to show up in the North End unannounced for a meeting and then make these demands. The South Boston Gustin Gang was known to be careless, stupid, and reckless. But this stunt took stupidity to a whole new level.

Lombardo's ego had him accept the meeting, and he grabbed Ernie and Cucchiara to protect him. Ernie believed he had already made up his mind to kill the Gustin brothers before they even made their way up the stairs to his office. They were probably already dead. Ernie assessed the situation and wondered about the blowback. Nobody liked them, not even their own kind. As agreed, there were three members of the Gustin gang in the meeting and three members of the Lombardo family in the room. Others remained downstairs.

Frankie Wallace, the leader of the Gustin Gang, walked into the office with his brother Stevie and his lieutenant, Bernard "Dodo" Walsh. He saw the weapons in the hands of the Italians, smiled, and raised his hands in the air. "I know you're upset Joseph, but hear me out. There's a lot more to this than you think." Lombardo bristled, and Ernie could see his face flush and his arm tense. Ernie spoke up quickly, "Maybe we should hear what he has to say, Mr. Lombardo." Stevie and Dodo looked at Ernie gratefully.

Gustin said to Ernie. "I heard you were a smart kid." Turning to Lombardo he began, "I guess you know who the prime minister is." Gustin was referring to Frank Costello, a highly placed and well-known New York gangster who, although born Francesco Castiglia, was closely aligned with the top Jewish and Irish gangs in New York City. He had forged a close alliance between the Irish and the Luciano crime family for the purpose of running liquor – a joint enterprise that came to be known as the Combine.

"So what?"

"Well, the Combine has made a close friend and benefactor of ours the head of everything up here in Boston relating to booze. And since we had a previous relationship with him, we are now your partners, and as such we get a piece of what is yours, because now it's ours too."

"Who is this benefactor?" asked Ernie. Anything to keep Lombardo from erupting. Even if there was a hint of truth to any of this, it wouldn't be smart to kill these Irish bastards, at least not now.

"Oh, he's a well-respected man with his hands in a lot of influential pockets in this city. I can't be telling you who, but you'd know him."

Ernie figured he was talking about Joseph Kennedy. Kennedy walked a fine line between respectability and racketeering. He was a Harvard-educated banker and investor who had made a fortune maneuvering in the cloudy area between what was legal and what wasn't. The son of a saloon owner and ward boss, he could grapple in the dirt as well as waltz in high society. Always the opportunist, he had married the daughter of Honey Fitz, cementing the support of the Irish bosses. Rumor was that he had been selling what was left of his father's ample stockpile of liquor to the Combine and running in more from Ireland, stacking up both money and favors. He was also known to be forging alliances and distribution channels with respectable liquor companies in Ireland and Britain that gangsters in America, particularly the Italians, could not.

"You buying any of this bullshit, Ernie?" asked Lombardo.

Ernie sized it up. If an alliance of this magnitude had been set up out of New York that included Boston, they would have heard of it. Gaspare himself would have been informed, and he certainly would have contacted Lombardo. The same Irish cops Lombardo paid would also be in the loop. No, the Gustins were trying to take advantage of a mix of truth and rumors involving Kennedy, Costello, Luciano, and the Combine. And these were all smart men who would certainly never have allowed these crazy punks to be part of anything that might be traced back to them.

"No, I'm not Mr. Lombardo."

"I'm telling you stupid wops, you'd better…" Gustin never got the chance to finish. The bullet from Lombardo's gun caught him in the neck. There was an instant of stunned silence as the four other men in the room were startled by the sudden gunshot. Then all hell broke loose.

Stevie Wallace and Walsh were pulling their guns while they dove for the door to the outer office. Ernie and Lombardo were unloading their pistols after them. Then a wild shotgun blast took out a piece of wall by the door that sent plaster flying and allowed the Irish the extra instant they needed to reach the hallway. Ernie took off after them and saw Dodo Walsh bleeding at the top of the stairs. His left arm dangled by his side, but he still held a gun in his right hand.

There was a commotion down below as Lombardo's men heard the gunplay and were rushing up the stairs. Dodo turned and saw Ernie, who had his gun pointed directly at him. There was panic and fear in his eyes as he backed away from the stairs. He looked at Ernie then looked at the stairs as the others got closer. He never raised his gun. Then Ernie heard Lombardo behind him shouting, "Shoot him! Shoot him!" And Ernie did.

1938

DOMMY BASSINI WANTED to crawl under his seat and disappear. It would have been tough to do, however, with his best friend Luigi "Lou" Molinaro, who was seated next to him, holding him in an enthusiastic bear hug. The auditorium at Cathedral High, filled for the end of the school year awards ceremony, had erupted into applause as Monsignor O'Hern announced that Dommy, who was just a junior, had been awarded that year's prestigious William Cardinal O'Connell Award for "outstanding achievement in athletics and scholarship." It was the first time an underclassman had won the award and also the first time the recipient was not Irish. It was also the first time that neither of the recipient's parents were there to witness it.

Cathedral High was founded by the Most Reverend William Cardinal O'Connell himself in 1926 with a generous gift from the estate of Mary C. Keith, a wealthy widow who sought comfort from the church, and the Cardinal himself, in her final days. It was created to serve immigrant and first-generation American youth of Boston by "developing them spiritually, intellectually, and socially to become Catholic leaders." In other words, to perpetuate the dominance of the Irish influence in controlling the Archdiocese of Boston.

The decision to attend Cathedral High had not been an easy one for the Bassini family. Dommy wanted to stay closer to the North End at the public high school with his friends from school and the neighborhood. Cathedral was located across Boston in the South End, next door to the Cathedral of the Holy Cross, the mother church of the Archdiocese of Boston. Domenic was torn between what might open up the best opportunities for Dommy and his distrust of anything having to do with the Irish. It was "Uncle" Joe Rossario who worked hard to convince them both that this was where Dommy should go to "broaden his horizons" and "open up more opportunities for his future."

Dommy was still resistant to the idea until Lou announced that he would go to Cathedral with Dommy, depending of course, if Joe could get him accepted as well.

It appeared to the world around him that Dommy had made the right choice. He flourished at Cathedral, becoming the star halfback on the football team and rising to the top of his class academically. He had even become somewhat of a celebrity in his neighborhood after being named to all-city football teams by both the Boston Traveler and the Boston Globe. But each day, when classes were over, he couldn't wait to hop on the trolley to Haymarket and home in the North End. Lou, who was as outgoing as Dommy was reserved, would always want to stay and join classmates at gathering spots around the school, or eschew the trolley in favor of making the long walk across town to home to breathe in the life of the city from the Back Bay mansions to the bustle of Scollay Square.

Dommy had no choice now but to stand and make his way up to the stage to accept his award from the Monsignor. As he stood, he could feel every eyeball in the hall on him and each one felt like a tiny burning pinprick. He couldn't hear any of the words of congratulations sent his way from students in the audience as he carefully made his way down the aisle and up the stairs to the stage and Father O'Hern at the podium. As Father O'Hern handed him the award, he was suddenly terrified that he might be asked to say something. But thankfully he wasn't, and he quickly made his way back to the stairs in a hurry to return to the obscurity of his seat. But the sure-footed halfback who could leave would-be tacklers grasping at air, missed the first step and slid down the remaining four stairs on his rump. Totally mortified, he bounced up and half ran back to his seat to a round of the same sardonic applause and laughter afforded the poor souls who dropped their tray in the lunchroom.

As he sat back in his seat, Lou turned to him and said, "Hey, at least you didn't fumble the plaque."

***

Later, the two friends were on the way home, Dommy giving in to Lou's insistence that they walk.

"I'm going to live in one of those big brick monsters someday, Dommy," Lou said to his mostly silent friend as they walked past the townhouses on Commonwealth Avenue. "You can live in the servants' quarters and bring me my cognac and cigars." When the gloomy Dommy didn't respond, Lou kept on going, "And the beautiful, big-titted, Mrs. Lou Molinaro, who we now know as Bridgett Ryan, will wonder how she could have ever been so crazy as to be gaga over that dope Dommy Bassini in high school who now sweeps her floors and serves her tea."

Dommy now turned and gave Lou a look of disgust. "You're so full of shit, Lou."

"Am I?" replied Lou. "About what? The fact that Bridgett Ryan has big tits or the fact that she loves your ass?"

Dommy stopped walking and looked at his friend. "You know what I think, Lou? I think it's been too long since the last time I kicked *your* ass."

Lou smiled. It looked as though he had finally broken his friend out of his doldrums. "You can't kick what you can't catch, Mr. All Shitty halfback." And with that Lou knocked Dommy's books out of his hands and sprinted down Commonwealth Mall toward the Public Garden, dodging pedestrians, bicycles, and dogs. Dommy quickly gathered up his books and took off in hot pursuit. Lou dodged cars as he crossed Arlington Street into the Garden with Dommy quickly closing the gap between them. As Dommy closed in, Lou tried to juke away but lost his footing and went sprawling down on the grass with his books and notebooks flying everywhere. Dommy stood over his friend laughing, and Lou didn't mind a bit.

***

After leaving Lou, Dommy's first stop upon returning to the North End neighborhood was, as usual, the Rossario Insurance Agency on Hanover Street. His godfather, Joseph Rossario, at thirty-three years of age, was more of a big brother to Dommy than the "honorary" uncle he proclaimed himself to be. His other unofficial title was "Mayor" of the North End, as he seemed to know every one of the forty thousand residents squeezed into the neighborhood which was ninety-nine percent Italian. More importantly, several years earlier he had become the first Italian-American to be elected to the twenty-two-member Boston City Council.

Joe's office was more of a neighborhood gathering spot than a place of business. It had once been a popular bar that had been forced to close during Prohibition. The owners moved to live with relatives in Medford, and Joe had purchased the entire three-story building with some financial help from Ernie Lentini. He lived in the apartment right above the office, and the top floor was empty but occasionally used by Ernie and his immediate crew, away from the prying eyes of his boss, Joseph Lombardo.

Joe's office was the normal bustle of activity when Dommy arrived. The large front space had two desks and a large sitting area, which was occupied by men from the neighborhood discussing anything and everything except, probably, insurance. Joe had a huge brass expresso machine set up in the sitting area that he had no idea how to use, but half the men in the neighborhood did.

At one desk sat the estimable Elisabetta Salvucci who essentially ran the Rossario Insurance Agency. Born and raised in the North End, she had been one of the few female underwriters for Boston's John Hancock Life Insurance Company before joining Joe and his fledgling agency six years ago. The fact that the agency had flourished was due equally to Joe's ability to bring in customers and Elisabetta's ability to do everything else.

The other desk was piled high with papers and folders, and a young, pretty girl, in her early twenties or so, was sorting through them. Dommy was used to seeing different young women at the second desk, as it seemed their position as Elisabetta's assistant lasted only as long as their relationship with Joe.

Elisabetta looked up as Dommy entered, giving him a motherly smile. Joe's office door was surprisingly closed, and Dommy raised his eyebrows toward Elisabetta and gave her a questioning look, to which she responded, "He's with a friend, but he said if you showed up to go on in."

There was a burst of laughter from Joe's office as Dommy opened the door and saw Joe seated at his desk and Ernie Lentini sitting in one of the two chairs facing it. To Dommy, the sight of the infamous Ernie "The Eel" Lentini always brought a touch of anxiety. He never fully understood how the two men he admired and loved most in his life, his father Domenic and his Uncle Joe, could have such starkly different opinions of the man.

This made him uneasy around Ernie, who his father always referred to as "Ermino" when he mentioned him, which was rarely. This same man who would send gifts to Dommy every birthday and Christmas was not welcome in Domenic's home. He could understand Domenic's reluctance to have any association with a known member of Joseph Lombardo's "family." Domenic had his rigid principles that Dommy knew all too well. But to many in the neighborhood, men like Lombardo and Ernie were heroes to be respected.

Both men looked up as Dommy entered and welcomed him with the same warm smile.

"Well, well, well," hummed Joe, "if it isn't Mister Cardinal O'Connor Award winner himself." Joe was beaming as he turned to Ernie and added, "Took that Goddamn award right out from under the noses of the Irish, Ernie. They had no choice but to give it to our boy."

Dommy wondered how Uncle Joe already knew he had won the award he received about an hour earlier.

"Hey, Dommy," said Ernie, "it's been a while." Then after a brief moment, as though looking at Dommy for the first time, he added, "Jesus but you look just like your father did the day I met him."

Dommy had grown to be taller than his father, with broader shoulders from which hung a slim frame begging to be filled in. And although he had a less-pronounced bend in his "Bassini" nose, he had the same dark, penetrating eyes, wavy, black hair, and strong jaw.

"Bullshit, Ernie," chimed in Joe, getting up from his chair, "The kid is way better looking than Dom ever was. Hell, I'm afraid to bring my girlfriend around him."

"Which one?" asked Ernie sarcastically.

"All of them, you jealous bastard."

Joe walked over, gave Dommy a hug and a kiss on the forehead, then whispered to him, "I'm proud of you, kid. We're all proud of you."

Dommy wasn't sure who "all" referred to, but was pretty sure it didn't include his father.

Ernie got up saying, "I gotta go. Good to see you, Dommy. Give my best to your father. Tell him he'll always have my respect, no matter what he thinks of me."

Instead of leaving through the office door leading out front, Ernie exited by the back door, which led to stairs going to the upper floors and another door that opened up into the alley. After he was gone, Dommy said to Joe, "I never know what to say to Mr. Lentini. My father never talks about him really. All I know is what you've told me, Uncle Joe. About how my dad helped Ernie get into America and how Ernie has never forgotten that."

"That's all you need to know, Dommy. But Ernie has many qualities your father can't see. He only sees Ernie the gangster."

"But isn't he?"

"Ernie makes his living doing many things that are illegal, but he is not like Lombardo and the Angiulos who just want money and power over others and will do anything to get both. He is not bound by any ancient blood oath to serve any family. He is smart, very smart, and he makes money for himself and his crew and shows the Lombardo family respect and, more importantly, profits from his various enterprises. But he is not a soldier, not a button man, not a servant…to anyone."

"Has he ever killed anyone?"

Joe dismisses the question with a shrug and wave of his hand and instead of answering says, "Let me tell you a story about Ernie. Remember when the building on Salem Street where the Marianos had their business burned down a couple of years back? They lost everything. They put every penny they had into buying that crumbling, two-story shithole of a building and opening their little grocery and butcher shop. Well, I had sold them on buying a fire insurance policy. God knows we have something burn down around here every week. Got them a policy through the New England Life Insurance Company. But when they had the fire, some claims manager at New England denied the claim because the Marianos were letting some relatives from Italy stay on the second floor while they looked for an apartment. Said that nullified the fire insurance.

"Well, nothing in the policy said anything like that, but it appeared the Marianos were pretty well fucked, pardon my language, Dommy, because big insurance companies never lose, which is why they have the biggest buildings. I got nowhere with them. Claims manager wouldn't even see me and stopped taking my phone calls. But then Ernie paid that claims manager a visit, at his house in Brookline, not his office. Next day the claim was approved. I didn't ask Ernie any questions. And maybe a law or two was broken, but I believe justice was served. And what did Ernie ask of me or the Marianos for this favor? Nothing. Not a goddamn thing. If that's a bad guy, give me more of them and maybe this neighborhood will stop getting stomped on by the bigots and other assholes in general who run this city."

Dommy said nothing but nodded his head to indicate he understood.

"But your father, who you know I love like a brother, can be very… strong minded."

"You mean stubborn, Uncle Joe," replied Dommy. "Tell me about it."

"Domenic has his standards, his impossibly high standards, and he doesn't hesitate to pass judgment on anyone who doesn't meet them."

"Like me."

"Hell no!" Joe exclaimed. "Your father is so proud of you. I've seen him beam when the men talk about you and ask about you. He would never show it or brag about you. But believe me he knows what you've accomplished and is damn proud of it."

"He has a strange way of showing it," said Dommy. "Today I was told he and Mama were invited to the awards ceremony but Papa declined. Went to work like always."

"That's Domenic," sighed Joe. "Go out and do what you're supposed to do, and do it right. Don't ask for help, don't expect favors, don't make waves, and don't get involved in anything you don't have to. But, believe me, he sees everything."

1939

IT SEEMED SURREAL to Lou to see Leverett Saltonstall, the governor of Massachusetts, sitting in Domenic's chair in the Bassini's tiny parlor. He appeared too large for the chair, the room, the entire apartment for that matter. Lou kept glancing over at Dommy hoping to make eye contact, but his friend sat stone-faced and polite between his parents on the small couch. Pasqualena looked terrified. Domenic, as always, appeared calm as he listened intently to what the governor had to say.

With all the sitting space in the small room occupied, Lou stood off to the side at the opening to the dining room thinking how lucky it was that he happened to be at the Bassinis for dinner that night. Of course, he was there most nights, so he supposed the odds of his being there had actually been pretty good.

For Lou, Saltonstall was the first well-known, old-money Brahmin he had ever encountered in such a social setting, and he was intrigued. Saltonstall was polite yet aloof. His suit was conservative and bland but hung perfectly on his tall, thin frame. He managed to sit impossibly straight in the soft chair and spoke with the ease and confidence borne from a life of privilege. His manners were impeccable as he complimented Pasqualena and Domenic on everything from their well-kept apartment to the wonderful job they had done raising such a fine son. But an air of condescendence hung on every word spoken, and Lou didn't trust him for a minute.

Saltonstall, for his part, really did not want to be spending his early evening in an Italian immigrant's apartment in the North End. But when you represented the tenth generation in direct descent to graduate from Mother Harvard, you were duty-borne to respond when she requested a favor. He had played football at Harvard, and the current powers-that-be wanted this young Italian boy now seated across from him to do the same. Harvard had just ended a three-year losing streak against Yale behind All-American halfback Clinton Frank. But Frank was graduating, and apparently this kid sitting on the couch in front of him had the talent to be the next Clinton Frank.

Saltonstall fully anticipated a brief visit ending with a grateful thank you from the family whose son was being handed the opportunity of a lifetime. He spoke directly to the father, who met his gaze and said little. Saltonstall wondered how good his English was and how much of what he was saying was really understood.

Speaking slower now, he said, "So you must understand, Mr. Bassini, in addition to the most superb education a young man could receive, a Harvard degree provides lifetime membership in an exclusive club. Your boy will be presented with opportunities throughout his life that I am sure you could never even imagine. Entrance into Harvard is granted to only a select few."

As always, Domenic thought, considered and weighed his words carefully before responding. Governor or not, this man was a stranger to him and his family. *Beware when strangers come bearing gifts,* he thought.

"I understand Harvard is a wonderful college and you want my son to go there," said Domenic. After nearly thirty years in America, his words were still soaked in a heavy accent. "And Harvard's offer to take care of all the costs is appreciated. Thank you. Now you haven't said it, but I know that you, that Harvard, is not doing this because you think it is best for Dommy. You are doing this because you think it is best for Harvard. For your football team."

Lou grimaced, and Dommy suppressed a smile. As surprised as he must have been by this response, Saltonstall for his part showed no emotion. It was now his turn to weigh his words.

"It is true, Mr. Bassini, that if Dommy were not so talented in athletics I would not be here. Now I do not know the specifics, but I would wager that he must also be accomplished in his studies and of strong character as well, or else he would not be considered for Harvard even if he were the next Red Grange."

Domenic had no idea who Red Grange was, but he understood the meaning and couldn't suppress a small prideful parent's smile.

"Thank you for the kind words about my son, Mr. Saltonstall, and your honesty." Turning to Dommy, he said," You have sat and listened, Dommy. Now I think we need to hear from you what you think about all this."

Saltonstall admired the respect shown his father by the boy. *Don't speak unless spoken to.*

Dommy had been listening. As always, he had been made uncomfortable by all the compliments paid him. He hated being the center of attention, and now it had been brought to an absurd level by having the governor in his home. The friggin' governor for Chrissakes! Still, a little of him wished his father could understand what a big deal this was and relish it a little instead of being his usual practical, unflappable, blunt self.

"Well, Governor Saltonstall," Dommy began, his proper addressing of the governor earning a thumbs up from Lou that no one else noticed. "To be honest, sir, I'm not sure how comfortable I would be at Harvard. I think as a first-generation Italian kid on scholarship I would stand out and not fit in."

Wise beyond his years, thought Saltonstall, *and probably correct as well.*

"Dommy, let me tell you about a classmate of mine back at Harvard. His name was Joseph Kennedy. He was one of the first of Irish descent to attend Harvard. And I won't lie to you that sometimes he was brushed aside as inconsequential, so to speak, by some of his classmates. Yet through his dogged determination he managed to become somewhat of a leader during his time at Harvard, earning entry into the Hasty Pudding Club and the prestigious Delta Upsilon fraternity. Today, he is the United States Ambassador to Great Britain and has one son who has graduated from Harvard and another there right now. He opened the door for others, so to speak, and you could well do the same. What say you to that?"

Lou thought that Saltonstall said "so to speak" too much.

Dommy knew what he wanted to say but could not. He wanted to say, "I don't want the scrutiny, the attention, or the expectations that would accompany me to Harvard. I don't want to always be the one singled out for being so goddamn wonderful when I'm not. I'm just lucky, and someday that luck will run out, and I'll disappoint everyone. I want to be left alone to be me."

But what he did say was, "Can I think about all this, sir? It's kind of overwhelming right now."

"Absolutely, you can, my young friend," said Saltonstall as he stood up, indicating his work at the Bassini home was done. Pasqualena scurried to get his coat, which had been set on the dining room table.

Turning to the Bassinis as he stepped into the stairwell where his driver stood waiting, he said, "I understand the fear of the unknown you all must have. But it is by venturing into the unknown and by accepting challenges that we become great. Remember that, Dommy."

And with that little inspirational speech, he set off down the stairs with the thought of getting home to Chestnut Hill, where the staff would have his dinner warmed and waiting.

※※※

Dommy spent a good part of the next day answering, or avoiding actually, questions about Saltonstall's visit. A special trip by the governor of the state to a four-story walkup in the North End could not go unnoticed in the neighborhood. Somehow, even his teachers at Cathedral had heard about it, and one brought it up in front of the entire class. Now, he wanted to get home and forget about it. But as he approached the Rossario Insurance Agency, there was his Uncle Joe standing out front. Joe waved to Dommy as he got near, signaling him to come over. *He's been waiting for me,* Dommy thought.

"So, Dommy, I hear you had a visitor last night."

"You know we did, Uncle Joe. Everybody seems to know."

Joe laughed. "It's a small neighborhood, Dommy, or a large family depending on how you look at it." This last sentence was spoken in all seriousness as Joe put his arm around Dommy. "Come on into the office. I want to have a talk."

They walked through the reception area into Joe's small private office. People said that Joe Rossario wrote every life insurance policy in the North End, and his office looked like every one of them was sitting on his desk or on the small table off to the side. Even the three chairs at the table weren't immune from the clutter, essentially serving as four-legged file folders. Joe lifted a pile of binders, folders, and random unattached papers from one chair and pulled it over by his desk, motioning for Dommy to take a seat. He then squeezed between some stacks on the floor and into his chair behind the desk.

"So, Dommy, I understand you don't want to go to Harvard."

"No, I don't, Uncle Joe. Can't see myself there."

"I guess I can understand that Dommy. And why is that? Because those are not our kind of people over there? Because you're afraid you won't fit in? Won't be accepted? Or is it because you're afraid that you're not good enough? Smart enough?"

"Maybe all of that, Joe."

"Which is exactly why you have to go! Because someone from around here has to be first so others can go someday without worrying about fitting in. Because people like my father, and Roberto Scigliano, and even your father in his own way have worked to get us to the doorstep of respectability and inclusion, and now its time for your generation to open that door. Whether you like it or not, people in our neighborhood look up to you. I know that's a weight you don't want to carry, but it's a responsibility you must. Go to Harvard, show the bastards what a kid from the North End can do, and serve as an example and, hopefully, an inspiration to all the other kids from here."

Dommy sat in silence, a little stunned by the forceful tone of Joe's words. But the familiar Joe smile returned quickly, and he said, "I bet if Saltonstall had offered Domenic a plot of land in Harvard Yard to plant tomatoes he would have sold you right down the river."

SEPTEMBER 1940

FOR THE FIRST time in years, the annual varsity-freshman scrimmage at Harvard was close. When Dommy Bassini weaved his way in for his second touchdown of the afternoon, the freshman section at Harvard Stadium exploded in cheers, and many of the students cast their crimson freshmen beanies with a white H in the air. One landed in the lap of Dommy's father, who sat by himself in the stands. He turned to look for its owner, but no one seemed to want to claim it, so he set it on the concrete bench beside him. He looked back to the field where the scrimmage was ending and remained there watching his son.

He wouldn't go down to the field as the players shook hands and milled about before making their way back to the locker room. He wouldn't even let Dommy know he had been there. Curious, Domenic had come to see Dommy's new world for himself. He had not accompanied Dommy when he set off for Harvard two weeks earlier. He was a man now at eighteen and should be able to travel three miles on his own. Hadn't he himself traveled across an ocean to a new country alone at the age of sixteen? As much as he loved the boy, he would not spoil him. His mother did enough of that. In fact, unknown to Domenic at the time, Pasqualena followed Dommy out of the apartment the day he left for Harvard, saying she was going to the market, and got into Joe's waiting car with him, and the three co-conspirators drove off together to Harvard. When a remorseful Lena confessed this to Domenic, the only time she had ever deceived him in their nineteen years of marriage, he was secretly relieved to hear that Dommy had settled in nicely despite expressing some feigned anger.

Dommy spoke little of this place that occupied so much attention in the consciousness of Bostonians. Harvard was like a mythical island to people like Domenic, one that existed nearby but allowed access to so few. He wondered what made it so special in the minds of so many.

At work, in the neighborhood, in the society, people asked him what it was like to have a son at Harvard. A football star at that. Dommy offered no answers, shrugging off question about college life behind the walls of Harvard Yard from him and Pasqualena. Mostly Pasqualena, as he refused to delve deeply into the obviously reticent responses from his son. So he came to see for himself.

As he walked down the steps, he caught pieces of a conversation from the group of students surrounding him.

"I have a class with him, and he never, never talks," said one of the girls.

"Maybe he no speaka da English," joked one of her male companions.

"Oh, he speaks English all right," said the girl. "When called upon, he always has the right answer."

Another girl chimed in, "Tall, dark, handsome, and mysterious. That's my kind of guy."

"Well, I'll grant you the dark part, but he's not a true Harvard man," objected one of the men. "What are we if all it takes to claim a Harvard pedigree is the ability to avoid tackles? We might as well welcome trained baboons and offer them degrees in exchange for amusing us on weekends. I'm sure they could run from tacklers just as well, if not better."

Most in the group laughed at this. Domenic bristled and felt a burn of anger that he quickly extinguished. So this was what his son endured living amongst what he perceived to be these spoiled and silly children. He gained some understanding of what made his son so reticent to speak about Harvard, not that he would ever consider asking him directly.

✳✳✳

Dommy went from the stadium to Dillon Field House, which housed the team's lockers, as quickly as he could, stopping only briefly to shake hands with some of the varsity players and accept congratulations on his play from others he didn't even know. He was eager to get changed and return to the North End, where he would spend the rest of his weekend away from Harvard, as he always did. As he neared the entrance to Dillon, Stanley Belinsky caught up with him, dropping one of his huge arms around Dommy's shoulders. "Great game, Dommy," he said. "And tonight will be even greater. There are parties all over campus waiting for us."

Dommy truly liked "Big Stan," as everyone called him. The non-pretentious farmer's son from Maine stood six foot three and weighed 220 pounds. He played tackle and loved to laugh and talk between plays, reveling in the ferocity of the game. He was at Harvard because his grandfather was a Harvard man who owned several of the largest paper mills in Maine. He was grossly disappointed when his only daughter married a "Polak," as he called her husband, against his wishes and chose to live on his family's farm. But he made sure through the financial largess he showed toward his alma mater that his only grandson would be admitted to Harvard.

"Can't, Stan," replied Dommy. "Going home."

"So what else is new?" sighed Stan. "Dommy, you are becoming known as somewhat of a hermit."

Ignoring Stan's comment, Dommy said, "Why don't you come? You won't believe my mother's cooking. Ever had real, I mean *real* Italian food?"

"No, thanks, I prefer to stay here among the living. But I'll take a raincheck."

After a quick stop at his room to gather a few things, Dommy set out on the walk home to the North End from Cambridge as he had every weekend since arriving at Harvard. It was a walk he always enjoyed, made even more pleasant by the perfect fall day with a clear blue sky and bright sun glimmering off the waters of the Charles River. He always marveled at how his starting point from the cloistered green dignity of Harvard Yard contrasted with the lively and loud asphalt streets of his destination. He took his time, dragging out his journey, alone with his thoughts away from his two roommates on one end and friends and family on the other. He found his two roommates to be well meaning but childish in their vapid pursuit of college rituals, politely refusing their constant invitations to join them. At home, he could relax and enjoy Lena's pampering while his father's taciturn nature provided a welcome respite from talking about school, or much of anything for that matter.

He was always on guard at Harvard, worried about saying or doing the wrong thing and being judged by people with whom he had so little in common. As he walked, he would often think about the future, concerned he had no idea what his place in it might be.

1941

THE WORLD CHANGED for all Americans on December 7, 1941 when the Japanese bombed Pearl Harbor. Four days later, the United States was officially at war not only with Japan but Germany and Italy as well. The result had a far reaching effect on all Italian Americans. In the North End, Italians who had not become citizens suffered the ignominy of being forced to register as enemy agents, no matter how long they had lived in the country. Ironically, many of these "enemy agents" had sons fighting for America in the war.

For Domenic, the insult was even more pronounced. After working at the Navy Yard for nearly thirty years, he was now prohibited from speaking Italian at work, a transgression punishable by termination. And the unfairness of the situation was magnified when Dommy announced he was leaving school to join the Marines.

Dommy's decision, along with the shame and anger he felt taking Pasqualena to register with him as enemy agents, triggered a fierce determination within Domenic to prove he was as much an American as anyone. He doubled the effort he had already begun to become a citizen, the dream of ever returning to his small town in Italy abandoned years earlier when he married Lena, whose only family were now all in America.

He also vowed that none of the workers at the shipyard would buy more war bonds than he to support the war effort. He not only saw this as a way of proving his loyalty, but he also felt if buying bonds aided the war effort, it also aided his son. Each day when he arrived at work, he would check the list by the main gate of the shipyard of those purchasing bonds to make sure his name, his very proud Italian name, remained at the top.

Dommy, for his part, had described his decision to join up to his father as "needing to do his duty," which was at least partially true. It was also an opportunity to escape the suffocating confines of Harvard Yard for a legitimate and noble reason that no one could question. Any fear associated with going off to war was softened through the haziness of distance, while his uneasiness at Harvard burned sharply every day.

For Ernie "The Eel" Lentini and the Lombardo family, the war offered opportunity. The Office of Naval Intelligence had reached out to the New York Mafia to help them weed out any Mussolini supporters among the heavily Italian fishermen and dockworkers along the Mafia-controlled waterfront. Deals were made, and the Boston families were ordered to follow suit. There would be no union strikes during the war, Italians of questionable loyalty would be identified by the families, and any helpful assistance, whether through firsthand knowledge or contacts in Italy, would be provided to the government to help plan the invasion of Sicily. In exchange, certain federal investigations and prosecutions would be put aside, and leniency recommended in existing cases. Normal, nonviolent operations could continue without fear of federal scrutiny.

Lombardo's role in the Gustin shooting, which made him something of a folk hero for helping to end the Irish mob's reign and cement the power of the Italian Mafia in Boston, had also made him untouchable by competing Italian family factions, including the Patriarca family of Providence and their allies, the Angiulo family in Boston. Both would prefer someone else to run a consolidated Boston operation, but Lombardo's popularity kept that prospect at bay. This was to Ernie's benefit as Lombardo, aware of his own limitations, had grown to depend on him for advice, despite each man's dislike of the other. They both prospered while Ernie did his best to keep the hard-headed Lombardo in check.

Also prospering was Dragatto Enterprises, mostly due to Francesca's innate management skills. In addition to his popular restaurant and wholesale fish business, Cologero now owned several highly leveraged buildings in the North End and Back Bay, partially financed by his Sicilian "investors." Although he and Francesca's relationship had grown distant, he valued and trusted her acumen. He could always find partners to satisfy his sexual desires elsewhere.

Colin O'Riley's mini empire within the BPD had been eroding prior to the war, as the old school superiors began retiring and new reform-minded supervisors took their place. But with the war came an attrition of officers, since many volunteered to serve, causing a need for auxiliary and reserved police units. Within these groups, Colin found volunteers still reeling from the deprivation of the Great Depression more than willing to join his cadre of officers loyal to him in exchange for some additional income and a permanent position within the force. His profitable relationship with Joseph Lombardo since being introduced to him by Ernie Lentini during Prohibition continued to flourish. All in all, he had his eyes set on a prosperous post-war run.

It seemed on the surface that normal life paused in the North End, as it did everywhere as the entire country focused on the war effort, but the unstoppable momentum built up over decades of tribalism kept many silent societal wheels in Boston turning in their same inescapable direction.

JANUARY 1942

SERGEANT JAMES DUNNIGAN sat behind a small, Spartan desk seemingly engrossed in paperwork. There were four other desks exactly like it in a room so small it would be nearly impossible for all of them to be occupied at once. Right now, Sergeant Dunnigan's was the only one in use. To Domenic, the sergeant was the toughest man he had ever known – mentally and physically. The sergeant didn't even look up as Domenic entered the room and stood in front of it.

"Private Bassini reporting as ordered."

Dunnigan slowly piled a stack of papers and pushed them aside before saying, "At ease private", still without glancing up. "Sit down."

Domenic sat and waited.

Dunnigan finally sat back in his chair and looked straight at Domenic, expressionless as usual.

"You like it here, Bassini? You like being a Marine?"

"Yes, sir, Sergeant, sir."

"You like me, Bassini?"

"Yes, sir, Sergeant, sir." Domenic detected a slight twinkle in the man's eye, as though he was enjoying this, and Dommy tried to figure out where this was going. The truth was he did like it at Parris Island, he did like the Marines, and he did, in fact, like the sergeant. It was the regimen, the lack of personal freedom that actually made Domenic feel free. More free than he had in years. He enjoyed being another anonymous piece of the platoon mosaic. They may have come here as individuals, but now they were part of something much larger, and each of them, all his brothers, were not only ready to accept their role in it but embrace it. The last four weeks were both the toughest and best weeks of his life. In two more weeks, basic would be over, and they would move along together to their next stop.

"Don't bullshit me, Bassini. I don't like it when people bullshit me," he said gruffly, but some of the usual intimidating edge was missing in the sergeant's voice.

"No bullshit, sir, Sergeant, sir."

"Know you can't bullshit me, Bassini. But apparently you can bullshit other people who aren't quite as bright as me."

Domenic was still confused, but this time he was sure he saw a hint of a smile. But he wouldn't know what a smile looked like on Sergeant Dunnigan's face, since he had never seen one.

"Seems the other ignorant assholes in your squad have elected you their squad leader."

Domenic was stunned. Since he arrived at Parris Island, he had done nothing to stand out, nothing to excel. He did not want to be a leader, he enjoyed being just another team member. As a college man, he could have enrolled in officer training and chose not to.

"Thing is, Bassini, I think you'll make a shitty squad leader."

"Yes, sir, Sergeant, sir. I agree."

"Don't be agreeing with me, private! I don't need you agreeing with me, and I sure as hell don't want you agreeing with me because you're no goddamn smarter than the mud on my boots, Mister Harvard Honey." That was how Dunnigan referred to Domenic since the day he set foot on Parris Island.

"Yes, sir, Sergeant, sir."

"Now because your squad members are such piss-poor judges of character, I have to protect them. That's why I'm getting you away from them and recommending you for the new Special Officer Candidate School they're starting up at Lejeune." Now the sergeant was definitely grinning.

"But, sir, I don't want to be an officer, sir. I just want to be a Marine."

Dunnigan was silent. It was almost as though Domenic's response was what he had expected and at some level wanted. But he stared at Dommy for a while, squeezing his lips with his thumb and forefinger as though buying time before speaking. When he did, his voice was serious and softer than Domenic ever imagined the gunner's voice could be.

"I know that, son," he said, looking Domenic straight in the eye. "I know that. But these days, an awful lot of people are being asked to be things they don't want to be. And I don't know much, but I do know the Marine Corps needs the best men in the right spots. Now any poor, loyal, stupid sonofabitch can carry a rifle and shoot at the enemy, and God bless him for it. And we're going to need a lot of them if we're going to win this war. But we need good men who can lead these poor bastards and maybe save some of their lives in the process. Leaders they will trust and respect and whose orders they will follow without question.

"The men trust you and look up to you, Domenic. Anyone can see that. You are going to be a much better lieutenant than most of the spoiled college shitheads showing up all around the corps. So do it. Just fuckin' do it." Dunnigan looked away, as though embarrassed at having spoken so honestly to a mere recruit.

Domenic sat stunned, not knowing what to say.

"You might as well get it over with now and learn what you can. You're only going to keep getting promoted anyway, if you live long enough that is." The twinkle was back.

MARCH 1943

AS DOMENIC LOOKED down for the first time at Lena in her open coffin in the viewing room of the Joseph A. Langone, Jr. Funeral Home in the North End, she seemed more at peace than she ever was in life. Life for his Lena always seemed to be one of great worry and great caring, neither of which allowed her the luxury of simple contentment. Her pleasure, her only real pleasure, came in taking care of him and Dommy. Even more so Dommy, who she fought so hard to conceive and bring into the world. God may have given her a weak body, but he also gave her the iron fortitude to overcome it.

He recalled the day he met her. Scared and hurt, covered in sticky molasses yet holding her nephew aloft with a strength that exceeded her own. That strength manifested itself every single day that he knew her, until one day it simply gave out. The doctor said it was pneumonia, but Domenic knew it was the stress from worrying about Dommy. She couldn't take him by the hand for his first day of school or make him a special dinner to lift his sunken spirits on a visit home from Harvard. She couldn't do his laundry or mend his socks or buy him a new football. He was at war and she could only worry and pray. And it killed her.

For Domenic, below the surface of grief was a sense of guilt. He felt he never loved her as much as he should. She deserved it, but in his heart he knew that although he admired her, respected her, appreciated her, and treated her as well as he could, he could never love her as much as she loved him. And it hurt. As he looked down at her, he cried for the first time in many years. And he promised her he would take care of Dommy, and she would always remain in his life through their son.

MARCH 1945

AS DUSK TURNED to darkness over Iwo Jima, Lieutenant Domenic Bassini struggled to remain conscious as he clung piggyback-style to the broad back of Sergeant Peter Keenan. The pain from the bullet holes in his shoulder and thigh throbbed with each rapid step Keenan took over the flat, hard volcanic island surface dotted with craters, foxholes, and bodies. His arms were draped around Keenan's neck, and he still held his M1 Grand rifle in his good arm, which bounced off the sergeant's chest as he scurried back toward the safety of the beach encampment.

Domenic's platoon had been making its way back when the Japanese suddenly sprung from the ground around them while unleashing a deadly assault. Domenic, Keenan, and two of his men took a position at the rear of the platoon and dug in while ordering the rest of the men to retreat back to the beach. Of the forty-five Marines in the platoon who had come ashore three weeks earlier on February 19, only twenty-three remained. The remnants of the platoon spent their days searching for Japanese tunnels and caves before returning back to the battalion encampment before nightfall. That was when the Japanese would silently emerge from underground to ambush and kill as many of the Americans as they could under the cover of darkness before returning like vampires to their labyrinth of hidden caves before dawn. Their only objective was to kill as many US Marines as they could before the inevitable defeat they faced.

Despite Dommy's pleas to leave him and head back to safety, the sergeant would scurry from foxhole to foxhole with his lieutenant on his back, trying to evade the enemy oozing out of the ground around them. After catching his breath, he would move on, half running, half crawling until collapsing into the next crater.

The sound of Japanese fire seemed to be further away as they fell into a large crater and landed amidst the bodies of several dead American and Japanese soldiers, enemies made equal by death. The bodies were half submerged in the muddy water at the bottom of the crater.

The two waited in desperate, panting silence for any sounds from above. None came.

"I think we may have lost the dirty bastards, Lieutenant," whispered Keenan as he lay on his back next to Dommy with his rifle pointed up at the ridge of crater.

"I ordered you back, you stubborn Irish bastard," Dommy spoke haltingly, the pain from his wounds growing worse.

"Now, Lieutenant, you know I never liked taking orders from an eye-talian. You should have ordered me to stay. Then I would have gladly left you for the vermin."

Despite the pain, Dommy smiled. He and Keenan had bonded through training when Dommy was assigned a platoon out of officer's school. Everyone liked the big Irishman from Brooklyn, who was a New York City police officer before joining the Marines after Pearl Harbor. Dommy lobbied for his field promotion to sergeant while on Guam and assigned him a squad.

In his rare serious moments, Peter would talk about how much he loved being a cop.

"Ya know, Dom, I shoulda been a thieving bum like most my buddies growing up, but a cop in the neighborhood kept me on the straight and narrow. For some reason, he was always there to whack me in the head or give me a boost of confidence, whichever I happened to need at the time. Everyone loved him. Now I'm returning the favor. Best part of the job though is cracking the heads of all the various scumbags I come across. I see that as a bonus." Always punctuated with a hearty laugh.

In the mud at the bottom of a pit surrounded by death, Dommy never felt closer to another human being. Keenan rolled toward Dommy to look at his wounds. Dommy grimaced as the sergeant pulled at his shirt to get a look at his shoulder.

"That's funny," said Keenan. "I always thought Italian blood would be more greasy." And he laughed at his own joke. "But I need something to stop that bleeding. Soon. Your leg is just a scratch."

"Doesn't feel like a scratch," muttered Dommy.

"I'm going up top to forage around to see what I can find to wrap those wounds. Medics are always leaving shit lying around these holes. Might get lucky and even come across some help."

"It's not safe, Pete. Best bet is to stay right here and keep our fingers crossed the Japs don't stumble upon us before daylight."

"Shit, Lieutenant, not to scare ya, but you might not make it to morning if we don't find a better way to stop this bleeding."

Before Dommy could mount a protest, Keenan was crawling up the side of the foxhole. At the top, he peered out into the darkness before looking back at Dommy and giving him a thumbs up as he climbed out. Almost immediately after Keenan disappeared over the side, the shots rang out. He heard his friend returning fire. Dommy couldn't lift his rifle and reached for his sidearm with his good arm, but it was gone. Then he heard Pete screaming. The screams intensified and seemed to go on forever until they finally stopped. He could hear the voices of the Japanese soldiers. Some were actually laughing. He wanted to help his friend but couldn't stand. The Japs were close to the top of the crater. He was ready to die.

Suddenly, Pete's naked body came flying back into the pit, his face landing inches from Dommy's. Dommy didn't move, he just stared into the blank, dead eyes of his friend. Blood flowed out of what was left of Pete's mouth, his teeth smashed away, his tongue gone. The muffled voices of the Japs moved away. As he choked on the stench of the death, mud and blood around him, he reached for the small wooden cross around his neck. He wanted to pray but could not. Pete's bloody face frozen in horror was the last thing he remembered.

DECEMBER 1945

THE CURTAINS PULLED tight to keep it out were no match for the morning sun, and it gradually and relentlessly sliced its way into the room. Lying in his bed wide awake, Dommy turned away from the window with its unwelcome brightness and forced his eyes shut. From the street he could hear the familiar sounds of the North End coming alive, the same sounds that used to be like a siren's call to a new day but were now like fingernails on a chalkboard, and he wished he could close his ears as well. But he knew the new day would be unrelenting and eventually force itself upon him.

The worst part of every new day was seeing Domenic for the first time. Wearing a mask of pleasantry had never been a strength of his father, nor was small talk. And although Dommy appreciated his father's valiant attempt at normalcy, all the pain, concern, and love in Domenic's face was revealed most starkly to him the first time he looked into it each day.

If he could wait until Domenic left for work, he could at least prolong that uncomfortable encounter until later in the day. So he remained in bed waiting and trying not to think. He wanted his mind to be blank so he would not have to dwell on the past nor make any decisions about the future. He wouldn't even deal with today until it became too intrusive to ignore.

He had lost much of himself in the war. He knew that, and he knew how different he must seem to everyone around him. But there was nothing he could do about that. He couldn't pick up his life where it had left off three years ago. It didn't make sense somehow that people's lives should simply go on as though the war had never happened. Or that they even could go on.

The one decision he had made even as his wounds healed in hospitals on Guam then Hawaii and finally Boston was that he was not going back to Harvard, or any college. His love of sports had been extinguished, rendered insignificant by all he had been through. And how could he ever worry about a grade on an exam while he could still smell the rancid sulfuric air of the beach on Iwo Jima? And he swore to himself that he would live his life from now on as he wanted, not as others expected. But now, although firm in his resolve, he remained dispossessed of any direction.

His strategy, for the time being at least, was one of simple evasion. People, decisions, life…anything and anyone could be evaded. He had learned to occupy himself with the simplest of distractions that kept him in the here and now. Jigsaw puzzles had become a favorite pastime. Reading had evolved from a love to a need. But other times he would just get behind the wheel of the 1937 Chevrolet Master Coupe his father and Joe had waiting for him when he got home and drive with no destination in mind, allowing his mind to wander into nothingness. He would sometimes find himself on back roads as far away as New Hampshire and wonder how he got there. He would avoid the streets of the North End as much as possible because there was always someone who wanted to stop and talk. He was okay, he told himself. He only needed some time.

Domenic for his part had not pushed. It tore at his heart to see the spark that had always burned so brightly within Dommy snuffed out, but he had his son back from the war while so many others did not. He would give Dommy all the time and all the space he needed.

JANUARY 1946

DOMMY SAT ON the top step of the stoop of the Bassini home, half hidden in the shadows of the early evening January darkness. He had returned home from a long drive to nowhere and wanted to avoid going upstairs for a while, where he knew his father would be preparing dinner. He had also spied Lou's car parked on the block and suspected he too was upstairs waiting for him. Since returning home, Dommy had avoided Lou as much as he could, but his old friend was persistent. Lou had managed to earn his degree from Boston College and was now in law school after spending three years stateside during the war in the Military Intelligence Service.

He would joke that it was ironic that "intelligence" was not actually a prerequisite for his job, which he would describe as walking reports from one office to another. "I was essentially a mailman with a very short route," he would say. Domenic loved the two people waiting for him but felt uncomfortable around them. They were concerned and compassionate and would talk about anything except what was really on their mind, him. Dommy knew it was time for him to pull together as many of the salvageable pieces of his past life as he could and get on with it. But too many of those pieces remained missing for him to become close to being whole.

The main one was a purpose. What was the purpose of his life? Of anyone's life for that matter? What he had seen, and what he still saw every night in his dreams, had made any earthly purpose seem trivial.

As he sat on the stoop, his thoughts turned to Peter Keenan as they usually did. He could not escape the crushing weight of a debt that could never be repaid. This, more than anything, kept him from moving forward.

Sounds from across the street pulled Dommy away from his thoughts. The voices of a group of kids who had been sitting on a stoop suddenly became louder and more animated as they bounced down from the steps and ran to an approaching figure. It was a cop. Dommy could hear the children's laughter and the deep baritone voice of the police officer but couldn't make out what they were saying. Then he saw the officer take a bag from under his tunic, reach into it, and start handing out what must have been candy to the kids. He then shooed them on their way with a grin and resumed walking his beat down North Street.

As he did, he happened to look up and see Dommy watching. He tipped his cap with a smile and said to Dommy in a strong voice soaked in a thick Irish brogue, "It's the best part of the job. Have yourself a good evening, sir." He continued walking.

Dommy continued to sit but found himself suddenly holding back tears. He gathered himself after a few moments, stood up, and said out loud, "Thanks, Pete." He then went up the stairs to the first floor apartment and entered into the living room to be greeted with an unnatural cheeriness from both Joe and Lou, who were seated there. His father, upon hearing him come in, came more hurriedly than necessary from the kitchen where he had been preparing dinner. Dommy sensed they were all relieved to see him.

"Just in time," said Dom, feigning normality as though everything in the world was okay. "Dinner is ready."

"Let me guess," said Lou, "gnocchi."

Joe laughed and replied, "The gnocchi remain the same, only the filling changes."

Over dinner, the banter remained light, while Dommy ate in silence, lost in thought. The others would look to him and try to draw him into the conversation, but he would respond only with a smile or nod.

"So, Joe," said Lou. "When the hell are you going to settle down with a nice woman? How old are you now, fifty-five, sixty?"

"I'm only forty-three you wise ass and still young enough to kick your culo."

"He's right, Joe," chimed in Domenic, only more seriously. "All this running around with the girls is no good."

"My dear friend, Dom," responded Joe. "You like to eat. No, you love to eat, right? But you don't eat the same thing every night, because then you would get sick of it. Well, I love to screw, but if I had to screw the same thing every night I would get sick of it too. "

Lou and Joe laughed, and Dom shook his head in disgust.

Then, even before the laughter subsided, Dommy suddenly stopped eating, sat back in his chair, and declared, "I'm going to be a cop."

***

Very little happened inside of Boston Police Headquarters that escaped the prying eyes of Captain Colin O'Riley. This included the list of incoming new recruits. As he perused the latest list, a name jumped out at him, *Domenic Giuseppe Bassini*. What was even more noteworthy to Colin was the accompanying notation. "…this Purple Heart and Silver Star recipient has been recommended and endorsed by Boston City Councilman Joseph Rossario."

The name Bassini alone was enough to spark some interest in O'Riley's mind. He still recalled the night he received the scar on his scalp, which he now unconsciously rubbed, courtesy of the elder Bassini and Ernie Lentini. But it was seeing that he was recommended by Joe Rossario, who had been a thorn in his and the department's side for years with his calls for transparency and reform, which were cause for outright concern. He mused to himself how he and Lentini, who he had never stopped hating, had become unlikely and uneasy associates due to their respective relationships with Joseph Lombardo, as he got up and opened the door to his small office to summon in Sergeant Billy Flynn. Flynn and Colin went back to the days when both were breaking laws instead of enforcing them, and he was the captain's most trusted confidant. The cadre of "O'Riley's officers" as they were known, received most of their orders from Colin via Billy Flynn.

"What's up, Colin?" asked Flynn as he entered the office, closing the door behind him.

"Have you a seen the list of new officers coming onboard?"

"I have not."

"Well, there's a name on the list, Domenic Bassini, who I never want to see assigned around any of our boys. In fact, I don't want him doing any real police work that could jeopardize our interests."

"Fine. So who is this guy?"

"He's Joe Rossario's godson, and he's got connections to our buddy The Eel. He could be a plant."

"Got ya." Flynn turned to leave and then stopped as he reached the door. Turning back toward O'Riley he asked, "Do you think he can ride a horse?"

O'Riley looked up at Flynn quizzically then broke out into a laugh. "Not a bad idea, Billy boy. The mounted unit. Perfect. He'll march in parades, write a few parking tickets, do some crowd control, and never ever get near a real crime scene. I love it. Make it happen."

SEPTEMBER 1946

DOMMY'S FIRST MONTH as a police officer was spent learning to ride a horse. He was shocked and disappointed upon being assigned to the mounted unit but quickly realized it was useless to protest. No one could, or would, give him a reason for it. "A roll of the dice, Officer Bassini," Captain Michael Fitzgerald, the commander of the unit told him his first day on the job, although Dommy doubted this. Fitzgerald then went on in lengthy detail about the proud history of the Boston Police Mounted Unit dating back to 1873, making it the oldest mounted police unit in the country. Domenic was assigned a large, brown eleven-year-old Percheron named Fitzy.

"No relation," joked the commander with a laugh as he introduced Dommy to his new best friend. "He's a good horse, strong and calm. He'll give you no trouble." Fitzy weighed nearly 2,000 pounds and stood five feet eight inches to his shoulders. When Dommy was mounted upon him, his head was an imposing ten feet from the ground.

In a short time, Dommy was riding the big draft horse with confidence while learning how to care for him. Each officer had their own mount, and no others would ride it. Dommy and Fitzy bonded quickly, and Dommy would often find his way to the stables on Stanhope Street on his day off to take Fitzy on a jaunt to the nearby Fens and Muddy River for fun, bringing him fresh carrots and apples from Haymarket.

Dommy's nine-hour shift was from four in the afternoon to one in the morning and normally began with an evening trot with his mount down Commonwealth Mall to Kenmore Square. As darkness fell on a warm September evening laced with a hint of fall, it was a pleasant trot to Commonwealth Avenue from the stables on Stanhope Street. The rhythmic clop of the horse's hoofs on the pavement echoed loudly, drawing the attention of the people he passed, and Dommy was sure to offer them all a smile and nod.

Kenmore Square had sprung to life over the years, evolving from little more than the point where Commonwealth Avenue and Beacon Street crossed after stretching out from the Back Bay into a bustling amalgamation of hotels, businesses, and nightlife at the doorstep of the rapidly expanding Boston University. With the opening of Fenway Park in 1912, it became a gathering spot for all types of Bostonians and eventually got so crowded that the trolley stop was moved underground to alleviate the congestion. On days like this when there had been a ballgame at Fenway, many fans tended to linger around the square into the evening, particularly in the hotel bars, of which there were many, putting traffic and pedestrians at odds. Thus the need for a mounted police presence to keep traffic flowing and crowds moving.

But as boisterous as Kenmore Square could become, it paled in comparison to where most of Dommy's nights ended, Scollay Square. As he made his return downtown along Commonwealth once the Kenmore crowds and traffic thinned, Dommy slowed his horse and soaked in the warmth and the sophisticated beauty and allure Commonwealth always held for him at night. It seemed so different now with fewer cars and pedestrians and bore little resemblance to the busy throughway it had become during the day, and certainly nothing like the route he would sometimes walk on his way home during his high school days. But this would end abruptly when he reached Scollay Square.

In the early 1800s, Scollay Square had become home to some of Boston's most prominent citizens as it was far enough away from the bustling docks and sordid alleyways along the waterfront. Its erudite beginnings included being the home of William Lloyd Garrison's abolitionist press and early experiments by Thomas Edison, Samuel Morse, and Alexander Graham Bell, who transmitted the human voice over wires for the first time from his Scollay Square laboratory. It was also the home to grand theaters, the Howard Athenaeum being the most famous. But just as the stately Howard Athenaeum evolved from hosting Shakespearian performances to the raunchy "Old Howard" featuring risqué burlesque shows, Scollay Square itself gradually evolved into Boston's most tawdry neighborhood filled with bars, tattoo parlors, whorehouses, amusement halls, and hot dog stands. It attracted an unlikely mix of seamen, servicemen, and college students, all seeking to engage in the vice of their choice, while a cadre of wily locals awaited to fleece them of anything they could.

It was this Scollay Square that awaited Dommy and Fitzy each and every evening. The worst time was midnight, when the city's "Blue Law" ordinances required bars to close, forcing their drunken patrons out into the streets. That was when the fights, stabbings, and robberies peaked. The imposing presence of mounted units gathered in the square, along with the paddy wagons parked and ready to shuttle their troublesome cargo to the Charles Street Jail, could only slightly mitigate the nightly mayhem.

This night seemed like any other as Dommy slowly walked Fitzy through the main streets and smaller alleyways, many reeking with the unmistakable scent of urine. Approaching the Old Howard, Dommy saw a commotion out by the street. There was shouting and what looked like some pushing and shoving in the center of a group of people standing about watching. Dommy quickened the pace and was soon able to see what was going on from his vantage point atop Fitzy. It appeared to be a disagreement between one of the locals, who Dommy recognized from past encounters, and a college boy, each backed by his respective friends. Such confrontations were not uncommon. Visits to Scollay Square were something of a rite of passage for Harvard men, many of whom would make the obligatory stop to pee on the plaque in the square commemorating the birthplace of Elihu Yale, the founder of Harvard rival Yale University. Dommy knew from experience that after their drunken fun in the theaters, bars, and amusement halls they would return to their dormitory rooms, many of which were larger than apartments in the West End housing entire families, and brag about their adventures among the unsavory locals.

Things were getting heated as Dommy rode up, but everything quieted down a bit as the intimidating presence of the huge police horse and his rider approached. "What's the problem here, boys?" asked Dommy authoritatively, eyeing the locals with a disgusted look that says *here we go again*. The agitated Harvard boy began shouting, "He scammed me. He cheated at the game and won't give me my money back!"

"What game?"

"The shell game. There was no pebble under any of the cups!"

Dommy looked at the local running the game, who shrugged his shoulders with a look that was half guilty and half defiant. "You and your buddies get out of here now and stay away." The group gladly obliged. Dommy knew they'd be back the next night.

The Harvard man protested, "But he has my money! Arrest him!"

Before Dommy could respond, a girl stepped up from behind the man and said to him with disgust in here voice, "Oh for God sakes, Benjamin, let it go! I told you not to get involved with that stupid game in the first place, but you wouldn't listen. It's not worth getting beaten or stabbed over a lousy ten dollars. My girlfriends are petrified and want to get away from this horrible place."

Then she looked up at Dommy and smiled. He noticed how the city lights danced off shining blonde hair that fell to her shoulders. It was not styled or curled, as was the look of the day, but worn naturally, confidently. The face was movie star perfect, as was the smile. She caught his eye and said, "I'm sorry officer. You know how boys can be."

Benjamin, however, was furious. Looking at Dommy, he shouted again, "I demand you do your job and arrest those crooks!"

Dommy responded, "I'm sorry, sir, but there's nothing to be gained by taking this further. You took a dumb chance and lost. This isn't Harvard Yard where gentlemen play fair and square, and I might add that it's no place to be taking young girls who I suspect are under the drinking age. So I could arrest you for contributing to the delinquency of minors or you could simply go home as your girlfriend suggests."

"I'm not his girlfriend," the girl quickly protested, keeping her smile aimed at Dommy.

"If you were to get down off that horse, I'd show you what a Harvard man can do fair and square."

Before Dommy could respond, a loud, strong voice from the group gathered about shouted, "And that would be a great mistake, son." A large man stepped from the crowd and spoke again. "That officer you've challenged is Dommy Bassini, the best damn Harvard football player I've ever been around. And probably the toughest."

It took Dommy a moment to recognize big Stanley Belinsky, his former classmate and teammate at Harvard. They left Harvard on the same day to join the war. Stanley was still as large as ever, but one arm was gone.

"I heard you earned a few medals, Dommy," said Stanley as he stepped aside Benjamin, grabbed his shoulder with his one good huge hand, and yanked him toward the street. "Now, as one Harvard man to another, collect your buddies and these girls and get into that lovely Caddy convertible of yours and get out of here."

"I'm not going anywhere with him," says the girl. "He's drunk, not to mention spoiled and stupid." She glared at Benjamin as he was dragged away by his buddies.

"I've got a car. I'll drive you and your girlfriends," said Stanley.

"Thank you, sir. You're a gentleman." Looking up at Dommy, she said, "Never would have figured you for a Harvard man."

"Why? Because I'm just a cop?"

"No, because you're too damn handsome."

Stanley bursts out laughing. Dommy said nothing but felt a slight burn in his cheeks.

"C'mon, honey," said Stanley. "Think you might be a little drunk yourself."

"Wait," she said, still looking at Dommy, "so your name is Dommy? Mine is Martha. I'm at Pine Manor. Ask for Martha Anderson when you call."

Dommy ignored her comment and started to lead Fitzy away from the retreating group. But he couldn't help from turning his head for a final look at Martha Anderson. At that same moment, she turned to look back and caught him watching. The smile she flashed remained etched in Dommy's head.

***

To Martha Anderson, the problem with growing up female, rich, and beautiful in old-school Chicago society was that you were neither expected nor required to be intelligent and ambitious. The Andersons were among Chicago's societal royalty with the family fortune dating back to Walter Anderson's investment in the fledgling Chicago & Northwestern Railroad in the 1850s. The Anderson fortune grew with the success of the rail line and led to Walter becoming a founding investor in the First National Bank of Chicago, where Martha's father now served as Chairman of the Board. They were one of the first families to build a mansion in the bourgeoning Gold Coast neighborhood in the 1890s, while maintaining a grand vacation estate on Lake Geneva in Wisconsin.

Growing up, the curious and mischievous Martha envied the attention lavished on her older brother by her father as he was being groomed to one day run the family empire. She found the societal niceties being taught to her by her mother and a series of nannies and private instructors tedious and uninteresting. She longed for some time with her father, to learn the intricacies of business and finance, which she found fascinating, but he had no desire to involve her in the family business or his life in general. Despite achieving grades in school far superior to those of her older brother, she was pretty much relegated to the myopic worldview of her mother in training for her future role in Chicago society.

The very qualities that caused teachers to label Martha "rebellious" made her popular and a leader among her peers. By the time she was enrolled at Ferry Hall, a private boarding school for girls in Lake Forest, she was able to maintain a record of achieving both perfect grades and multiple disciplinary actions. Because of her looks, she was a magnet for the boys across the way at Lake Forest Academy and enjoyed toying with their hormonal desires. Still, she found most of them immature and boring, as were most of the boys her parents would arrange for her to meet from among the sons of their aristocratic friends. At her coming out débutante ball at the Palmer House, her parents were thrilled that she would be escorted by a grandson of Potter Palmer himself. But they would later be humiliated by her drunken behavior.

Her senior year at Ferry Hall, Martha took a group of friends to the Lake Geneva house without permission for a weekend party where the drinking and merrymaking eventually wound up with the local police being called to the estate. The Andersons were greatly embarrassed by the whole thing. Walter Anderson declared it "the last straw" and essentially sentenced Martha to "house arrest" for the remainder of her senior year. He then declared that immediately upon graduation Martha would be sent to Pine Manor Junior College in Boston to learn "how to be a proper woman worthy of the Anderson name."

For Martha, this was a godsend. Despite the gifts of privilege, wealth, and beauty, she was deeply unhappy with her life. The outrageous behavior belied the inner fear of never being able to find happiness on her terms. All her friends were quite satisfied with the way their lives were unfolding. The girls would happily and gradually become their mothers. The boys would traipse into a world of privilege along a path determined by wealth and connections. What they did now would have no bearing on where they would end up, their paths predetermined. Martha meant to achieve something of substance on her own, and getting away from Chicago seemed like a great first step. Maybe in Boston she could also find someone who appreciated her for her mind and ambition, and not just her social standing and looks.

Pine Manor Junior College catered to young ladies of privilege who required some "finishing" of their social and academic endeavors. There, Martha was surrounded mostly by the same type of girls she had been around all her life. The mixers with the Harvard men were at first somewhat exciting as she ventured into a more intellectually interesting world. But at the root the boys who pursued her were slightly older, worldlier versions of the boys back in Chicago. Like them, she could easily control these Harvard men with her beauty and will.

When she suggested to Benjamin Madison, heir to a hotel fortune, that she would like to see the infamous Scollay Square, he at first hesitated. But she cajoled him and some of her friends from Pine Manor to go. Once there, she was intrigued by the sights and the brazen flaunting of any sense of propriety. She loved the amusement halls and was disappointed to be blocked from attending a burlesque show at the Old Howard. But they had no trouble getting served alcohol in the bars to compliment the flasks carried by all the boys.

But by the time Benjamin got himself into a roil with a local con man over a silly shell game, she'd had quite enough of his increasingly drunken and surly behavior and the whining of her girlfriends who wanted to get away from "this disgusting place."

She saw the police officer on the horse approaching before anyone else and watched transfixed as he calmly diffused the situation. Sitting high atop his mount he looked almost princely, and she was impressed by the confidence and dignity he displayed as much as by his dark, handsome looks. When the man she knew as Stanley, who was almost like a father figure to the Harvard group, identified him as a Harvard man, she was enthralled. He *seemed indifferent to her obvious flirting though, until she turned to catch him watching her as she left. Then she knew she had to see him again.*

***

Martha gave Dommy a week to call her, and when he didn't she cajoled his address from Stan Belinsky. It took her another week to summon up the courage to go see him. She would tell herself this was a stupid idea, but then her vision of Dommy looking almost regal upon his great mount and looking down at her would stir a desire that pushed her forward. Once she found the apartment, she walked up the few steps but then retreated to the street before entering the outer door. The next time, she made it through the door into the small hallway and just stared at the interior door with the numeral 1 on it, unable to touch it, the fear of the reaction she might encounter behind it holding her prisoner. She turned to leave again but suddenly stopped and surprised herself by knocking loudly on the door.

***

"I got it, Pa."

It was after dinner, and there had been a knock at the door. Dommy opened it expecting to see either Lou or Joe, who were both prone to dropping in unexpectedly. He was stunned to see Martha Anderson.

"Hello, handsome," she cooed in an exaggerated, playful, sexy voice she hoped would hide her anxiety.

"What, how did you…" he stammered.

"Your friend Stanley. Didn't realize you were such a celebrity."

"Who is it?" asked Domenic walking into the room.

There was an awkward moment of silence as Dommy stood looking into Martha's face that had on it a forced half smile and eyes that seemed to be pleading with him. "Please," she whispered, "may I come in?" His own slow smile was the only answer she needed.

"You must be Dommy's father," said Martha suddenly striding right by a flabbergasted Dommy. "So pleased to meet you, Mr. Bassini. I can see where Dommy gets his good looks."

Domenic was startled as much by her boldness as by her beauty. This wasn't how a strange young girl approached and spoke to an old man she didn't even know. But something about it was both charming and disarming. He looked at her and asked, "And you are…"

"Martha Anderson, and your son is crazy about me, but he's too damn stubborn to do anything about it, so apparently I have to take matters into my own hands." Then they both looked back at Dommy, Martha for a reaction and Domenic for an explanation.

Dommy stood shaking his head slightly but not taking his eyes off Martha. Then the corners of his lips rose and his expression became one of bemusement. It was a look that Domenic hadn't seen in a very long time, and it warmed his heart.

Dommy started to speak, but Martha cut him off.

"He promised to call me but never did, Mr. Bassini," she said while taking Domenic's arm as if it were the most natural thing in the world. "What do you think of a man who steals the heart of a young, impressionable, innocent girl and then disappears?"

"Innocent?" says Dommy with feigned astonishment. "Ha!"

As always, Domenic thought before speaking.

"Dommy, first you don't even introduce me to your friend Martha, then you don't offer to take the poor girl's coat, and now you aren't even offering her something to eat or drink. How could I have raised such an *individuo ignorante?*"

"I don't know what that means, Dommy, but it doesn't sound very good," said Martha.

"So now it's the both of you picking on me?" replied Dommy playfully, still keeping his eyes on Martha. "Okay. Martha, may I take your coat, and would you like something to drink or eat, perhaps?"

Domenic hadn't seen his son act like this since long before he left for the war. He thought to himself, *this girl clearly makes him happy.* And that was all he needed to know about her.

"Got any wine?" asked Martha, taking off her coat.

"Yes, but you're not going to like it."

"Try me."

"Come on, our vast wine selection is in the kitchen. Some of it is aged nearly three days."

As they walked to the kitchen, Martha actually turned back, smiled at Domenic, and mouthed, "Thank you." She punctuated it with a wink. And at that exact moment, Domenic fell in love with Martha. And he would always love her for breathing life back into his boy.

DECEMBER 1947

WALTER GIFFORD ANDERSON III sat on the bed in the best suite the Parker House had to offer and still felt cramped. Compared to the spacious splendor of the McCormick Suite at the Palmer House in his native Chicago, the room, in his mind, seemed rather mundane. In fact, Boston itself felt tiny and cramped. The narrow winding streets and lack of buildings of any real height or breadth made the city seem archaic compared to the wide avenues and soaring skyscrapers of Chicago. His view of the room and the city, however, might have been tempered by the fact that he really didn't want to be there.

This whole business of his daughter Martha and the Boston cop, an Italian no less, should have never risen to the point where he was forced to intervene. For this, he blamed his wife. He had groomed his son to be a fitting heir to the Anderson family fortune and in this he had succeeded magnificently. The raising of his daughter Martha, on the other hand, had been pretty much left up to his wife, and she had failed miserably. For all her beauty and alleged intelligence, Martha was rebellious, disrespectful, and reckless. She seemed to have no interest in, or understanding of, what it meant to be an Anderson in Chicago. To be his daughter.

Walter got up and walked to the large mirror in the bedroom, one the hotel claimed once hung in the room preferred by Charles Dickens. That was Boston for you, all about the past while brawny Chicago, the city of the Andersons, was paving the way into the future. Looking into the mirror, Walter saw a large, some might say overweight, imposing figure of a man. A crumple of white shirt poked out from below a vest that looked like it might burst at any moment, and Walter did his best to tuck it away. He checked to make sure there were no leftover crumbs from lunch in his ample mustache and then checked his gold pocket watch. He had kept the boy waiting long enough in the lobby to establish who was in charge here.

He walked out to the parlor where his two traveling companions were waiting. William Meers, his personal attorney was hunched over some papers spread over the coffee table in front of him and peered up over his glasses as Anderson entered the room. Gene Marino, standing beside the marble bar, finished the whiskey he had been nursing and placed the empty glass down.

"Meers, call down to the lobby and have the boy sent up," he said. "Let's get this over with."

***

Moments later, Dommy knocked on the door to the Beacon Hill Suite on the 14th and top floor of the Parker house with a feeling of resignation. He was about to meet the father of the woman he loved, and she knew nothing about it. This could not go well, but he was determined to weather whatever was in store for him on the other side of this door with as much dignity as he could muster.

"Mr. Bassini, I'm Walter Anderson. Come in, please," said the man opening the door without offering either a handshake or any hint of a smile.

"Nice to meet you, sir."

Dommy was introduced to the two men who had been sitting in chairs set around a large coffee table. Meers, the attorney, was a small, meek-looking thing who stood quickly, flashed a very insincere smile and sat back down. The other man was powerfully built and looked out of place on the ornate Queen Anne chair, its fragile curved legs looking ill-suited to the task of supporting his bulk. The sharp suit couldn't mask the rough edges of the man called Marino, who stayed seated and barely nodded when introduced. *Muscle,* thought Dommy. *Not a good sign.*

Dommy took the chair apparently reserved for him, the middle one between the other two men. The chairs were arranged in a semicircle facing the large sofa, which Anderson had to himself. Walter looked directly at Dommy and was taken by the young man's self-assurance, which he was determined to strip away.

"First off, I can only imagine what Martha has had to say about me, and I assure you I am not the ogre she has made me out to be," began Anderson, pulling a cigar from his pocket and inspecting it while he spoke.

"Actually, sir, she has never spoken about you at all. Or her family."

Appearing mildly agitated, Anderson responded "Well, let me tell you a little about myself then and the family she seems determined to embarrass at every opportunity." To Dommy, the word "embarrass" was like a pin prick.

"My grandfather went from operating a small tool shop in Chicago that made locomotive parts to a major shareholder of the Chicago and North Western Railroad. He was one of the founders of The First National Bank of Chicago, where I now serve as chairman of the board and where my son, Walter IV, is being groomed to become president." Anderson took a cutter to the end of his cigar as he spoke. "What I'm getting at is this. The Andersons have earned a certain stature in Chicago, and beyond I might add. And with that stature comes great expectations and much scrutiny. Facts that Martha has never quite grasped." Anderson stopped to finally light his cigar and then went on.

"Now, you claim not to know anything about me, Mr. Bassini, which I find a little hard to believe, but I know a lot about you," he said smugly. "I know you started at Harvard, joined the Marines when the war broke out, and were wounded on Iwo Jima."

At the mention of Iwo Jima, Dommy noticed Marino, who had appeared largely uninterested to this point, glance up at him.

"I also know that as a police officer you make around four thousand dollars a year."

"Four thousand three hundred and twenty-seven last year," interjected Meers.

"Now you seem like a smart young man, Mr. Bassini. You went to Harvard, for God's sake. And for the life of me I don't understand why you chose to leave. You could have been so much more."

Dommy bristled at this. Then he calmed himself and asked, "Did your son happen to serve in the war, Mr. Anderson?"

"No, the work he did on the home front was of much more value than any he could have provided by carrying a rifle."

"Then I guess you wouldn't understand."

Dommy thought he saw Marino suppress a slight smile, but his comment seemed to inflame Anderson, who did not like being told what he could and could not understand.

"Let's cut to the chase, shall we, Mr. Bassini. You are little more than a diversion for my daughter and a nuisance to me. Mr. Meers here has a check made out to you for a year's salary of four thousand and whatever it is sitting in front of him. Take it, leave, and stop seeing my daughter."

Dommy was astounded by the arrogance of the man and fought to control the rising anger that suddenly burned behind his eyes. It must have shown, because Marino fidgeted in his chair. *Calm is the virtue of the strong*, he told himself.

But before he could say anything, Anderson went on, "And if you choose not to take this offer, you should know there will be consequences."

Dommy simply glared at Anderson. He could see that Anderson was enjoying this and wanted him to react. Marino casually patted his side to indicate he was carrying, more as a heads-up than a threat. The fat bastard was sitting there thinking he had his goon and his money to protect him, and for an instant Domenic wanted to show him he was wrong. But instead he answered as calmly as he could.

"First you try to bribe me, and then you threaten me. Thank you, Mr. Anderson, for showing me the type of man Martha has had to endure as a father. Now I can see why she adores my father so much." And with that, he got up and headed toward the door.

Determined now to spark a confrontation and with a glance toward Marino, Anderson shouted at Dommy as he walked away," Have I upset you, Mr. Bassini? Have I hurt your feelings? Have I made you angry?" His own anger was palpable as he practically spat out his words.

Dommy had his hand on the door knob but turned back to face the room. "If I were truly angry, Mr. Anderson, you wouldn't still be talking. You'd be spitting out your goddamn teeth."

"Oh, is that so? And you think Mister Marino here would have allowed that?"

"I think it might have become very interesting," said Dommy with a glance toward Marino, who replied with an almost imperceptible nod.

"This won't change anything, boy. If I stop paying for everything, Martha will have no choice but to come running home."

"Oh, she'll have a choice, Mr. Anderson."

***

The next morning, Dommy dropped by Joe's office and recounted his meeting with Walter Anderson.

"So let me get this straight," says Joe, "the sonofabitch actually comes here to Boston personally to try and buy you off, and then when that doesn't work he threatens you? Stupid bastard. A smart guy would have sent someone else."

"I think he wanted to show how powerful he is and how insignificant I am. Some type of ego thing. I got to say the privileged class here in Boston is much more subtle about their superiority complex."

Joe laughed. But as soon as Dommy left, he placed a call to Ernie.

***

Later that same day, there was a knock at the door of the Beacon Hill Suite. Walter Anderson peered through the eyehole and saw a man wearing an expensive suit and stylish fedora. He opened the door, and the man introduced himself.

"Mr. Anderson, my name is Ernie Lentini. I understand this belongs to you."

Ernie stepped aside, and a huge cop led Gene Marino into the room. His hands were handcuffed behind him. Ernie then stepped into the room and closed the door.

Anderson was suddenly confused and a little scared. The cop spoke.

"My name is Officer Flynn. Billy Flynn Badge Number 761. You've got very large balls but very little brains to think you can come here and threaten a Boston cop. I don't know who the fuck you think you are, but that shit don't fly around here. Now, Mr. Lentini here is about to tell you exactly, and I mean exactly, what is going to happen, and you better listen and do exactly what you're told."

Ernie spoke, "First off, I want you to call your son. He's at his home by the way." Anderson looked confused but placed the call through the switchboard to his son's home. A strange voice answered the phone.

"Who is this?" asked Anderson.

"This is a friend of Mr. Lentini, who I understand is with you."

"Where's my son?"

"Oh, he's right here, sitting in a chair."

"I want to speak to him."

"Father, who are these guys? They showed up out of nowhere. They have guns," a panicked Walter the fourth said. "I don't know…"

Ernie grabbed the phone away from Anderson and hung it up.

"So, Mr. Anderson, you should now understand that we have friends in Chicago and how easy it is for us to find you or anyone in your family. Correct?"

Anderson nodded.

"Good. Now you and your lawyer are booked on a 4 PM train leaving South Station for Chicago in less than two hours. First class sleeper car, I might add. You're welcome. You will make that train, which will give you a couple of days to think about how lucky you are to be going home at all.

"And once you are gone, you will not attempt to contact Dommy Bassini again. Is all this understood?"

"Yes."

Ernie drew close to Anderson and spoke with emotion for the first time, "And I would just like to say that Dommy Bassini is a war hero with more integrity and balls in his little finger than you have in that entire grossly overinflated body of yours."

Anderson said nothing, quietly enduring the ignominy of the repudiation and insult.

Then he asked, "What about Marino here?"

"He stays. I'm about to offer him a job."

FEBRUARY 1948

DOMMY'S SHIFT WAS ending as it usually did around one in the morning with a quiet ride through mostly deserted downtown streets back to the stables. He took his time as he enjoyed the quiet solitude after the cacophony of Scollay Square a few blocks away and believed Fitzy did as well. It gave him time to think, reflect, and unwind. He was satisfied with the way his life was now progressing, but neither was he content. He was optimistic about the future but still bore an overwhelming sense of uneasiness.

What moved him forward and gave him purpose was Martha. He loved her deeply, and when he was alone with her was when he was truly happy, the nightmares and the anxiety dissipating for longer and longer periods of time. That happiness had begun to extend to other people in his life. He could converse more with his father, laugh more with Lou, and confide more in Joe.

Much to the chagrin of Domenic, to whom appearances meant much, Dommy and Martha, though unmarried, had moved into the second-floor apartment of the building. They spoke of marriage but seemed to be in no hurry. Martha left school, determined to sever ties with her family and begin taking care of herself. She found a job working as an assistant to the banquet and entertainment manager at the snobbish Ritz Carlton Hotel, a job well suited to her upbringing, personality, and beauty. It was a world far removed from that of their neighborhood, and Martha was much more comfortable dealing with the demands of her upper-crust Ritz clientele than the scrutiny of her nosy North End neighbors.

As he trotted down Washington Street, Dommy's thoughts were interrupted by what sounded like an alarm going off. He hastened his pace in the direction of the noise and determined it was coming from inside a small jewelry store. The front door to the store was locked, and the security shutters were down, blocking any view of the interior.

Dommy galloped back to Winter Street and turned down the alley that ran behind the store. When he got to the back entrance, the rear door was open. He dismounted, removed his weapon, and entered the darkened store with his flashlight while calling out, "Police!"

He quickly realized that whoever had broken in was gone, probably scared off by the alarm. The back of the store was a shambles, as the burglar or burglars rummaged through anything they could looking for valuables, and there were rings, watches, bracelets, and necklaces scattered about. The front display case was intact. Dommy went back out to get to the nearest call box to inform the station of the break in, but as he did a patrol car turned down the alley. The car came to a stop, and the two officers stepped out, one of whom Dommy recognized.

"What's going on, Bassini?" the patrolman Dommy knew as Jimmy Broderick asked.

"Seems like someone broke in, grabbed what they could with the alarm going off, and took off. No sign of them."

The two officers looked at each other and started to enter the store.

"Aren't you going to call it in?" asked Dommy. Patrol cars were equipped with radios, while foot patrolmen and mounted officers still depended on call boxes and telephones.

"In a minute," responded the second officer tersely.

The three policemen entered the store while Broderick and his partner surveyed the scene. Broderick said to the other two, "Okay, grab what you can, and then we'll call it in." The second cop then began picking out watches and jewelry and filling his pockets.

"What are you doing?" exclaimed Dommy.

Broderick turned and gave Dommy a severe look. "We're taking what we can, Bassini. That's what we're doing. No one knows how much the thieves got, and I'm sure they aren't going to report it."

"But we're not thieves. We're cops, for Chrissakes!"

"Don't give me that choirboy bullshit, Bassini. This is how it works. Now grab what you want. We don't have a lot of time."

"I'm not taking anything, and I'm going out to call this in right now."

"Don't be an asshole," shouted the other cop, who was headed out to the front of the store. "You want to be one of us or do you want to be someone who can't ever be trusted by other cops? You get on O'Riley's shit list, and you'll never go anywhere in the BPD. And be sure to grab something for O'Riley. He'll expect it."

"I think he's already on O'Riley's shit list," laughed Broderick.

Dommy stood there dumbfounded. He knew about O'Riley and his cadre of corrupt cops, but he never saw such brazenness firsthand. Before he could speak again, Broderick's partner shouted from the front of the store. "Jimmy, come take a look at this."

Broderick and Dommy went out to the front of the store and found the other cop eyeing the display counter. "Looks like all the good stuff is out here."

"Break it," said Broderick. "Hurry up."

The cop took a large vase and did as he was told. Then the two partners grabbed at the rings and bracelets like hungry dogs digging up bones. Dommy just watched.

After a minute or so, the two had filled their pockets and headed back out to the alley. As they walked by a stunned Dommy, he said, "I'm going to report this."

Both turned and glared at him.

"No, you're not," said Broderick, the threat in his words unmistakable.

"That would be a big, big mistake," added the other.

✱✱✱

"So what do you think I should do, Joe?"

Uneasy after the evening's events, Dommy found himself buzzing Joe awake at two in the morning. When a sleepy and startled Joe let him into his building, Dommy confided in what had happened at the jewelry store. He planned to report the two other officers to his superiors the next day and wanted to know what Joe thought.

"Let me ask you this," responded Joe, as they sat at his kitchen table, each with a sambuca-laced coffee in front of them. "Do you like being a cop? Do you see yourself making a career of it?"

"I do. I want to do some good. I'm not doing much now, but I plan to finish my degree with night classes and move up in rank. Probably take the sergeant exam next year."

"And I'm sure you'll do well on it, just like you did on the civil service exam you took to join the force. But did you know that of those getting the twenty top scores on that exam, you were the only one to get an appointment to the force? And that, if I may say so, was only because of my involvement. The other two dozen new recruits getting selected were well down on the list."

"What are you getting at, Joe?"

"I'm getting at the fact that merit has little to do with advancement in the Boston Police Department. It's all about politics. Why do you think that asshole Colin O'Riley gets away with what he does? He's Curley's man inside the department, and his brother KO is currently the acting mayor for Christ's sake. You get on O'Riley's shit list, and he'll make your life inside the department miserable. If you want to get ahead in the department, you need to keep your head down and go along to get along. At least for now."

"For now?"

"Yes, for now. Change is coming. If things work out, as soon as next year there will be big changes in how this city is run. KO wants to do things differently, and if he runs for mayor next year he'll probably win, as long as Curley remains locked up that is. I've promised him my support but with conditions. If everything works out, I'll have more power and be right beside KO as he starts to make some reforms."

"So your advice is not to report what happened last night, let these crooks get away with it."

"As I said, for now, Dommy."

***

Leaving Joe's, Dommy was still uncomfortable with the idea of not reporting the theft by fellow officers. It ran counter to everything he believed in about policing. Dommy completed the short walk to his apartment and after letting himself in found Martha asleep on the sofa in the front room. Try as she might to stay awake to greet him, most nights he found her like this and would proceed to quietly wake her with a soft kiss. Her eyes would slowly open, and she would offer him a sweet, sleepy smile as she pulled him down for a longer, more passionate kiss.

They would embrace, and the outside world and any problems in it would vanish, replaced by the comforting, all-encompassing warmth of their love.

But tonight, Dommy did not want the stench of his night near Martha. He walked past her and into the kitchen, where he poured a glass of wine and sat at the table sipping it and thinking. He had lived with guilt for too long and did not want to start again. If he did nothing about the travesty of public trust that he had witnessed this night, he would feel guilt every time he thought of Pete Keenan. And he would never get over his disappointment in himself. Still, Joe's words resonated, and he needed to consider them. Joe had never given him bad advice.

"What's wrong?" It was Martha standing in the doorway watching him.

"Nothing. I'm fine," Dommy replied, looking up at her and trying to force a smile. "Just tired."

"You're a lousy liar, Bassini."

This time it was a sincere smile. God, how he loved this woman.

She walked over behind his chair, leaned down, and put her arms around his neck, her cheek next to his. "Tell me about it," she said.

"It's the same old bullshit. Bad cops, and I have to look the other way."

"Well, do it."

"Do what?"

"Look the other way. For your own good." Then she added softly, "For the good of all three of us."

Dommy was momentarily confused. "You mean you, me, and my father?"

"No, I mean you, me, and our baby."

"What!" Dommy was stunned.

"I'm pregnant, Dommy."

Dommy turned in the chair and looked up at Martha. His lips seemed to stop working as he tried to speak. Finally he sputtered, "I'm going to be a father?" It was more of a question than a realization.

Martha nodded, her eyes were wet, and she had a soft quivering smile that tore into Dommy's heart. He stood up, and they embraced, neither one saying another word. Dommy knew right then he would listen to Joe and Martha and not report what happened this night. He would live with it for the sake of his family. He heard his father's oft spoken words in his head, "Other things may change us, but we start and end with the family."

When they finally pulled apart, Martha said, "I guess we'd better get married. Domenic will kill us both if his grandchild is born a bastard."

***

The next day when Dommy reported to work, there was a squad car sitting outside the stable. In it sat Billy Flynn. He called to Dommy, "Get in, Bassini. You've got an appointment down at Berkeley." He was referring to police headquarters on Berkeley Street.

Dommy looked toward the stable entrance, but Flynn read his mind and said, "Captain Fitzgerald has been informed. Let's go."

Ten minutes later, Dommy entered the office of Colin O'Riley, who was seated at his desk. He motioned to a chair in front of it without saying a word. The two sat facing each other for a moment, neither one saying anything as Dommy met O'Riley's icy stare with his own.

"So, Officer Bassini, I understand you had a little misunderstanding with two of your fellow officers last night."

"No misunderstanding, sir. They stole a number of valuable items from a crime scene."

"Hmm. That's not how they described it. They say that when they arrived at the scene they found you inside filling your pockets with all manner of things, watches, rings, bracelets."

"With all due respect, sir, you and I know that's not true."

"Watch yourself, boy. Know who you're talking to. The truth is what people will believe, and if you decide to make a stink about this, the people who matter will believe the version given by me and my officers."

"So if you have nothing to worry about, why am I here?"

O'Riley made a face that said it was a good question. "You're here because I'm going to give you a chance, for old times' sake."

"Old times' sake?" Dommy was confused.

"Oh, you don't know the history the O'Rileys have with your family?" He feigned great surprise. "Well, you see this." He pointed to a scar running down his temple to his eye. "Your good friend Ernie 'The Eel' Lentini gave me this one night."

"Ernie's not a friend."

"Oh, but your godfather Joe Rossario and your dear old dad were both there too. Now I don't begrudge them. I've let bygones be bygones, particularly since my own dad, retired Superintendent of Police Brendan O'Riley to you, gave your dad a lesson in manners shortly after this unfortunate event occurred." O'Riley again pointed to his scar.

Domenic had never mentioned this incident to Dommy, but Joe had told him the story many years ago. He didn't give O'Riley the satisfaction of a reaction as the captain went on.

"But all that is neither here nor there. What is here is that little envelope sitting on the corner of my desk right there." O'Riley nodded to an envelope in front of Dommy. "In that envelope is your share of what went missing from that jewelry store last night. I'd like you to take it, go back to work, and never say another word about it. In good time, I'll see that you get a better assignment in the department, something you might like a little more than getting saddle sores on your arse."

Dommy sat looking at O'Riley, forcing himself to remain calm despite the disdain he felt for the man. But he gathered himself and slowly responded. "You can relax, Captain. I made up my mind already not to say anything about the events of last night. I want to stay out of your dirty world and concentrate on being a good cop. So I'll keep my mouth shut, but I'm not taking that envelope. If I do, it will define me for the rest of my career, and I'll be no better than your other scumbags who disgrace the uniform."

"Scumbags? You think my men who put their lives on the line daily arresting the really bad characters in this city, busting drug dealers and pimps and breaking up gangs and facing down crazies with guns are scumbags for taking a little when they can? Don't you think they've earned it? They take shit from the newspapers, politicians, rabble-rousers, everyone, and they wade through all the political bullshit in this very department while barely making enough to support a family."

"You can rationalize it all you want. It's not right." Dommy stood up to leave. "Am I dismissed, Captain?"

"Take the goddamn envelope, Bassini."

Dommy stood there, unflinching as he met the fury in O'Riley's eyes without flinching.

"If you don't take that envelope, you'll never be trusted around here by anyone. You'll be a marked man."

"Am I dismissed?"

"Go to hell."

"I've been to hell, Captain. I'm not going back."

"Have it your way, you naïve, sanctimonious, Boy Scout piece of shit. Get the fuck out of here and go enjoy cleaning up horseshit for the rest of your miserable career."

***

Joe Rossario sat back in his chair and thought what an unlikely threesome this was as he pointed to a plate of pastries on his desk and offered them to his two guests, Kevin "KO" O'Riley and Ernesto "The Eel" Lentini. Ernie, took a sfogliatella, as he usually did and Kevin politely declined, "I'm good with the coffee, Joe. Thanks."

"So you believe you can beat Curley?" Joe started the conversation. Since Curley's unexpected release from prison and his firing of KO, much had changed in the city's political landscape.

"With the right people behind me, yes," replied Kevin.

"The right people?"

"Basically, that's all the good people fed up with James Michael, and there are a lot of them. People like you, Joe. People of influence who think Boston can be a better place if we break Curley's corrupt grip around the neck of the city. We're stuck in the past, stagnant. There's no city planning, projects are haphazardly awarded to the highest bribe. The business community, which should be our greatest partner in rejuvenating Boston, is totally disengaged by Curley's continued bashing and disinvestment. He threatened to open water mains and flood the basement and vaults of the First National Bank because they wouldn't give the city a loan for God's sake."

"You know, KO, if I can call you that…"

"You can. I sort of like it," Kevin answered with a grin and a glance toward Ernie. "It makes me sound tougher than I am."

Joe continued, "Oh, we know you're plenty tough, KO. So as true as everything you've said may be, what would a Mayor O'Riley do for us if we were to rally the ninety thousand citizens of Italian descent now living in Boston to support you?"

"What do you want?"

"Glad you asked. We want you to stop this so-called reform movement to reduce the size of the city council from twenty-two district members to nine at-large members. It could likely rob us in the North End and East Boston of any council representation, and it would be filled with Irishmen and Brahmins. I'd also like you to back me for president of the council."

KO looked at Joe with no expression, as he seemed to consider his demands. After a moment he said, "I think you'll make a damn fine council president, Councilor Rossario."

Joe smiled, as did Ernie. "There's one more thing."

"What's that?"

"Get your asshole brother to lay off my godson Dommy Bassini over at the BPD. He's making his life miserable."

Kevin frowned. "Your first two requests I can do. This, I'm afraid, I can't promise. My brother and I are not on good terms. He, in fact, will do everything he can to get his protector James Michael reelected." Turning to Ernie, he added, "I understand you do business from time to time with my brother, Mr. Lentini. You must know what he's like."

"I don't like your brother, O'Riley. He's a ruthless, selfish, greedy sonofabitch, and I do business with him because Joseph Lombardo asks me, no make that *orders* me to."

KO nodded his unspoken agreement with Ernie's frank opinion of his brother. He turned to Joe and asked, "Why exactly is Mr. Lentini here?"

"Ernie can be of great assistance in an election campaign. He knows the important union leaders and a lot of people with deep pockets."

Kevin made a face and said, "No offense, Mr. Lentini…"

"Call me Ernie."

"No offense, Ernie, but I don't want to be beholden to you and Joseph Lombardo."

Joe interjected, "Oh, you won't be, Kevin. Anything Ernie does, he does for me, not you. And Lombardo has nothing to do with this. The fact that Lombardo hates Curley, hell he hates every Irishman in this city, but Curley in particular, certainly helps. Anything else you have concerns about?"

"Not really. One thing I'd like to know while I have the opportunity," responded Kevin, who turned again to Ernie with a wry smile. "So, Ernie, was it really you who shot Dodo Walsh back in '31?"

Ernie was surprised at the question but said nothing.

"Okay, this meeting is over," said Joe, reaching for a cannoli.

***

Martha was miserable. Her life seemed to be spiraling downward so quickly from its joyous heights just a few months back. After some subtle cajoling from Joe, some not so subtle cajoling from Ernie, and a sizable donation to Sacred Heart from Domenic, Father DiPetro agreed to forego quite a few rules of Catholicism and permit Dommy and Martha to be married in the eyes of the church. The ceremony was basic. Father DiPetro drew the line at having a full mass and saw Domenic walk Martha down the aisle where Dommy waited with his best man Lou. Sofia DiBona from the upstairs apartment was maid of honor. Although the hastily arranged proceeding was simple and lacked many of the traditional trappings of a formal wedding, to Martha it was perfect. Hearing Domenic whisper, "You are now my daughter forever," as he handed her to his son nearly made her cry. Then seeing the love in the soft eyes of the strong, handsome man who would be her husband finished the job, forcing her to wipe away tears of happiness throughout the ceremony.

Domenic spared no expense on the reception, which was held at the Sons of Italy Grand Lodge. With his co-conspirator Joe, he overruled the pleas of Dommy and Martha for a small reception comprised of close friends and family. "Let me have this," he said. "Pasqualena and I would talk about how Dommy's wedding day, the day our only child takes his wife, would be the finest party the North End has ever seen." And he made sure it was. Martha had never before heard so much singing, seen so much dancing, tasted so much food, or had so much fun. She was kissed by a hundred people she did not know and danced with dozens more. It was a totally exhausting and totally rapturous evening she would never forget.

Then, a few short months later, her life took on new meaning with the birth of Peter Domenic Bassini. Dommy had insisted on the name "Peter" and tried to explain why but could never quite bring himself to go into detail, as he would become emotional and change the subject. "He was a friend who died in the war," he only said. And it was about the extent of what he ever had to say about his time fighting overseas. He never talked about the war, but the nightmares he still had from time to time spoke volumes.

Having a baby gave Martha so much, but it also took away much of what made her life bearable. The social mores of how Italian wives and mothers were supposed to act were the antithesis of how she wanted to live her life. Their lives were subjugated to the needs and desires of their husbands. They seemed to be happy cooking, cleaning, caring for the children, and gossiping. She had no female friends in the neighborhood, where she would often feel, real or imagined, the universal disapproval about how she lived. Before Pete, she had the escape of her work at the Ritz, which occupied many of her days and evenings. She would be around people she enjoyed, and it filled the time when Dommy was at work. Now, once Dommy left for his shift, she was totally alone with Pete until her father-in-law would come home from the shipyard. Domenic would always come up to their apartment after stopping at his own on the first floor to shower, and he would always ask if she and Pete wanted to come down for dinner. Since Martha was so inept at cooking, Domenic had assumed responsibility for feeding her and sending her back upstairs with leftovers for Dommy to have when he got home from work. He was always eager to help with Pete, proving to be adept at changing his diaper and giving him his bottle while talking and singing to him in Italian.

She would fill the time waiting for Domenic to come home by taking walks with Pete around the neighborhood, often finding herself at Joe's office where he would always make time to see her and gush over Pete.

"Who would have imagined a blond Bassini?" he would say with a laugh. "But by God he does look like his father. And how is Dommy? I seldom see him anymore."

Martha frowned, which did not escape Joe's notice, and replied, "What's that expression the Italians use, "*cosi, cosi?*" On one hand, he's the most loving father and thoughtful husband a girl could want, but on the other there's an unhappiness within him that sometimes consumes him. We hardly talk about anything besides Pete. When we're alone, Dommy is mostly silent, and I can see he is on edge, almost struggling to keep up a positive front for me and Pete's sake."

"Does he talk about the job? I know it's been rough on him."

"Never, but I can see it weighs on him. I ask him to quit, but he won't hear of it. I worry about him every minute."

Joe nodded, taking it all in. "Dommy's never been a quitter. And how about you? How are you coping?"

"Not as well as I should, frankly. I should be happy having a devoted husband who absolutely cherishes me and a healthy, happy baby. But I'm lonely, Joe. I don't fit into the North End very well. I want more out of life than taking care of Dommy and Pete. I want my own career, which makes me sort of a pariah among the women in the neighborhood. When I'm around, they speak in Italian, and I can only guess what they're saying."

"They're jealous, Martha. You're smart and beautiful and more independent than they will ever dare to be, so they make excuses to demean you. They don't really care that you lived in what they call "sin" with Dommy or that you got pregnant before getting married. Hell, you stole away the neighborhood hero any of them would have loved to land. They see you looking like a million dollars going off to work in a world they can only dream of, and they're simply jealous."

"You forgot to mention that I don't cook," Martha responded with a slight smile.

"Now that," laughs Joe, "that is a legitimate sin. For Italians, the 11th Commandment is thou shall not NOT cook!" They both laughed as Joe gave Martha a fatherly embrace.

PART 2

APRIL 23, 1950

SOMEHOW, TWO THINGS *were able to penetrate the sudden spinning blackness that slowly and relentlessly tightened its suffocating grip. He knew he held a gun in his hand, and he could see the face of his son. Everything else was gone from his consciousness. No other thoughts, no feelings. There were no questions about where he was and what had happened.*

His open eyes stared blankly as they looked up into a light he couldn't see. The shouts around him were soundless as he tried to reach out and touch his boy through the growing darkness. Then the sharp, unmistakable sound of a gunshot pierced the shroud of heavy silence and brought him partway back.

The comforting sense of his son being there was gone, replaced by dark fragments of disjointed images that blurred then and now. And, for the first time, he felt fear. As he fruitlessly tried to move, he saw his wife and felt the same pang in his heart as he did the day they met. A sadness more numbing than the fear engulfed him. He instinctively tried to lift his gun, but it was too heavy. Then his father was there, and he kept repeating the same phrase in his native Italian that he had been hearing all his life. "Other things may change us, but we start and end with the family." He clung to the comfort of his father's voice as the words echoed in his head. And he began to remember. The hallway, the door, the sergeant behind him and in his ear. "Take out your gun. Take out your goddamn gun." He remembered being confused. He remembered the gunshot. There was a gunshot.

Now he could hear the voices, the shouting. There was someone over him speaking, though he couldn't make sense of it. But it was a familiar voice that gave him a sense of hope. The haze started to lift. His father's reassuring words were becoming fainter. He heard his name leap out from all the other meaningless words being spoken to him. But then the voice suddenly screeched, "What the fuck are you doing?" The blast of the gun and the total blackness were one in the same.

JANUARY 1950

NOISY AND BUSTLING during the day, the corridors of city hall were cloaked in an eerie silence at night. The cacophony of voices and footsteps clacking on the marble floors outside the mayor's office were replaced by a peaceful, encompassing quiet that was only occasionally interrupted by a stray worker or watchman making their way by the ornate wooden double doors that opened into the office where Mayor Kevin O'Riley now sat alone. The door to the reception area was open, and he could see straight through to those large doors, each featuring a meticulously carved lion's head at its center. He found those strange-looking heads to be unwelcoming and inappropriate for the office of a public servant who should embrace the intrusions of his constituents, but he also saw them as his guardians of the silence at night. It was at night, alone in his inner sanctum, that he could best reflect on all the things requiring his attention, foresight and leadership.

This night, as he put the finishing touches on his first major address to the city council, he was drawn into thoughts of the twisting road that brought him to this office.

***

For nearly thirty years, since he first became James Michael Curley's eyes and ears during the turbulent term of Mayor Peters, Kevin "KO" O'Riley seemed to live his life within the five blocks that ran from city hall to the Massachusetts State House. As James Michael's protégé, he managed to be elected to the Boston School Committee and then the Massachusetts House of Representatives. He was Curley's confidant and advisor when his mentor served three terms as mayor of Boston, a term in the United States Congress, and a term as governor of the Commonwealth of Massachusetts. When Curley served five months in prison for war profiteering and mail fraud in 1947, Kevin served as acting mayor. So to many it was surprising that it was Kevin who ran against and defeated James Michael for mayor in 1949.

He knew that many in the old school world of ward bosses saw him as a traitor. But for the first time in his career in politics, he felt free. For years, he walked a fine line between satisfying the demands of the Curley machine and doing what was best for the people he served. His had been a life of compromises. He would turn a blind eye to Curley's corruption in order to use his influence to push Curley away from the stagnation of the past and into an era of urban modernization. After Curley was elected to Congress in 1943, it was generally assumed that Kevin would run for mayor in 1945 with Curley's support. But in 1945, Joseph Kennedy offered Curley a small fortune to vacate his seat in Congress to allow his son John Kennedy to run for it. Facing mounting debt and indictments by Federal prosecutors, Curley agreed and decided to once again run for mayor and won handily.

When sentenced to six to eighteen months in prison in June of 1947 for mail fraud, accepting bribes, and war profiteering, Curley named Kevin to serve as acting mayor. Kevin immediately set about trying to build relationships with the business community, which had been attacked and alienated by Curley's "divide and conquer" approach as the self-proclaimed "mayor of the poor." Kevin saw businesses as an essential partner in moving Boston forward. He worked to reform and codify tax assessments on businesses, a heretofore random process that saw Curley assess the highest rates business could tolerate, only to lower them through payoffs paid directly to him and his political partners. Kevin himself had benefited from this practice at times.

When President Truman suddenly commuted Curley's sentence after only five months, he returned to Boston furious over the reforms Kevin had initiated and proclaimed after his first day back in office, "I have accomplished more in one day than has been done in the five months of my absence." He immediately fired Kevin, severing all ties with him and banning him from city hall.

Wounded, Kevin retreated to the home in South Boston his family now shared with his widowed father. He was sitting alone on the same worn sofa in the same den where his father had years before assigned him the role of Curley's spy in Mayor Peters's administration, launching his career in Boston politics. Little had changed over the years. It was still void of any decoration. The small table by his father's chair might have had a few more round glass stains, but it still held just an ashtray and his father's private phone, which he insisted on keeping despite it being rarely used anymore. As he sat contemplating his future with a bottle of Irish whiskey, the doors to the small study slowly opened and his father Brendon stepped in. Without a word, the seventy-five-year-old former superintendent of police, weakened by time and illness, shuffled to his chair and plopped down with a grunt. He took a glass from his bathrobe and reached it out to Kevin, who obliged by filling it to the top. He took a swig, closing his eyes for a moment while savoring the happy burn it made while he swallowed.

"So, feeling a bit sorry for yourself, huh?" Brendon rasped then coughed a few times to clear his throat.

"More angry than anything."

"Yea, James Michael can be a real bastard sometimes."

"Sometimes?"

"He wasn't always this bad. He's old, tired, and scared. He's fighting best he can to cling to what he has…or had. The power, the adulation. But he's not feeling invincible anymore. Probably because he isn't."

Kevin looked at his father with a sullen expression. "He's not? He got the goddamn president of the United States to let him out of prison."

"So what?" Brandon shot out as loudly as his worn-down vocal chords would allow. Kevin was startled by the suddenness of his father's reaction. "Are you telling me that my son, the great K.O. O'Riley, is backing down from a fight with this bedraggled seventy-five-year-old shell of what used to be the great James Michael Curley? No, you won't. We won't. We're the O'Rileys of South Boston, and we've never backed down from a goddamn fight. We're owed favors, and we have friends. We'll make James Michael rue the day he double crossed an O'Riley. You were to be mayor of this city, and by God you will be. And I'll see it before I die. That's a promise."

Kevin sat silently, taking in his father's words, gripped by the passion with which he delivered them. He found himself suddenly believing he could defeat James Michael Curley, and he was already plotting his strategy before he even replied to his father. He knew he could be as ruthless as the man who had mentored him. And if that was what it would take, he would do it. For himself, for his family, and for the good of the city he loved.

"We've got to get the businesses and the old money on our side without alienating Curley's popular base. There's all kinds of dirt about James Michael we'll leak to the press, stuff that only me and a few others know about."

Brendan slowly smiled. "And there's deals to be made with the Italians now that they actually vote. And a lot of them vote Republican because Curley and the old bosses have shit all over them for so long. Then there's that shameful brother of yours to lean on to get his people on the force behind us, not to mention all those undesirables he deals with."

"Are you sure Colin would help me? He's flourished under Curley's protection."

Brendan shot his son an angry look. "He damn well better help us. There's been a lot of dirty water run under the bridge between us, but we're still family. He'd be nothing without me looking out for him all those years. Sullied my own reputation to keep him out of trouble many a time. He will fall in line, or I'll make his sordid life miserable."

"I'm sure he'll expect my support and protection if I get elected."

"Of course he will, and you'll provide such. But that's a small price to pay."

✱✱✱

Kevin was thinking about how wrong his father had been about Colin as he gave the four pages of the speech he had completed a quick read, making a few notes and changes as he went. Normally he would have spent more time reviewing it and practicing it out loud in the solitude of his office, but he was running late for a meeting with his brother. A meeting he was dreading. He put on his suit jacket, folded the papers in half, and put them in the breast pocket to go over again once he got home. Then he put on his topcoat and left city hall.

Unlike Mayor Curley, Kevin enjoyed neither a driver nor an entourage. He preferred to walk through the city alone, often with his fedora tilted forward and his head bent low to avoid being recognized, a strategy seemingly being practiced by many others this frigid January evening. He would walk in step with the heartbeat of the city, absorbing its quiddity while feeling both powerful and humbled as he traversed the streets he knew so well. It was a relatively short walk from city hall across Boston Common to the bar Colin had selected near police headquarters on Berkeley Street. Kevin was surprised when his brother reached out to him for a meeting and even more surprised that he selected such a public place. He had taken the meeting solely to appease his ailing father, who encouraged him to make peace with his brother.

"For all the things he isn't, he's still your brother," Brendan told him. "I'd like to die knowing the two of you have made your peace."

As Kevin entered the bar, he immediately spied his brother, sitting brazenly in full uniform at a booth with some other police officers. Colin saw him, ushered the others away, and rose to greet him, making sure everyone in the place saw.

"Why, it's my brother, the mayor," he exclaimed with a sly smile. "What a pleasant surprise." There was a smattering of applause from the patrons.

Kevin slid into the booth facing his brother. "Why am I here, Colin? You made it clear when I asked for your help during the election that you were a James Michael man and had no intention of supporting me. In fact, I think your exact words were, 'I'll do everything I can to keep you from being mayor.'"

Kevin replied, "That was just good business. James Michael was always good to me."

"And our father wasn't? You nearly put him in an early grave many a time with all your bullshit, but he always stood by you. Then you ripped his heart out by standing against me."

"What he did for me he did out of guilt, because we all know you were his favorite. Do you want a beer, brother?"

"No, thanks. Just get to it."

"Well," began Colin, "it's like this. After you beat him, James Michael shared with me a number of things that transpired over your years as his butt boy that wouldn't make you look too good if they were to come out."

Kevin felt a shiver go down his spine. "Anything I did, I did on Curley's orders, and he's the one who benefitted. He's got as much to lose as I."

"Actually, brother, he's got nothing to lose. He's been to prison. He's out of office. He's paid for his crimes. While you, you're some kind of saint in the eyes of the cherished electorate."

"What do you want, Colin?"

"I want to be left alone to go about my business. I want no interference from my higher ups, from outside agencies, from no one. I might want favors from time to time, and I want them granted."

"And if I say no?"

Colin smiled and took from inside his tunic a piece of paper and began reading, "Thomas Medville, owner of Coastal Development gave you $5,000 in cash on May 14, 1946 to expedite a blocked permit. Swears he never met or spoke to Mayor Curley. Got the permit. Same month, Guido Alongi had his tax assessment for his land along the waterfront lowered by $9,000 after handing you $2,000. Good deal for the guinea, saved $7,000. Not a bad deal for you either."

"That money went straight to Curley."

"Prove it, brother. Like everyone on this list, the wop says he never met Curley."

Kevin quietly fumed as he thought how to respond. Truth was he was guilty. He would often benefit from Curley's corruption over the years. It never felt right to him, but he never refused. To do so would make Curley distrust him.

"And while you mull it over, brother, there's a couple more things. Number one is that you will not make that troublemaker Joseph Rossario president of the city council. And you will not oppose the proposal in the state legislature to reduce the council to nine members."

Kevin was aghast that his brother would blackmail him like this, but he had no choice. He could never be the productive mayor he yearned to be with a corruption scandal hanging over him. "Okay," he finally said, "but I want you to come to the house and see our father. And we will act as though all our fences are mended. Like brothers. So he can die in peace."

"I suppose I can fake that, if it makes you happy, brother."

FEBRUARY 1950

THE WET SNOW blew directly into the faces of Dommy and Fitzy as they trudged back toward the stables at the end of a shift, man and horse of the same mind as they both looked forward to getting in out of the cold. With his head bowed against the oncoming wind, Dommy would have missed the figure darting away from his approach if it hadn't knocked some metal trash cans to the ground in the process. Almost reluctantly, Dommy gave Fitzy the signal to pick up the pace as he headed after the person fleeing down a side street.

Catching up to him, Dommy could see it was a boy, and he shouted for him to stop, but he kept on running, turning into an alley. Dommy and Fitzy followed in time to see the boy clamber up over a fence and get away. "I'll guess we'll never know what he was up to, Fitzy," said Dommy, as he turned the horse around and headed back to the barn

Later, Dommy crawled into his warm bed, snuggled up against a sleeping Martha, and fell almost immediately into his own deep slumber. But then the dream invaded his sleeping consciousness. He was chasing the boy from earlier, and as the boy was climbing over the fence he took out his gun and shot him dead. He fell to the ground, and Dommy could see his blood flowing into the fresh snow. With a shudder, Dommy awoke. He knew it was a dream, but it seemed so real that he couldn't put it out of his head. *It was just a dream,* he told himself as he got out of bed and walked around the apartment. "It was just a dream," he said out loud as he found himself getting dressed and heading back out into the night to look for a body he knew was not there.

MARCH 1950

JOSEPH LOMBARDO WAS barely paying attention to Colin O'Riley because he was more focused on Mary DePalma. They sat in the small downstairs private dining room of the Piccolo Nido restaurant, where Mary brought them their food and drinks from upstairs. Mary was one of those rare natural beauties who seemed oblivious to the gifts God gave her.

Her natural blonde hair and deep blue eyes, courtesy of her Northern Italian mother, stood out in stark contrast to her perfect olive skin. Her full breasts and ample round behind would not have seemed nearly as enticing if not exaggerated by a thin waist and long, perfect legs. When she leaned over to pour more wine into Lombardo's glass, he casually placed a hand on the small of her back, a small gesture she seemed not to even notice while arousing him greatly. When she left to go back up the stairs, his eyes followed.

Colin O'Riley followed Lombardo's stare and smiled to himself. The two men had come to know each other well. They both knew that at their core they were natural enemies, and neither had any illusions that the other could be trusted not to turn on him if there were an advantage to be had. But they had come to understand where to give and where to take to further their own objectives, and each meeting was like a probing of intents and limits. They hunted for a weakness in the other like foxhounds on the scent of a prey. But both seemed to enjoy the game. Perhaps it was because they were alike in so many ways. Each demanded respect and loyalty from their people, rewarding both qualities generously while punishing any transgressions severely.

"That's quite the arse, ain't it, Joseph?" commented O'Riley, following his dining partner's eyes.

The remark brought Lombardo back to the business at hand, and he turned his attention to the cop seated across from him. "Yes, it is, Captain O'Riley. Yes, it is," he replied. "I can't believe she's married to that stupido Jimmy DePalma. The bum works for me and The Eel and is a complete fuck-up. But still, wouldn't look good if I moved in on her."

The admission from Lombardo was no surprise to Colin. He knew this already, and he knew Joseph. He was perspiring, and that meant something large was about to be discussed.

"Oh, ya think she'd be interested in you, you horny prick?"

"Fuck you, O'Riley."

"So what do you need from me? I know we're not here for the ambience," said O'Riley as he gestured around the converted basement, which barely had room for the one table surrounded by restaurant supplies, some broken chairs, and a small bathroom. But the food was excellent, and the entrance directly from the alley behind the building, guarded by one of Lombardo's men, ensured they could dine and speak in total privacy.

"I need a favor, a big one."

Colin smiled. Whatever it was Lombardo needed could only strengthen his leverage in the profitable relationship he enjoyed with the man. The cost of the protection and information he provided would increase, as would the many gifts and privileges bestowed upon him by the grateful head of one or Boston's largest crime families. Along with his hold over his brother the new mayor, Colin was looking forward to a profitable and powerful run in the new year. With a new, smaller city council, he would control enough members to quash any police reform initiatives. Now he only needed to silence the growing calls to eliminate corruption coming from within the Boston Police Department itself.

APRIL 1950

CAPTAIN FITZPATRICK GRABBED Dommy's attention as soon as he entered the stable for his evening shift, waving him over to his office and saying, "I need a word with you, Patrolman Bassini."

The unfamiliar formality of the request sparked a sense of apprehension as Dommy walked over.

"You won't be taking Fitzy out tonight. He's being assigned to another officer," the captain said brusquely.

"What?" exclaimed Dommy.

"You heard me. Make yourself busy around the stable. I understand you're to be reassigned soon."

"Understand from whom? O'Riley?"

"Can't say. Simply passing along the word."

"With all due respect, Captain, you're full of shit."

"Watch your tone, Bassini. I'll write you up if you keep that up."

"Oh, you're going to write me up?" responded Dommy, his voice rising along with his anger. "How about I write you up along with your boss O'Riley? How about I go to people I know and let them know how friggin' corrupt you all are? I've been watching and listening, and the shit I know I could fill a book, you wormy little lackey. I'll bury you and your friends."

"You better calm down and think about what you're saying, Bassini."

"Or what? You'll go running to O'Riley?" shouted Dommy, grabbing Fitzpatrick and shoving him against the wall. The commotion got the attention of others in the barn.

"Let go of me, you crazy bastard," croaked the captain, grabbing hold of Dommy's arms.

196

"I will. And then I'm going to get my horse. My horse. And I'm going out there to do my job."

"No, you ain't. You're going to follow orders. You're never riding Fitzy or any other horse in here again. Go home. I'm suspending you right here and now." He was still holding Dommy's arms that had him by his shirt when Dommy threw the captain to the ground. Two other officers rushed in and restrained him. One said, "C'mon, Dommy. You'd better go before you get yourself into even more trouble."

Dommy turned and looked at the officer who had spoken to him. He was confused. What had he done? His eyes were burning, and his head throbbed. He patted his fellow cop on the shoulder as he walked by him as if in a daze and headed over to Fitzy's stall, where the big stallion gave a snort and a bob of his head as he saw Dommy approaching. Dommy hugged the huge animal's neck for a moment and then turned and walked away and out of the stable.

He soon found himself back in the North End but didn't want to go home to Martha, not right now. He headed to the Torre de'Passeri Society clubhouse where the few old men gathered there at this early hour were surprised to see him. He was in full uniform as he sat at the small bar and ordered a beer, oblivious to the stares of the others. One of the members sidled up beside him and said, "It's on me, Dommy." Then he adds, looking at him, "Are you okay?"

Dommy turned and looked at him as though he didn't understand the question. After a moment, he responded, "I'm fine." And then he turned back to the beer that had been placed before him, leaving no doubt that he was in no mood for company or conversation. Three hours later, he was still there.

✱ ✱ ✱

Martha was having a rare good day. With the walls of the small apartment suffocating her, the phone call from the Ritz was like a lifeline thrown to a drowning person, rescuing her from boredom and depression. She had been holding little Pete in her arms for what seemed forever as he fussed and refused to nap. Her old manager begged her to come over as soon as she could to help with an important client who insisted that Martha was the only one who could arrange the type of event she wanted.

Martha and Dommy had agreed that she could not work. Taking care of Pete was her full-time job now, but she had come to see it as more of a prison sentence. It would be years before Pete could start school, which would still only leave her a little time for some type of menial work, not a career. For now she was alone with an infant in a foreign world with no friends to speak of while she changed diapers and worried about her husband. The thought of being back at the Ritz, even for a little while, was invigorating.

She prevailed upon her upstairs neighbor Sofia DiBona to let Pete stay for what she guessed might be an hour or two at the most.

Arriving at the Ritz, Martha felt transformed. She was thrilled to be wearing a favorite dress she hadn't been able to fit into since shortly after becoming pregnant. She had worked hard since Pete was born to lose the remaining "baby weight" as she called it, and although the stylish dress was a little snug, she loved the way it emphasized her ample breasts. With her hair styled and makeup applied, she felt pretty for the first time in months.

The meeting went well. Her client was a wealthy Beacon Hill matron in charge of planning a Daughters of the American Revolution banquet to honor Harriet Hemenway, a prominent Boston socialite and founder of the Massachusetts Audubon Society, on her ninetieth birthday. Martha was able to offer a number of suggestions that the woman loved, including having live birds in the room in honor of Hemenway's campaign to ban the wild bird feather trade.

"This is exactly why I insisted on having you manage my event, my dear," she gushed, and then insisted they retire to the Ritz bar after the meeting to relax and catch up. Martha knew she should get back to Pete with dinner time approaching but couldn't resist extending the seductive pleasure she was feeling from being back out in the world. *I'll stay Cinderella a little longer,* she thought. *Midnight will strike soon enough.*

An hour later, Martha arrived home with conflicting emotions heightened by the two glasses of Chablis she enjoyed at the Ritz. Although the sight of the building where she lived saddened her, a lonely fortress in a desolate land, the thought of holding Pete gladdened her heart as she walked straight up to the third floor to gather him from the DiBona apartment. As soon as Sofia DiBona opened the door, Martha knew from her surprised reaction to seeing her that something was wrong.

"Martha, are you here for Pete?"

"Yes, of course, is he all right?"

"Well, yes," Sofia replied with some hesitation, "Dommy came up looking for him and you over an hour ago. He took Pete back downstairs."

Surprised that Dommy was home, Martha thanked Sofia and turned to go when Sofia stopped her. "Martha, Dommy doesn't seem to be himself. I hope he's OK." It sounded like a warning.

Martha heard Pete crying as she opened the door to the apartment. Sitting there, staring straight at her was Dommy, who held Pete on his shoulder while rubbing his back. The chair had been turned to face the door, and Martha was at first startled and then frightened by the look on Dommy's face. It was a look she had never seen before, so menacing it rendered Dommy almost unrecognizable. His jaw was clenched tightly shut, his dark eyes wide and glaring. One leg was bouncing, his heal rapidly tapping the floor. On the small table next to the chair was a half-empty liquor bottle of some type she had never seen before. They never had hard liquor in the house.

"Dommy," she uttered, "what are you doing home?"

Dommy continued glaring, saying nothing.

"Dommy?" she repeated. "Are you okay?"

"No, I'm not okay. I come home and can't find my wife and son. Then I find my boy being taken care of by a neighbor with three small children of her own and my wife off gallivanting somewhere. So I'm not okay!" Dommy shouted.

The shouting frightened Martha even more, and she started to explain, "The Ritz called. They needed me, and I had a chance to make some money, which we could use, so I decided…"

"You decided to leave your baby because your disappointing husband doesn't make enough money for you," interrupted Dommy, still shouting.

"No, that's not it all," protested Martha.

"Oh, that's it, alright. You're a spoiled rich kid at heart and always will be."

"That's unfair," Martha snapped back. "I've given up everything for you. I live in your closed-off Italian world where I don't fit in. I take care of you and our son. I wait here alone every night worrying about you. And when you're home, you just sulk around the apartment. We never make love. We never go out. We have no friends. What more can I do, Dommy? Tell me and I'll do it!"

"If your life is so terrible, why do you stay?"

"Because I love you, you stupid, selfish bastard. Because I love you."

This silenced Dommy for a moment. Then he said slowly, closing his eyes as he tried to gather his thoughts while battling his emotions. "You're job, your only job, is to take care of Pete. Just take care of Pete."

"And what's your job, Dommy? To save the world while I rot away in misery?"

"Martha, I think you should go. Me and my father will take care of Pete. Go. Leave."

In disbelief, Martha grew furious. "If I go, I'm taking Pete. I won't leave him alone with you. You need help, Dommy. Get some help. The war and the job took away the best part of you, and you need to get it back."

"Go, Martha. I can't handle this right now."

Enraged, Martha shouted, "You can't handle this? You can't handle this? What about me? What about me, Dommy?"

There was a loud pounding on the door. They both stopped and looked. There was another short pound, and then the door opened. It was Domenic. He was still carrying his lunchbox.

"What is going on here? I could hear you shouting from the sidewalk. The whole neighborhood can hear you. What is wrong with you two? You're arguing, and your baby is screaming." Domenic put down his lunch box, walked over to Dommy, and took his grandson from him. "I'm taking Pete downstairs. You two work out whatever the problem is, and please do it quietly."

A few moments later, Domenic was still holding Pete as the door opened and Martha stuck in her head. The mascara she had been so proud of a few hours earlier was running down her tear-streaked face. "I'm leaving, Papa. But I'll be back for Pete as soon as I'm settled."

Before Domenic could say anything, she took a few quick steps into the room, kissed Pete, and told him she loved him. She looked up at Domenic and said, "I love you too, Papa. Please take care of him and Dommy." And then she was gone.

***

Eight hours later, Martha was on a train headed for Chicago. Before the train reached each stop along the way, she would pick up her small bag stuffed with things she grabbed as she fled her apartment with the intent of getting off and returning to Boston. But she never did. She wanted to hold her child and to be held by Dommy. The old Dommy, the one she fell in love with and married knowing that as long as she had him by her side she could deal with anything that life threw at the two of them. But that Dommy was gone, drowned in some mysterious black sea of self-loathing and paranoia she could not fathom nor penetrate. She would remember the look on his face the night before and be frightened. She knew she had to get away and knew she had to take Pete with her. And the only way out was to stay on the train and get to Chicago, no matter how much she dreaded the prospect of returning home like this.

The night before, she did something she swore she would never do; she called her father for help. She needed money to get a place to live and a lawyer. She should not have been shocked when her mother answered and her father refused to speak with her. She half expected such a reaction. At her mother's insistence, her father finally took the phone and without allowing her to say a word said, "I warned you, and you wouldn't listen. I don't want to have anything to do with you or your guinea son. Not now, not ever." Then he hung up.

Her next call through the switchboard at the Ritz went to her brother, who was more sympathetic. "Come home and stay with me until you get your feet under you," he offered. "I'll talk to father and try to get him to come around. I'll wire you money for your ticket now."

As the train kept moving relentlessly westward, her head was making plans for Chicago while her heart remained in Boston.

***

Domenic barely slept. It wasn't so much that the couch in Dommy and Martha's apartment was uncomfortable as the gnawing fear he felt. He was worried about his son, his grandson, and his daughter-in-law.

He wanted to make everything right again but did not know how, and he fretted he could never fix what was now broken. He heard Dommy moving about and got up. Pete was still sleeping soundly.

As he was making coffee, Dommy walked into the kitchen red-eyed and looking like he may have slept even less than his father. The sight of him did little to alleviate Domenic's anxiety, but then Dommy offered up a forced half smile and said, "I guess I really fucked things up, Dad. I'm sorry." He sounded more like himself, and that was a relief.

"I'm making coffee," Domenic replied. "Do you want some? I have to leave for work soon."

"Dad, I was wondering if you could take today off and watch Pete?" Dommy asked sheepishly, knowing this was a huge request. Domenic never took days off from work." When his father didn't answer immediately, he explained, "I have to fix some things today. I have to find Martha and apologize. I've got to mend some fences at work, if they can be mended. I don't know why I do things and say things I don't really want to do or say, but I do. Martha is right. I need help."

Domenic can see that Dommy was about to start crying. He went to him, and father and son embraced with unfettered emotion for the first time in a long time. "It's going to be all right, Dommy. Of course I'll stay with Pete," Domenic whispered to his boy.

***

Dommy's first stop was the Ritz, where he learned that Martha was, in fact, there the night before and then took a cab to South Station, information given to him reluctantly by a desk clerk intimidated by his police uniform. Dommy could only guess where she was headed and left hoping he would hear from her soon. Next he headed over to the stables to learn what the consequences might be for his assault on Captain Fitzpatrick. He was surprised at what he was told.

"You're to report to the One right away," Fitzpatrick said, barely looking up the moment Dommy entered his office.

"The One?" Dommy was surprised. *The One* was the District One Station in the North End. He started to ask a question, but the captain shut him off immediately.

"That's it, Bassini. I've nothing more to say to you. If I had my way, you'd be put off the force. You must have someone upstairs looking out for you. Now get out of here, and might I add that I hope I never see your face again."

Domenic offered a weak salute that was more like a wave goodbye, turned, and left. Since the captain didn't offer to have an officer drive him over, he set out walking to the District One station on North Bennet Street, a few blocks from the Bassini home. He didn't get very far when a squad car pulled up beside him. "Would you like a ride Officer, Bassini?" the driver inquired. It was Billy Flynn.

"So I understand you're going back to police the streets of the old neighborhood," Flynn said sarcastically as Dommy got into the car. "You should thank Captain O'Riley for that. He got wind of the complaint Captain Fitzpatrick filed against you for that stunt you pulled yesterday and intervened. Thinks the change of scenery would do you good. Not that there's much to do over there. You know what they say, 'there's not a lot of crime in the North End, just a lot of criminals.'" Flynn laughed at his own joke.

A few minutes later, Dommy was standing at the desk of District One Commander Captain William Richardson. A twenty-year veteran of the force, Captain Bill, as he was referred to around the station, was known for his tough, no-nonsense approach to policing.

"I'm glad to have you here, Officer Bassini. You know the neighborhood, the neighborhood knows you. That's good. You'll be walking a beat the next couple of days with Sergeant O'Shea during his day shift, and then you'll be on your own evening shift after that. Any questions?"

"No, sir."

"I just want to say, Bassini, that I understand this is your last chance. I don't know what happened between you and Captain Fitzpatrick, but nothing remotely approaching that will be tolerated here. "

"Yes, sir. I understand."

"Now go to work. O'Shea is waiting for you."

As Dommy left, a big, ruddy-faced officer approached him and introduced himself. "I'm Sargent O'Shea. Going to show you the ropes, but I guess I don't have to show you the neighborhood," he said with a laugh.

It was the same cop that Dommy saw from his front steps the night he decided to become a policeman.

1 PM
APRIL 23, 1950

MARTHA WAS ANXIOUS as she sat in the Grand Hall of Chicago's Union Station awaiting her train back to Boston. She felt she'd been away too long wasting time talking to lawyers and planning her next steps when she should be back in Boston with her child. Her brother has been kind, allowing her into his home and giving her enough money to get back to Boston and restart her life, but she felt he would be relieved when she was gone. It caused tension between him and their father, who still refused to see or speak to her. Martha looked up at the huge barrel-vaulted skylight that soared high above the station floor and swore she could see the beams of light coming through moving, slowly marking the passing of each long minute.

Her one phone call with Dommy over the past three weeks did not go well. She could tell he was genuinely happy to hear from her and missed her greatly while begging her to come home. But when the conversation turned to her plan to find her own place for her and Pete unless some things changed, Domenic became agitated and then angry.

"I love you, Dommy, but we can't have a life together as long as you're on the force. You need to leave the department, we need to leave the North End, and you need to talk to someone about your…your issues."

"My issues? My issues are my wife has left me and our son and now wants to dictate how I'm supposed to live my life. And what happens if I don't agree?" Suddenly the tender man she loved was turning back into the monster that drove her away.

"Then I sue for divorce and custody of Pete."

"Go ahead and try." Then he hung up.

4 PM
APRIL 23, 1950

PETE SQUEALED WITH delight when Domenic produced the small container of gelato from his lunchbox that he had picked up on his way home from the shipyard.

"Mrs. Luongo made it with bananas especially for you," said Domenic, kneeling on the floor to accept Pete's show of appreciation, which took the form of a tight hug around his grandfather's neck.

Domenic looked up at Sofia DiBona, thanked her for looking after Pete, and presented her with some gelato as well. When Dommy worked his ten-hour evening shift, Sofia would watch over Pete during the hour or so from the time Dommy had to leave until the time Domenic arrived home.

Pete enthusiastically followed his grandfather down to Domenic's apartment on the first floor. For both of them, this was a special part of their day. Pete would have the unfiltered attention of his grandfather for the rest of the night. The two would spend the evening together until Domenic would put Pete to bed in Dommy's apartment and sleep there himself until Dommy arrived home.

Pasqualena's death had left a void in Domenic's apartment as well as his heart, and both were filled in a way by having Pete there. Domenic felt that he, Dommy, and Pete had adapted as well as could be expected to life without Martha or Pasqualena. There was still love in the house; there was still family. And for Pete, it was like having two fathers, one for the day and one for the night, both entirely dedicated to making him their center of attention.

7 PM
APRIL 23, 1950

ERNIE SAT AT a small table by the bar in the back of Villiano's Ristorante with Big Quiet. After Gaspare Messina had essentially bequeathed the impassive Sicilian to him, Ernie found Big Quiet to be the ideal dining companion, since true to his name he seldom spoke. This allowed Ernie to enjoy his food and think during meals. For his part, Big Quiet would gulp down his wine and attack his own food seemingly oblivious to Ernie's presence. But even as he ravaged a double order of Villiano's famous veal chops, his dark eyes never stopped surveying the room from beneath the cover of his furrowed brow and thick black eyebrows.

Even with his increased stature and notoriety in the Lombardo Family, Ernie refused to think of Big Quiet as a bodyguard. But neither was he a friend. Big Quiet had no friends and seemed to like it that way. Friends might require feelings, and as far as Ernie could tell Big Quiet had none. But he would kill for Messina and die to protect him. And Ernie had no doubt he would now do the same for him. He recalled how furious Joseph Lombardo became when Messina requested that Big Quiet become part of Ernie's fledgling Caporegime. Ernie was sure it was because the foresighted capo de capos knew that the hot-headed Lombardo would misuse this powerful resource.

Big Quiet's taciturn nature was never more appreciated than it was tonight, as Ernie tried to come to terms with the grim missive given to him by Lombardo earlier in the day. *Someone was going to die tonight*, he thought. Probably even more than one, Ernie suspected as he rolled the strange orders given to him by Lombardo over and over in his head.

Ernie's thoughts were interrupted as a family with small children settled into a nearby booth. The banter and laughter drew his attention, and he watched for a few moments like the poor boy with his nose pressed against a store window captivated by some expensive toy he knew he could never have. He never understood how glimpses of a life he never wanted, a life he shunned at every opportunity, could make him feel so hollow. He knew he would never marry and have children. He could not be what he was and have a family. He didn't deserve one.

He caught the eye of the little girl at the table and gave her a smile. She slid her head behind her father while keeping one sparkling eye on Ernie. The father turned to see what the girl was looking at, and when he saw Ernie and Big Quiet, the smile he had been wearing vanished. It wasn't fear, nor was it outward disdain. But it was a look that chilled Ernie by reminding him how he was seen by others. The father gave Ernie a respectful nod and then turned and whispered to his wife, and suddenly the aura of familial joy that had filled the booth a moment before was gone, extinguished by Ernie's mere presence.

He turned his gaze toward Big Quiet and said, "We've got to stop coming here. Too many damn kids." His dining partner offered up a soft grunt and a nod of agreement as he pushed aside the bone of his first veal chop and slid the second into place.

Ernie's thoughts returned to Joseph Lombardo. Earlier in the day, he had summoned Ernie to his office, and after keeping him waiting as he always did he brought Ernie in and gave him his strange orders.

"I want Jimmy DePalma looking after the game on Margaret Street tonight," he declared without offering any welcoming pleasantries. "You should stay away. I want to see how he does."

Ernie was startled. First of all, DePalma was actually one of Ernie's soldiers. And although technically this meant Lombardo was DePalma's ultimate boss, Ernie couldn't remember any Caporegime being told how to deploy his own men in one of his own enterprises. Secondly, the high stakes poker game on Margaret was more of a diversion than a serious moneymaker for Ernie and the Lombardo Family. It was also a small enterprise at a very low risk for a robbery or a bust. Anyone could man the door. Even DePalma, who Ernie saw as one of his least able men. But most importantly it was Ernie's game. He had started it, he ran it, and he gave Lombardo more of a cut than he should.

But Ernie had learned never to question Lombardo. Whereas Gaspare Messina would have explained his reasons to Ernie, Lombardo never felt the need to explain anything to anyone. He would take any questions as a challenge to his authority, so Ernie simply nodded.

As he sat, waiting for more, Lombardo stared at him for a moment and then finally said, "That's it, Eel. You waiting for a special invitation to leave?"

Ernie got up and headed toward the door. As he opened it, Lombardo said, "Remember, just DePalma. Alone. No one else." Ernie nodded without turning and left.

The strange encounter had bothered him all day, and common sense told him to stay out of it. Lombardo must have his reasons. But Ernie's instincts were sending out all kinds of alarms, and he was never one to simply do what he was told. He recalled how he had hijacked one of Messina's own trucks to get his attention. Something was up, and as he sat there sipping his Limoncello he mulled making his way over to Margaret Street. It was his game and his reputation on the line.

He paid the bill and told Big Quiet he was done for the day, wondering what the silent Sicilian actually did on his own time. On the way out the door, he handed the headwaiter a hundred dollar bill and asked him to send a tiramisu cake to the little girl's table. It was after eight, and the game wouldn't start for at least another couple of hours. He could wait around to check it out or go home to Swampscott.

***

Jimmy DePalma arrived early at 13 Margaret Street. He was excited, scared, and a little drunk. The first-floor apartment and the basement of the house had been converted into a lounge and gambling area. The house was owned by the Lombardo Family, and the top two apartments were rented to two Lombardo soldiers and their families. DePalma let himself in through the front door and made his way down into the basement where the gambling took place to begin getting ready. As he surveyed the layout, he felt his hands shaking, so he went over to the bar to pour himself a calming drink. He wasn't going to let Mr. Lombardo down.

"The first one through the door," Lombardo had emphasized several times. "Don't fuck this up."

8 PM
APRIL 23, 1950

DOMMY ENJOYED THE interactions with the people as he walked his evening beat. This was home to his great extended family, and he was protecting it. He made sure to stop in at Joe's insurance office where his godfather was always happy to share the latest news on everything going on in the neighborhood. This night though, his mind was on Martha. She arrived back in Boston tomorrow, and he was determined to make things right. He missed her deeply and vowed to remain calm and empathetic when he saw her. He wanted to convince her that he just wanted to be a good cop now and put all the troubles within the force behind him. If she wanted to work, that was fine. They'd figure something out for Pete. And if she cannot live in the North End, he wouldn't stay here without her.

As he walked past the storefronts and restaurants on Hanover Street, he saw a familiar face up ahead waiting for him beside a parked police car. It was Billy Flynn.

"How's the beat going, Bassini? Enough excitement for ya?"

"Everything is fine, Sergeant. Nice and quiet," replied Dommy suspiciously, wondering why Flynn was there.

"Well, I have a job for you to liven things up a bit. We're going to bust up an illegal gambling operation together, and since this is your neighborhood, I think you're the right man for the job. Get in."

2 AM
APRIL 24, 1950

LATER THAT NIGHT, Domenic was awakened by the sound of car doors and voices coming up from the street beneath the windows. The streetlamp outside cast a gloomy gray light through the thin curtains into the front parlor of Dommy's apartment, but everything else was black and still. He had fallen asleep in Dommy's big lounge chair with Pete on his lap, and his grandson did not stir as he struggled to stand up while still holding him.

He started toward the boy's room, but the voices outside weren't right, and this caused a twinge of uneasiness. Except for the voices, the quiet emptiness of the night signaled it was very late. And the voices themselves were too soft and muffled, lacking the life beat of normal conversation. Still holding Pete, he walked to the windows, pulled one curtain back slightly, and peered out. What he saw froze his heart. He squeezed his grandson tighter and instinctively kissed him on the forehead.

There were two police cars parked outside the building with several uniformed officers milling about them. Dommy was not one of them. An icy wave of fear broke over Domenic. He started toward Pete's room to put him into his bed, but suddenly it was more important to know the time. He walked to the kitchen, and the big clock there indicated 2:20. Dommy should have been home from his evening shift around midnight. Domenic could feel Pete's soft breaths as he stared blankly at the clock, its relentless ticking seeming to grow louder and faster in the suffocating stillness of the room. He turned to head back to the parlor, not knowing why, on legs that were suddenly unsteady.

Then he thought he heard the phone in his own apartment below ringing, and still holding Pete he poked his head out the door and into the stairwell. Yes, it was his phone.

The ringing phone was like a lifeline cast from somewhere beyond the heavy mist of fear engulfing him, and Domenic reached for it with all his might. It would be Dommy calling. He would explain why he was late and why the police were huddling outside his door. He scrambled down the stairs as quickly as he could with Pete in his arms and through the unlocked door into his own apartment. The ringing stopped well before he got to the phone, but he picked it up nevertheless and pleaded into its silence, "Hello? Hello? Hello?"

He put the phone down slowly and looked out his own first floor windows at the policemen gathered outside. They were much larger from this closer vantage point, making them all the more real, all the more ominous. And there were more of them now. What were they doing? What were they waiting for?

Domenic decided to go and confront them. He stepped out toward the door leading to the street but thought that he should put Pete to bed first and turned to head back up the stairs. Then he hesitated, one foot on the bottom step, as all the dizzying thoughts spinning in his head rendered him incapable of holding on to a single simple one. Should he get Pete to bed, should he go outside, should he call the station? As he stood in the hallway his phone started ringing again, awakening him from his stupor. This time he reached it in time.

"Hello, hello," he shouted into the phone.

"Domenic, it's Joe." The tone of his old friend's voice reached into Domenic's chest and put an icy grip on his pounding heart. "It's Dommy. He's been shot, Domenic. He's dead."

Joe was still talking as Domenic hung up the phone without saying a word. Outside his window, he could see the officers now stepping aside to make a path to the door for a grim-faced Father DiPetro, who was rushing up the sidewalk. Domenic went to the street door and unlocked it. He didn't want them ringing the doorbell and waking Pete.

Shivering uncontrollably, he took a few unsteady steps backward and sat down on the stairs, burying his face and quietly sobbing into the chest of his sleeping grandson.

APRIL 30, 1950

THE ENDLESS FLOW of faces circling around Domenic all seemed the same. Mannequin faces painted by an artist who captured only sorrow. Anything behind the faces no longer existed, no longer mattered to Domenic. They were familiar only in a strange, distant way, but they were all the same.

The Torre de'Passeri Club was filled with those who had come following the burial of Dommy Bassini. Domenic found himself surrounded by people he had known for many years, but none of them mattered to him today. Except one. He instinctively kept looking beyond the faces for his grandson Pete. Pete had hardly been more than an arm's length away from Domenic since the moment he heard of Dommy's death.

Instead, Joe caught his eye from the middle of the room and nodded toward the kitchen. Domenic walked through the faces without excusing himself, without saying a word. Although many were spoken at him, they were nothing more than a dull, distant murmur. He caught up with Joe and immediately asked, "Who has Pete?"

"He's fine, Dom. He's with Martha."

Domenic acknowledged this with a slow, gloomy nod. His fear of losing his grandson so soon after his son had been growing ever since Martha returned. He feared she would take him with her back to Chicago. Whenever the shock of Dommy's death lessened, even for an instant, this new fear rushed in to fill the void. He and Martha had not yet spoken about Pete.

"Come with me, Dom. There's someone waiting for us out back."

But Domenic wasn't listening. He was staring off across the room where a sea of blue uniforms were gathered around the bar. Unlike most in the room, they were loud, sometimes even shattering the low hum of reverence with laughter.

"Bastardos," he muttered under his breath.

"I know, Dom." Joe put his hand gently on Domenic's shoulder to direct him to the kitchen.

But Domenic didn't move, he turned his head and surveyed the room. "We had Dommy's First Communion party here. Remember, Joe? His confirmation too."

"Of course I remember, Dom. He was my godson."

Domenic didn't feel the need for any more words and slowly turned to follow Joe to the kitchen. As they headed off, Joe looked back and glared at the contingency of policemen as he tried to catch the eye of Giuliano, who was behind the bar serving drinks. He wanted to signal him to shut down the bar but couldn't get his attention.

Joe led Domenic through the swinging door into the kitchen. Some of the neighborhood women were in there preparing the food they'd brought, and they looked at Domenic with the same painted faces and uttered the same meaningless sounds as he and Joe passed through.

As they went out the rear door and into the alley, Domenic was shocked to see Ernie standing there. For the first time in days, Domenic felt an emotion beyond the numbing sorrow and fear that had entombed him. He felt anger. A quick intense flash that exploded like a bomb in his chest and then shot throughout his entire body. He stared quickly and accusingly at Joe and then glared at Ernie while walking toward him.

"You!" he screeched. "You killed my boy!" Then he felt himself being restrained by Joe.

"Dom, I didn't. I swear, Dom. I didn't know anything about it." Ernie was pleading with his hands held out as though trying to reach through the hatred separating him from his old friend.

"Listen to him, Dom. Please just listen to him," pleaded Joe as he tried to calm and restrain him at the same time.

"It makes no sense, Dom. That game is protected. It never gets raided," said Ernie. "The cops take a cut and everybody's happy. That's how it works. It's the cost of doing business. There's no way DePalma would have started shooting at the sight of a few cops coming through the door. No fucking way."

Domenic was trying to process what Ernie was saying but couldn't. There was too much raw emotion blocking him from the words. Seeing this, Joe interjected, "Ernie thinks that this whole thing stinks. That there's more to this. That maybe DePalma was set up. Or maybe Dommy was set up. That someone wanted him dead. That this was planned and Dommy wasn't just in the wrong place at the wrong time."

"Listen to me, Dom. I think the other cop, Flynn, went in there to get DePalma. Dommy never fired his weapon. But Flynn Swiss-cheesed DePalma. Seems to me he knew what was coming. DePalma never would have just started blasting away. The friggin' game hadn't even started yet. What the fuck was he protecting?"

Domenic found it hard to speak or even react. He sat down on a wooden crate in the alley and rested his forehead in his hands. "What are you telling me, Ermino? Why are you telling me?"

"Because I promise you that I will find out what really went down and why. And I swear to you whoever did this will be punished."

"I promise too, Dom," said Joe. "No one is getting away with taking Dommy from us right here in our own neighborhood."

"And I want you to know, Dom," said Ernie. "DePalma wasn't working for me. He was working directly for Lombardo."

"And so do you work for Lombardo," snapped Domenic, looking up suddenly and directly at Ernie. "He is a leech who sucks the blood from everyone around him, and he is a killer, and he is your boss. You serve him." Domenic spat on the ground.

"But I don't love him, Dom. I loved Dommy. You must know that. You must believe that."

Somewhere deep within his broken heart, Domenic knew this to be true. But he refused to acknowledge it. Not now. Instead, he said, "You live in a black, dirty world, Ermino. You will do this for me and for Dommy, and then you will crawl right back into it, and we will never speak again." Then he looked away, and all three knew they were the last words they would have on the subject this day.

Ernie reached down, put a hand on Domenic's shoulder, and said, "I am so sorry, Dom." Then he turned and walked up the alley to the street.

✼✼✼

Martha refused to give these damnable women whatever it was they wanted from her. It might be an apology, a confession of her sins, or to simply leave. But she would give them none of these things. They made it clear to her for two years that she didn't belong here, and they were making it abundantly clear now. She sat in a corner of the Torre de'Passeri Club with Pete on her lap, looking straight ahead and saying nothing. Some of the women actually came over and spoke to Pete without even acknowledging her. They might cast a slight disdainful glance in her direction, but that was the extent of it. Other than Joe, the only ones showing an interest in Martha were the cops who kept coming over with glasses of that godawful wine she never liked. But today it helped. Anything to get through this.

When her former upstairs neighbor Sofia DiBona approached, Martha was hopeful, as they had always had a cordial relationship. But as soon as little Pete saw her, he started calling her name, which sounds like "Soya," and holding out his arms. And when it was apparent she was not going to take him with her after fussing over him, Pete started to wail and scream her name louder and louder. The whole room turned to look. Even her own child wanted to escape her, and it destroyed any shred of stoicism she had remaining.

"Here, Sofia, please take him for a while. I need some air."

The front door was jammed with cops who spilled out into the street, and she didn't want to run that lecherous gauntlet, so she headed for the kitchen. She startled the women in there and went directly for the door out to the alley, where she ran straight into Joe and Domenic, who were coming in. There was a brief instant of pregnant silence before Martha broke down. The raging river of emotion that had been rising steadily since she first heard about Dommy finally burst the last remnants of the dam of pure resolve that had been holding it back. Sobbing uncontrollably, she stammered, "I'm so sorry, Papa. I'm so, so sorry."

Domenic stepped forward and wrapped his arms around his daughter-in-law as she sobbed into his chest.

"I'll leave you two alone," said Joe, kissing Martha on the top of her head. Then looking sternly at the women in the kitchen staring at the scene, he added, "We'll all leave you alone."

Moments later, Domenic still held Martha, but the sobs had slowly turned into words long burning inside her but never spoken. "I was suffocating, Papa. I had nothing here. Dommy would never leave this neighborhood. He needed it too much. He carried something inside him, something from the war, and it was like a weight that kept him anchored here. It was his cocoon, but it offered nothing for me. We'd never have a real home. I'd never have a career or a life. The women all hated me because I wasn't like them. I had no friends. We never went out. I was slowly suffocating. I kept hoping Dommy would go back to school, but then Pete was born, and I knew nothing would ever change. Dommy would never change. He loved me, but I didn't really know him. He didn't want anything more out of life than what he had. What we had. And I needed more."

She stopped briefly to catch her breath and fight back the last of her tears. "But the worst of it was the fear that one day he wouldn't come home and I'd be left all alone. And I knew it would happen, because Dommy didn't want to just be a cop. He wanted to be a saint. And it wasn't the bad guys I worried about. There were other cops who hated him, Papa. They hated him because he wasn't like them. He wouldn't lie or steal. And he was so proud of that."

Martha stopped talking. As she caught her breath and began to breathe and think once again, she was ashamed that she had dropped so much emotion upon a man who was already burdened with so much. But there was one more thing she needed to say again.

"I'm so, so sorry, Papa.

Domenic kept his arms around her in silence, but it felt to Martha as though he was not so much holding her as leaning on her. He felt heavier. She knew she needed to wait until he was ready to speak, walk away, or scream. She had done enough talking. Too much. But then he started to speak. He struggled at first, and she could feel him fighting to gather himself. And as he summoned the strength he needed to go on, she could feel his weight on her lessen. Then it was he who was holding her again.

"I just wish, I just wish…I don't know. I just wish I could have seen him truly happy. And maybe if you had stayed that might have happened someday. He was better with you. But I don't blame you. I know you loved him. I know he loved you. And he loves, I mean loved, Pete so much. But I don't think he could be happy, Martha. My boy died never really being happy. For that I blame myself. And that hurts so much."

"I'm so sorry, Papa."

"It's okay, Martha. But what about you? Are you okay?"

"I think I can probably make it through the day."

"I mean, with everything. Your life?"

"For now I'm just thinking about making it through today. That's all I can hope for. And, please, Papa, let's not talk about Pete today. I can't do it. I know that's a lot to ask, but please give me some time."

"I will, but…"

"Please."

"Okay. I understand."

"As for my life, I don't even know what I will do once I wake up tomorrow." She hesitated as tears once again began to fill her eyes. "But I know I'll miss Dommy then and forever."

***

Ernie lit a cigarette as he walked up the alley. When he reached the street, he was startled to see Colin O'Riley standing there, apparently waiting for him.

"I'm surprised to see you here, Mr. Eel," says O'Riley with a smirk. "But you're probably surprised to see me too."

Ernie said nothing. He just looked at O'Riley and took a long, slow drag of his cigarette. But at the same time he was surveying as much of the street and alley as he could while also using the silence to listen for any sound of movement behind him.

Seeing he was not going to get a response, O'Riley went on, "I got eyes everywhere, Mr. Eel. Seen you talking to the father and the councilor. You should understand it's a fragile thing we've built together, me and you and your…family. A very fragile thing. And I don't think Mr. Lombardo would like to see it broken. Once broken, it won't be easily fixed. And too many questions, too much talking can break this very mutually beneficial thing."

Ernie took a slow, final puff of his cigarette and then flicked it to the ground. "You know, Captain O'Riley, you'd think that ugly fucking scar I gave you might have gotten a little better over time, but I think it's actually gotten worse. Course, even without it you'd still be an ugly fucking bastard, so I guess it doesn't really matter."

Then he turned and walked away as O'Riley shouted after him, "Do I need to tell Mr. Lombardo we have a problem here, Mr. Eel?"

***

After leaving Martha and Domenic in the kitchen, Joe headed straight to the police contingent gathered around the bar in their dress uniforms. He meant to put a stop to their loud, disrespectful outbursts and drunken toasts. No one understood the clash of the cultures better than Joe, who had cultivated a career out of walking a fine politician's line between them. But this was an Italian funeral on Italian ground, and their rules needed to be respected.

But as he approached the bar, he saw a reporter from the *Herald Traveler* standing with Captain Callahan, so he reigned in his anger and approached with a practiced smile.

"Captain Callahan, we all appreciate you and your men being here today."

"We take care of our own, Councilor," said Callahan. "I assume you know Bill Duggan from the *Herald*?"

"Of course," he said, shaking Duggan's hand. "Would you mind, Mr. Duggan, if Dennis and I had a brief word?"

They moved a few steps from the bar, and Joe put his arm around Callahan. The smile never left his face as he whispered into his ear, "You ignorant sonofabitch. The bar is closing, and I want you to get every single one of your drunken hyenas out of here in the next ten minutes or you'll be entertaining a huge shitstorm of problems raining down on the department from the city council. We're mourning the loss of a good man today. A war hero, a son, a father. Your men are treating it like fucking prom night."

Callahan was startled. "With all due respect, Councilor, this is how we honor our own."

"He wasn't yours. He was ours. And this isn't how we do it here in our home. So you either get your men to show some reverence for the son we've lost, or get the hell out of here." He then shook Callahan's hand and flashed a bright smile for Duggan or anyone else to see. But only Callahan could see the venom in his eyes.

Five minutes later, there was not a blue uniform to be seen in the room.

JUNE 1951

JOE ENTERED THE basement of L & G Imports through the side door off the alley. The basement setup was like that of many mutual-aid society clubhouses, with a bar on one end and tables and chairs spread around between the many floor-to-ceiling beams in the room. The walls were framed with wood paneling with the bottom stained from when water had flooded the room over the years. Cases of wine and beer were stacked in one corner opposite the bar while a pool table sat impossibly close to the wall in the other.

In the middle of the room, Ernie sat alone at a table. There was a bottle of wine in front of him along with two glasses and a brown bag streaked with grease stains. Lunch.

Ernie looked up with a slight smile and said, "Welcome, Mr. Mayor." He began pouring a glass of wine. Joe sat down and commenced to probe the contents of the bag. They were the only two people in the room.

"Eggplant parmesan from Mama's?" guessed Joe, pulling out the meal on top that sat on a paper plate wrapped in wax paper.

"What else? You're such a creature of habit."

"Me? I'll bet you a thousand dollars the other meal is veal with marsala sauce specially made with no mushrooms."

"No bet," replied Ernie, stifling a grin. "Here, this is a new Montepulciano we are importing. I understand the vineyard is not far from Torre. Teramo?"

"Teramo is nowhere near Torre, my Napolitano friend," said Joe, taking a sip. "This is good though."

Ernie took his meal from the bag, and the two men settled into lunch and conversation. After KO O'Riley reneged on the deal they had made, Joe was furious and decided he would run against him in November. He was a popular voice on the city council and among many of the rank and file voters sick of the Irish control of city politics. He felt he could easily win a seat on the new nine-member city council in November, but that opportunity would always be there. For now, there was a score to settle. Even if he failed to win, which was likely, he would be laying a path for future Italians in the city. He recalled what he had once told Dommy when the boy was hesitant to attend Harvard and decided to take his own advice, *someone has to be first.*

"So you never told me what Domenic has to say about all this. Especially with Martha helping you," said Ernie while licking a small taste of sauce from his spoon to make sure there were no traces of mushroom.

"If Dom knew you were helping me, he'd probably kill the both of us."

"That sounds like Domenic. Always so goddamn…"

"Righteous? Honest? Noble? Stubborn?" interrupts Joe. "Stop me when I get to the right one."

"How about holier than thou?"

"How about you tell me how you plan to motivate our union people."

Ernie looked at his old friend and smiled. Joe was probably the best known and most respected man in the North End. In fact, he, Domenic, and Gaspere Messina were the only three men Ernie ever felt were worthy of his respect. Joe was known for his humor, his compassion, his intelligence, and his leadership. But Ernie knew him for his iron will and his willingness to take whatever steps were necessary to achieve what he thought was right. Even if he knew those steps were wrong.

"*Our* union people?"

"Okay, your union people. But you split hairs."

Ernie laughed. "So who do you think the *facoltoso* on Beacon Hill and in the Back Bay hate more – you or O'Riley? The wop or the Mick?"

"The question should be who they like more in the working neighborhoods. The old money doesn't like O'Riley, but they hate change. They've gotten used to working with Irish mayors. And I'm promising change. But if we can get enough of all the pissed off mulignans and Jews and non-Irish working people in the western neighborhoods to get off their asses and vote we have a chance. A few bucks spread around those neighborhoods would go a long ways."

"I'll see what I can do. I've also got some pretty good stuff on some people close to O'Riley. Also got some old Curley people might spill some dirt on O'Riley from his Curley days for the right price…or the right coercion. Sonofabitch himself seems pretty clean though. Good family man, no whoring or drinking like some other candidate I know," he said, grinning at Joe.

"We don't need to discuss that, and they're not whores," said Joe with a dismissive wave.

"And I can pretty much guarantee the organized heckling will stop."

Joe tried not to laugh at this but couldn't help himself. He nearly choked on his food and started coughing. Finally he gathered himself and said, "You don't think fracturing a reporter's jaw was a little excessive?"

"Reporter, my ass. We all know he's a paid shill for O'Riley. Besides, it was all a misunderstanding."

"A misunderstanding! Some friggin' misunderstanding."

"Seriously. So Repucci's standing there at the back of the room with Martha while you're shaking hands after your big announcement, and this asshole starts shouting out shit questions like, 'Hey Joe, are you taking money from the Mafia? And 'Hey, Joe, any truth to the rumors about you and prostitutes?' You're ignoring him, but Martha says to Repucci, 'I'd like to see someone punch that jerk in the mouth.' Now we all know Repucci's not the brightest guy, but he follows orders well. And remember it was you who wanted someone watching over Martha. So to him it was simple logic. I'm supposed to take care of the lady, and the lady wants this guy's face broken."

Both men laughed hysterically at Ernie's version of the event and his impersonation of the dull-witted Repucci, even though both knew he wouldn't have acted without Ernie's blessing. "At least he had the decency to wait until he caught the jerk outside in the alley," said Joe, erupting into another fit of laughter.

Then, earnestly, Joe asked, "Why you really doing all this, Ernie? I've promised you nothing. And you're risking a lot by getting involved. What's Lombardo think? You fucking with his cozy relationship with KO's bastard brother Colin like this?"

Ernie looked at Joe then looked away, struggling with the question. He wanted to say, Lombardo's not my brother, Joe. He's not the closet thing I've ever had to a family like you and Domenic. He wanted to say if you knew what I knew you'd want to fuck Lombardo and Colin O'Riley a thousand times over. But he didn't. Not yet.

"Let's just say I'm as sick as you are of the bastards who really run this city. I'm sick of paying them off in private and then having them come after me in public. I'm sick of having to kiss asses or break asses to get what I've earned. I'm sick of the crooked cops and the crooked Feds who are tight with the Irish thugs but come after us with both barrels."

"There's got to be more to it. You've always been a good businessman, Ernie. This isn't good business. Could even be bad for business by pissing off some of the wrong people."

Ernie looked away again. "Let's say I owe a debt to the Rossario family and leave it at that. Now eat your eggplant. We can discuss that other thing after lunch."

SEPTEMBER 1951

EVEN THOUGH IT was an unseasonably warm Saturday for October, Domenic packed an extra blanket into Pete's stroller as he prepared for the walk to the Back Bay. Martha's apartment was the basement unit in a four-story townhouse on Commonwealth Avenue between Dartmouth and Exeter Streets. Domenic had been overjoyed when Martha announced she would be staying in Boston. "I can't be that close to my father, Papa." And he offered her an apartment in his building. She refused, saying being in the North End would only bring back bad memories she would have to relive every day.

Dommy's visit to the Ritz in search of her upset her employers enough to let her go. Cops showing up and intimidating employees in front of guests couldn't be tolerated. But she quickly found a job at Arnold & Company, an advertising agency, with an office in Park Square, a short walk from her apartment. She loved her job, and even though she was technically the receptionist, her looks, which she believed were the main reason she got the job in the first place, also got her access to some of the all-male meetings, which she found fascinating. The men in the office were flirtatious but harmless, and she was able to strike the right balance between playing along with their innuendos and keeping them at arm's length.

Pete spent his days upstairs with Sofia DiBona until Domenic arrived home from the shipyard, usually by 4 PM. Most weeknights, Martha would come directly from work for dinner, which Domenic enjoyed preparing, staying well into the evening before heading back to her apartment. Some nights, Lou would join them for dinner, and it seemed to Domenic that these visits were becoming more and more frequent. Those dinners were pleasant enough, but the grief shared by all three that hovered over those meals like a shroud never allowed the conversation to stray too far from the mundane. Lou was doing well at his law firm and had been resisting Joe's prodding to enter politics. Martha would talk excitedly about the latest client advertising campaign being nurtured at Arnold. Domenic would mostly listen but would reluctantly dole out some local neighborhood gossip his two North End expatriate guests seemed to crave.

Anything was fair game at dinner, except any talk about Dommy.

Pete usually returned home with Martha Friday evenings, but last night Martha had to work late and went straight home from the office. She was given the opportunity to work as an account assistant on a new project and was happily pouring everything she had into it. So Domenic offered to take Pete by first thing Saturday morning. It was a walk he enjoyed. He would take his time walking along the familiar streets of the North End, often holding Pete's hand while pushing the empty stroller with his free hand.

There were frequent stops as acquaintances would go out of their way to greet Domenic and fawn over Pete, who loved every minute of it. Pete was nearly three years old and wanted to walk like a big boy to his mother's, but he rarely made it past Scollay Square before his tired legs triumphed over his dislike of the stroller.

They would meander through the Haymarket on their way, and Domenic would always pick out some fresh vegetables and fish for Martha and Pete's weekend meals as well as for himself. He was always invited to join them for dinners but felt that Martha was doing it out of courtesy and would prefer to spend the time with her son alone. As they passed through Boston Common with Pete nodding off in his stroller, Domenic's thoughts turned to his meeting with Joe later that morning. It was not unusual for Joe to drop by Domenic's unannounced at any time, but it was unusual for Joe to ask him to his office. "A little something I need to go over with you, Dom, and I have to be in my office all morning, so could you come here?" But he felt that his friend was trying too hard to sound casual, and in his gut he suspected that there was something of importance to be discussed. He both hoped and feared that it might be about Dommy.

***

Domenic entered Joe's office and was greeted by several men he knew from the neighborhood who were gathered around the espresso machine. They exchanged pleasantries as he slowly made his way over to Elisabetta Salvucci's desk. She was genuinely happy to see him.

"Domenic! What a pleasant surprise." She got up and came around the desk to give him a hug. "Where have you been? That beautiful grandson of yours keeping you busy?"

"Nice to see you, Elisabetta," he replied. "I hope all your family is doing well."

"Everybody's fine, Domenic. You looking for Joe?" Then adding in a whisper loud enough for the other men to hear, she said, "Or did you just drop by to see me and mooch some free espresso like all those sfigatos over there?"

"Ahh, we know you love us, Betty," responded one of the men. They all laughed.

"Go on in, Dom."

Domenic still knocked first and waited to hear Joe's voice from behind the door. "You can come on in unless I owe you money."

"Hello, Joe."

"Hey, Domenic! You came."

"You ask me to come and then act surprised that I'm here."

"You're right. I'm a stupido." He walked over and hugged Dom. Then he whispered while still holding his old friend, "We need to talk." The way he said it gave Domenic a chill.

"OK, Joe, go ahead and talk."

"Not here, upstairs. Our old friend is waiting."

✱✱✱

Domenic, Joe, and Ernie sat around a small kitchen table in the sparsely furnished third floor of Joe's building. It was rarely used except for clandestine meetings Ernie sometimes held to avoid the prying eyes of the Lombardo family. As it was approaching lunchtime, Joe had offered to run across Hanover Street to pick up some sandwiches, but Domenic quickly and firmly declined. He had not said a word yet directly to Ernie, barely acknowledging Ernie's greeting when he had entered the room with Joe. Domenic sat quietly waiting for his hosts to get around to whatever it was they had to say to him. It was clear to Ernie and Joe that there would be no small talk, no reminiscing. This was business.

Finally, when Joe accepted the futility of drawing Domenic into conversation, he said sarcastically, "Well, Dom, I get the sense you are not disposed to friendly conversation today, so I suppose we should get down to what Ernie has to tell us. But if we're going to starve, I at least need a glass of wine."

He got up, pulled a bottle of chianti off a small rack in the kitchen, and opened it. He brought it back with three glasses and filled them. "Here's to three Italians who walked from Commonwealth Pier to the North End together nearly forty years ago and became…" he paused. "…family. Salute." Domenic glanced at Ernie and hesitated.

Joe looked at Domenic as he held his glass in the air and said, "Ernie has put himself at great risk, Dom, to find out what really happened to Dommy. Very great risk. And he is prepared to do more if you say the word. He has never forgotten what you did for him and has always been like a brother to me. We all do what we have to do. We start from very different places in life, so it is very hard for everyone to end up the same. You have said many times that many things may change us, but we start and end with the family. Well, maybe we're a different kind of family, but we are still family. Salute."

Domenic slowly raised his glass, nodded at Joe, then looked directly at Ernie and quietly said, "Salute."

"Thank you, Dom," said Ernie in a whisper.

***

"I knew from the beginning this stunk," began Ernie. "Nothing leading up to what happened on Margaret Street made any sense. Why did Lombardo insist that DePalma, a friggin' nobody, cover the game that night? Why would the cops even bother to raid a game they've known about forever and were paid through Billy Flynn to leave alone? And what was Dommy doing there at all? Why was someone who Colin O'Riley didn't trust suddenly ordered to go with his right hand man Flynn to raid a small-time card game? And how could a jamope like DePalma get the drop on two cops, one with twenty years on the force and one a combat veteran? None of it made any sense, and the cops were only too eager to accept the idea that DePalma was able to shoot them both before Flynn got a few shots off. Even if he panicked like they say and pulled a gun when Dommy and Flynn showed up, there's no way he gets them both. I don't think he ever shot a gun in his life. And why would DePalma even have to shoot?"

Ernie paused and finished off his wine. He refilled his glass and topped off Joe's from the bottle. Domenic had not touched his. He sat silently and listened.

"I thought at first it was all set up by Lombardo to get rid of DePalma without anything leading back to him. I knew he had a thing for DePalma's wife—everybody did—but it wouldn't look good him moving in on the wife of one of his men. He would lose the respect of a lot of his own guys, not to mention give Jerry Angiulo and the Patriarca Family more reason to move him completely out like they want.

He had to get someone outside his own organization to do the job. Then when O'Riley warned me at Dommy's funeral to stay out of all this, I knew he had to be involved. But this was a big ask by Lombardo, so what did O'Riley get in return?" Ernie stopped a moment to take a long sip of wine. Then he looked directly at Domenic and said, "The answer is Dommy."

The hardened, stoic look on Domenic's face changed in an instant. His eyes widened, and his chin began to quiver. He looked at Ernie who slowly nodded in confirmation. He then turned and looked away from them both to gather himself as he said, "So my son was assassinated."

"Yes, I'm sorry, Dom," said Ernie. "He was targeted. It wasn't just a bust gone bad."

Joe stood, took a step, and put his hand on Domenic's shoulder. "I'm sorry too, Dom."

Domenic said nothing as he tried to grasp what he had learned. As horrible and as devastating as Dommy's killing had been, somehow there had been some closure. He knew what had happened, who had shot him. He'd thought it was bad luck, the wrong place at the wrong time. Now even that small blanket of consolation had been taken away. He shuddered out of fear at first, thinking about where this might all take him. But the fear was quickly replaced by a burning anger he had never felt before. It swelled up rage behind his eyes, and he shook. He tried to compose himself, but his next words came out in a loud cry, "He killed my boy. The Irish bastard killed my boy." And he broke down in sobs, burying his head in his arms on the table.

Ernie and Joe exchanged a look. There was more Domenic needed to know, and they wondered how to proceed. Then Domenic sat up, and they were both surprised to see how quickly he seemed to compose himself. He looked at them both and was about to say something, but the look on their faces gave them away. He cleared his throat.

"There is something more you haven't told me?"

"There were others," said Joe. "Others who had a hand in having Dommy killed."

They expected another strong, emotional reaction, but Domenic slowly swallowed, gripped the edge of the table and calmly asked, "Who?"

"Martha's father and Cologero Dragotto."

Ernie and Joe saw Domenic's eyes widen, and he slowly shook his head from side to side. He then closed his eyes and thought to himself, *Calm is the virtue of the strong. Be strong, Domenic. Be strong so you can get through this and do what you have to do.*

✱✱✱

"Here is how I think it went down," continued Ernie. "At some point, Lombardo asked for O'Riley's help in getting rid of DePalma. O'Riley came to see this as a way of killing two birds with one stone."

Joe grimaced at Ernie's choice of words. They had opened a second bottle of wine, and Domenic insisted on knowing everything, every detail on how his beautiful boy wound up being assassinated.

"Dommy was the first one to get to the big break-in at DeAngelo's jewelry store on Washington Street. He was close enough to hear the alarm as soon as it went off. The next cops on the scene were two of O'Riley's guys, and they started filling their pockets with anything the thieves left behind and told Dommy to do the same before more cops and detectives showed up. Dommy not only refused—he told them to put the stuff back or he'd report it. They took it anyway. They knew O'Riley would protect them. Dommy never filed a report, but he went from simply not being trusted to being a threat in O'Riley's eyes. A threat that had to be dealt with.

"But being greedy by nature and smart—God knows he's a sly bastard—he saw even more opportunity here. He saw a way to get money out of some others he knew would want to hurt Dommy... and you."

"Martha's father?" Domenic asked.

Joe jumped in.

"That's on me, Dom," Joe jumped in. "That asshole came to town about a couple years ago and tried to bribe Dommy to get him to stop seeing Martha. Then he threatened him if he didn't. Dommy told me about it, and I mentioned it to Ernie. Ernie borrowed Billy Flynn, and they showed up at the Parker House and scared the bejesus out of the jerk and sent him packing back to Chicago. He never got over it, Dom."

Ernie picked up the story. "I know Flynn told O'Riley all about it. Probably both had a good laugh. I also know from my man Marino who used to work security for Anderson that O'Riley was in touch with Anderson a couple weeks before Dommy was killed. And that Marino's replacement traveled to Boston to personally deliver a package to O'Riley. It's my guess that..."

"Anderson paid O'Riley to have Dommy killed," Domenic suddenly interrupted in a quiet voice, the words spoken clearly and slowly, giving life to the realization at the same instant it came to him.

"Yes, that's my guess. The sonofabitch decided to double dip so to speak. He was doing Lombardo a favor, getting rid of Dommy, and getting paid for it."

"It's not a guess, is it, Ermino?" asked Dominic.

Ernie didn't hesitate. "No, it's not."

"And Cologero?" Domenic closed his eyes and rubbed the bridge of his nose. The tears had dried but left a stinging in his eyes. He wanted to know everything, but he had to calm himself to be able to withstand it. "What about Cologero?"

Ernie and Joe exchanged glances, as though saying, "You or me?" Joe knew it should be him and indicated this by holding his palm up toward Ernie and giving him a slight nod.

"Francesca came to me, Dom," started Joe.

"You spoke with Francesca?" Dom asked with surprise.

"We spoke a lot over the years, Dom. Most of it was business. I insured a lot of the Dragotto's properties. There was also a big life insurance policy on Cologero. But some of it was personal. We became friends, almost confidants. We had a common interest...you."

Domenic shuddered. *Dear God, what have I done? Did my feelings for Francesca somehow play into this? Did they somehow make Dommy a target?*

"Dragatto hates you, Dom. He knew about you and Francesca for a long time and always threatened her with what he would do to you if he ever caught you with her again. He was always convinced the baby they lost was yours."

"It wasn't!" protested Domenic.

"But he believed it was. And when it turned out that was the only child Francesca could ever have, he went a little crazy and became obsessed with getting revenge. But he was too much of a coward to do anything himself, so he went to O'Riley, who refused for a long time even with all the money Dragatto offered. But when he hatched the deal with Lombardo, O'Riley figured what the hell, why not get something out of Dragatto too? I can hear him telling Dragatto that he would make it so you suffered like he had suffered over losing a son."

Joe stopped, and the room was suddenly silent. Joe and Ernie looked at Domenic, and Domenic stared blankly at nothing. Then he slowly rose and went to the small kitchen window and stood there looking out but seeing nothing. He did not want the others to see him cry. After a long while, he finally gathered himself and spoke calmly and slowly.

"Ermino, I want them all to pay. And I want to be looking in O'Riley's eyes when it happens, and I want to be the one who does it. The others I leave to you, Anderson and Dragatto. Lombardo is a pig, but he didn't know it was Dommy. That means he's none of my business."

"But he is my business," said Ernie. "And he's got to answer for what he did."

"Wait," Joe protested, "this is a little bit crazy. Dom, you're not a killer. As much as he deserves it, you can't be killing a cop, any cop. Put that out of your head. Your life will be ruined. Pete's life will be ruined. Leave it to..." He looked at Ernie with a quizzical glance.

"Me," said Ernie firmly. "Leave it all to me."

Domenic seemed not to hear as he gathered his bag from the market and began heading for the door. He opened the door and without looking back cried out, "I told you what I want!" It was more of a wail than a command, and it startled the other two men. "They killed my boy." The words came out muffled in a sob. Then he repeated almost in a whisper, "They killed my boy." He hurried down the backstairs and to the door to the alley, not wanting them to see him cry again that day.

After Domenic left, Ernie and Joe sat in silence for a while, each seemingly focused on their wine glass. Then Joe spoke, "You've got to admire him."

"Who, Domenic?"

"No, O'Riley. He's a real bastard but a smart one. Figured a way to get paid twice for something he was going to do for free."

Joe looked at Ernie. "You almost sound envious."

Ernie shook his head. The wheels were already turning. He was going to make this right. Or at least as right as it could be.

***

"What's all this about, Eel? Why all the secrecy?" asked Colin O'Riley as soon as he walked up to Ernie.

It was after midnight, and the two were meeting in a seldom-used parking area beneath the Neponset River Bridge on the Quincy side. The area was littered with debris from fishermen, bums, and underage drinkers. Crabgrass broke through the old asphalt, and the smell of the brackish water where the river entered into Dorchester Bay permeated the air. *A really putrid spot,* thought Ernie, *appropriate for this putrid business.*

"I'm about to do you a big favor, O'Riley."

"And what is that, Eel?" O'Riley had a way of squeezing out the word "eel" that grated on Ernie.

"I'm going to do for you with Gennaro Angiulo what I did for you with Joseph Lombardo twenty years ago. I'm going to get you in and set you up for a very profitable relationship."

"And why would I want to ruin the good thing I've got going with your boss?"

"Because Lombardo is on his way out. I know because Angiulo's people have approached me. He's got Patriarca behind him, and they're tired of Lombardo. Too reckless, too impulsive, and they want all of Boston, not part of it."

"And you're doing this out of the kindness of your heart?"

"I'm doing this because it's good business. Good for me for making the introduction, good for you for the money you're going to make."

O'Riley thought for a moment and walked a few steps, kicking at an empty beer can.

"So how do you see this all happening, Eel?"

"Come to my house in Swampscott next Tuesday night. Come alone. It will be me, you and Angiulo. You two can take it from there."

"Let me think about it."

"Don't think too long. Things are going to move fast. And you cannot say anything to anybody. I'm out on a limb here, O'Riley."

"Next Tuesday, huh? That's election night, you know."

"Ya, I know."

"I'll let you know." O'Riley turned and headed back to his car.

Ernie could tell by the bounce in his walk that he would be there.

NOVEMBER 6, 1951

THE BIG HOUSE was filled with a suffocating, dark stillness as Francesca walked from her bedroom to the stairs, headed for the greenhouse. *Lifeless,* she thought, *just like me. I live in the dark, I stay silent. I am no more than a symbolic testament to the success of Cologero Dragatto. Just like the damn house.* As she made her way through the empty house, she felt the deja vu that came with dreaming of something for so long you felt you've actually lived it before. But this was real. She would finally end her living nightmare, consequences be damned.

Cologero had always been ruthless in his ambitious pursuit of money and prestige. And once they learned she would never bear him a son, she became nothing more to him than an ornamental enhancement to his social standing, much like the mansion he had built in Newton. She always knew of the wretched things he did that could ruin him, and her, and she kept silent. Maybe because she was scared. Maybe because she was able to rationalize that the philanthropic good she was able to do as Cologero's wife somehow evened out the cruelty he inflicted upon the world. But in her most private moments, she had to admit to herself that the poor girl from the hills of Sicily adored all the admiration hoisted upon her.

But what Joe Rossario had revealed to her was too devastating to allow her to keep living in her insulated pretend world. She saw Cologero now as pure evil. There were tears in her eyes as she made her way through the kitchen and out the short hall to the rear kitchen door and then into the greenhouse. Were they for Domenic, for his son, or were they for her? *Pray for me, dear Jesus,* she thought. *For what I've done and what I have to do.*

"Belladonna." Such a beautiful name for such a deadly plant. Belladonna. Translated, it meant "beautiful woman," from ancient days when Italian women would use small quantities to dilate and enlarge their pupils to appear more seductive. And like a skilled seductress, every part of the plant, from its roots to its leaves to its flowers with black berries, was toxic and deadly. Small doses of belladonna were used back in Sicily to treat anything from menstrual cramping to nausea and vomiting. But just two of her small berries could kill a small child, ten or fifteen for an adult. But her deadly leaves were even more lethal if ingested.

Tomorrow, Cologero would be served one of his favorite meals, pasta with fresh herbs from Francesca's garden. But along with the oregano, basil, and parsley would be a leaf from Belladonna. The wine will hasten the drowsiness, and Cologero will fall asleep full and contented, never to awaken again.

10 PM
NOVEMBER 7, 1951
CHICAGO

GENE MARINO ENTERED the huge mansion facing Lake Michigan he knew so well through the rear door used by the servants. The chilly wind blowing off the lake shook the folded canvas awnings that stretched out over the large stone patio in the summer and caught the door as he opened it, forcing him to use both gloved hands to close it behind him. Once inside, he made his way to the kitchen, avoiding the servant quarters, and up the back stairway to the second-floor bedrooms. He knew that the man who had replaced him as Walter Anderson's personal bodyguard was dangerous, a freelancer who often worked for Chicago mob boss Louis "Little New York" Campagna. And ever since Anderson's incident in Boston with Ernie Lentini, he lived in the mansion for added security. But he was out tonight drinking and dining with members of the Campagna family, an invitation extended by Campagna as a favor to The Eel.

Walter Anderson and his wife had separate bedrooms at opposite ends of the floor. While Walter was well known to turn in early, Mrs. Anderson would stay up late reading or writing letters accompanied by a bottle of sherry. There was a light shining from under her door, so he had to be quiet as he reached Walter's bedroom. The room was dark as he entered, and he was relieved to hear Walter snoring. Gently closing the door, he took five quick steps across the room to the bed and lifted a pillow from beside the sleeping tycoon. Anderson's eyes opened for a brief instant as Marino brought the pillow down over his face. In that flash, Marino saw surprise, fear, and panic but felt no remorse.

He held the pillow over his struggling victim's head with the full weight of his upper body resting on his strong outstretched hands as Anderson pounded fruitlessly at Marino with his fists. After a few moments, the pounding stopped, and Anderson's arms fell lifeless beside him. Marino kept up the pressure on the pillow for another full minute, counting off the seconds to himself slowly. When he removed the pillow, Anderson's eyes seemed to be bulging out of their sockets, and his tongue stuck out of his open mouth.

Satisfied that he was dead, Marino lifted and dragged his portly corpse to the bathroom, where he slammed Anderson's head as hard as he could against the granite sink and let the lifeless body fall to the floor, making sure fragments of skin and blood remained on the sink. The gash in Anderson's head did not bleed enough to satisfy him, so he lifted the body upside down as best he could so more blood would flow to the wound, allowing gravity to do the job Anderson's dead heart could no longer perform. He turned the bathroom light on and then went back to the bed and rearranged the disheveled pillows and bedsheets. Then he checked that nothing was disturbed when he dragged the corpse across the room.

Satisfied that the only thing out of place was Anderson himself, he opened the bedroom door, peered into the hallway to make sure no one was about and quickly made his way back down the rear stairway. A minute later, he was scampering across the backyard to his car parked nearby on Astor Street.

When the body would be found the next morning, there would be no reason to believe anything other than an aging, grossly overweight man stumbled as he made his way half asleep to the bathroom in the middle of the night. A shame for sure, but no reason to suspect foul play.

7 PM
NOVEMBER 7, 1951
SWAMPSCOTT, MASSACHUSETTS

THE TWO MEN sat in silence in the overstuffed leather chairs in Ernie Lentini's study. Not a word had passed between them for nearly an hour. Domenic had turned his chair to face out one of the two windows overlooking the long driveway that split the expansive front lawn and ended in a circle at the house. Ernie would occasionally get up, stretch, and walk about the room. But Domenic simply sat and stared out the window, barely moving and seemingly oblivious to Ernie's presence. The light from the lampposts nearest the house illuminated a portion of Domenic's face as he watched and waited. To Ernie, it seemed like a death mask set in hard resolve with only the sadness of the eyes offering any sign of life behind it. Dominic barely blinked as he looked off trancelike into the growing darkness.

Ernie decided to stand once again, placing both hands on his knees and rising slowly with a soft grunt. He had hoped the sound would at least elicit a glance from Domenic, but apparently it was not strong enough to penetrate the heavy barrier of history Domenic had dragged into the house and planted firmly between them. It signified there would be no discussion, no compromise.

After stretching his back, Ernie walked to the second window of the study, pulled back the drapes, and looked out. He cast a quick sideways glance at Domenic, as though even looking at his old friend would violate the unspoken rules that had been set. While still gazing into the night and without turning he said, "It's not too late, Domenic. I can take care of this. You don't have to be involved. I swear to you the result, in the end, will be the same."

Domenic said nothing, not that Ernie expected him to. They had covered this ground before. "Please, Dom, I beg you…"

Domenic replied without looking at Ernie, "This is about family, Ermino. You should understand."

To Domenic he would always be Ermino, never Ernie and definitely never The Eel, a nickname Domenic had always despised. In a way, it was comforting. It had been so long since he had been simply Ermino, and it reminded him of a very different time. An all-too-fleeting time it seemed to Ernie, when the future was still a hopeful, mysterious place waiting to be explored.

"Why should I understand?" he replied. "Where is my family? You think these *pagliacci* around me are family? They are soldiers, mercenaries. They're not family. You, you have family. Which is exactly why you should leave this to me."

"You understand family, Ermino, or we wouldn't be here now."

"Bah, you're a crazy old man," muttered Ernie, even as he accepted the truth of Domenic's words without acknowledging them. Then he made one last attempt at changing his mind, "So you think this will be an easy thing to do? An easy thing to live with?"

"I don't know. Why don't you tell me?" It was spoken calmly but laden with the same steely anger that Ermino had come to know so well over the years. Ernie had faced the uncontrolled wrath of furious, vicious men, but somehow he always found the quiet, controlled anger of this peaceful man to be more chilling.

"Oh, so you think this is something I do all the time?"

"Having others do it for you is the same thing."

Ernie felt his own rush of anger but quickly forced it aside and shook his head in surrender. No sense pushing any further. Things might be said that best remain unsaid. There was no need, and now was certainly not the time to enter the caverns of the past. Besides, he had never won an argument with Domenic and knew he never could. Maybe no one could. Domenic saw things in black and white with no acknowledgement of shades of gray, so being right was always easy for him.

Domenic spoke again, slowly and quietly, almost as though talking to himself, "I can live with it. I could never live with doing nothing."

Accepting the inevitable, Ernie walked over to the desk, opened a drawer, and took out the small handgun he kept there. As he was handing it to Domenic, lights appeared in the driveway. "That would be O'Riley," he said with resignation. "Here, the safety is off. Just point and squeeze the trigger."

Domenic took the weapon without a word. It was the first time he had held a gun of any type since the old shotgun his father would sometimes let him carry when they would hunt in the hills of Abruzzo, so many, many years ago.

***

Ernie stood silently in the shadows of the basement watching Domenic. His arms were crossed, and he held his own Beretta in one hand as he watched Domenic hold his pistol firm and steady and aimed directly at the head of Colin O'Riley. His heart broke as he could feel the turmoil roiling within the soul of his friend even as his exterior remained calm as always.

Domenic's eyes gave him away. Even though they displayed an emotionless, blind stare, they could not hide the emotion behind them. While pleading with Domenic, O'Riley still managed to cast quick, hateful glares in Ernie's direction. O'Riley knew, as did Ernie, that he would die tonight. There was no way Ernie could permit him to walk away after this. If Domenic could not pull the trigger, Ernie would not hesitate to pull his. Still, O'Riley continued to plead for his life, hoping that he could convince Domenic to let him go and then convince Ernie somehow to do the same.

"You pull that trigger, Bassini, and you're ending your own life, not just mine. You think you or anyone can get away with killing a policeman? Even your buddy The Eel over there couldn't be that stupid. That's why he's making you do it. The bastard is going to get you to kill me, and you'll take the fall. The sonofabitch always wanted me dead. I didn't have anything to do with your boy getting killed, no matter what he's told you. He was a good boy. I had no beef with him. It was a simple raid got out of hand. He's a hero now killed in the line of duty. But you kill me, and your family name will be turned to shit forever."

But Domenic remained silent, caught in the grip of a paralyzing anxiety that, try as he might, he could not suppress. It seemed as though he was being forced to relive the past before he could face the present. His exterior passiveness finally caused O'Riley to explode.

"You fucking wop! Are you hearing me at all? You stupid fucking guinea bastard, do you even know what you're doing? You are pointing a gun at a Boston police captain. You'll fry in the chair for sure. And your grandson will pay the price the rest of his life. He'll be known as the grandson of a murdering cop killer."

The mention of his grandson seemed to awaken Domenic. His eyes broke free from the trance that had held them and became alert. He began to focus…and think. The hatred did not subside, but he knew he could not shoot this pathetic, lying man. This was not him, and this was not how he wanted to be remembered by Pete. He would not be a killer. But this man who plotted to take away his Dommy, his precious son, had to pay for it.

While slowly lowering his gun, he simply and softly said, "Ermino." He closed his eyes.

The sound of Ernie's gun was much quieter than Domenic had imagined it would be.

***

The return to Ernie's study also marked a return to silence. Ernie poured himself a shot of Irish whiskey and was somewhat bemused by the irony of his choice as he drank to the soul of Colin O'Riley. *May he rot in hell.* As he drank, his eye went to the worn copy of *Moby Dick* that had left the orphanage with him so many years ago, a book he had read several times over the ensuing years. It was now time for him to face his white whale. He turned and watched as Domenic walked over to his desk and laid the gun on top. Then Domenic turned and cast a glance filled with sadness at Ernie, before reaching to retrieve his coat from where it rested over the back of one of the chairs. Not a word spoken.

Ernie broke the silence, "He'll never be found." He poured himself a second shot.

Domenic looked at him quizzically.

"O'Riley," said Ernie. "Don't worry, his body will disappear."

"I wasn't worried. I assumed you knew how to take care of these things."

Ernie bristled a little at the tone. After all he'd done, Domenic was still judging him. "I don't make a habit of this, Domenic. I have killed only three people in my life and regret none. Dodo Walsh, Colin O'Riley, and…" He hesitated as he downed the whiskey. "Billy Flynn."

It took a moment for the impact of what Ernie had confessed to begin to register in Domenic's weary head. Then he stopped with one arm in his overcoat as it struck him. "But Flynn died with Dommy…" His voice began to break. "Ermino, no, please don't tell me you were there. Are you telling me you were there when Dommy died?" Confusion slowly turned to anger. It swelled up from some hollow place in his chest, slowly growing into fury. He screamed, "What are you telling me Ermino!"

8 PM
APRIL 23, 1950

AFTER LEAVING VILLIANO'S *Ristorante, Ernie dismissed Big Quiet with a perfunctory "Buona notte," which was acknowledged with a slight nod from his large friend, who then quickly turned and walked away without a word. Turning up the collar of his topcoat and pulling his fedora down as tightly as he could against the wind, Ernie thought about getting out of the city to the new house in Swampscott. He had come to enjoy the solitude of his new home. It afforded him an expansive quietness in which to think and relax.*

But his mind couldn't put aside thoughts of Margaret Street, Jimmy DePalma, and Lombardo. It was still early, although total blackness already engulfed the city, making it seem much later. The game would not begin for several hours, as the regulars would start showing up around 10 and settle in for an evening of gambling that often lasted until dawn.

He stepped into a doorway out of the wind to light a cigarette, a delaying tactic, as he debated in his head whether or not to check in on DePalma. It was not only that he didn't trust Lombardo—he had to admit to himself that he hated the man. And if it was that hate that was driving him to Margaret Street, to find out what Lombardo was doing and maybe get something on him, then he told himself he shouldn't go. Because when you acted out of emotion, you inevitably acted foolishly. You made mistakes. But if something was up tonight at Margaret Street, he would suffer the blowback. It was his game, and if something was going down he deserved to know about it. Lombardo's sudden interest in the game and in DePalma was troubling. While still thinking about what to do, he found himself crossing Hanover Street and turning down Prince Street. He soon stood at the base of Margaret Street, which extended steeply uphill. He finally admitted to himself that the decision was made and started up the street to number 23 near the top of the hill.

The innocuous front to the old brick townhouse was no different from most of the others on the street. There were a few steps up to a small entranceway and a door that led into a small hallway with stairs up to the apartments on the second and third floors. Those apartments were rented or given to Lombardo's most trusted men. To the left of the stairs were two doors. One led to the small first-floor apartment that was mostly empty, save for a well-stocked bar and a few sofas, chairs, and tables. It was used as little more than a lounge for gamblers and friends of the Lombardo Family to relax and take a break from the action of the big stakes games, which took place in the basement below. On game nights, Ernie would arrange for prostitutes to mill about the first floor to keep the players entertained, and one or both of the two small bedrooms were often in use.

The second door off the hallway led down into the basement where three poker tables stood out in stark contrast to the drab stone foundation and concrete floor. Each stood on its own bright oriental carpet surrounded by six ornately carved mahogany and leather padded chairs, as though too proud to come in contact with the common concrete beneath them. Their shining mahogany and green felt surfaces were the only real color in the room. It was a room set up for serious gamblers only. No need for frills outside of the best gambling tables in the North End and maybe all of Boston.

Buying the house and setting up the game had been Ernie's idea, but when he approached Lombardo about it to get his blessing, his boss had insisted on receiving twenty percent of the gambling profits and owning fifty-one percent of the building, essentially making it his even though only Ernie's name would appear on the deed. Ernie would run the operation, and over time Lombardo became less and less interested in having much to do with it beyond sitting in on a game occasionally – more to enjoy one of the prostitutes upstairs than to actually gamble. But he never stopped expecting his weekly cut of the profits, which in Ernie's mind were almost too small to care about.

There was also a seldom-used entrance directly into the basement from the narrow alleyway behind the house. Not wanting to be seen snooping in case any of Lombardo's men were around, Ernie decided to continue up to the top of Margaret and then back down the narrow alley *that ran the length of the street behind the row of converted townhomes. Ernie was the only person who knew the old rusted metal half door off the alley actually worked. He had had the old lock taken out and replaced when he bought the building, and he had the only key.*

Stooping down, he ducked under the door fame and into the far end of the basement away from the stairs and tables. The room appeared empty, but as he took a few steps he was startled by a loud crash as Jimmy DePalma suddenly jumped up from behind some chairs with a gun pointed at him.

"What the fuck, Jimmy?" Ernie shouted. A wide-eyed and confused-looking DePalma stood there, sweating profusely with two very shaky hands on the gun pointed in Ernie's direction. "Jimmy, what the fuck is going on?"

"Ernie, is that you?" he finally replied, slowly lowering his weapon. "What are you doing here? He didn't tell me you'd be here."

"Who you talking about, Jimmy?"

"Lombardo. He told me to shoot the first guy through the door. But the other door. I thought the other door. I don't know. How'd you get in here? Lombardo sent you, didn't he? To check on me to see if I could do this. Well, I can. I'm going to..." DePalma's voice trailed off as he seemed to become more confused, slowly shaking his head as though it might help him think.

"Listen, Jimmy, nobody sent me. Nobody knows I'm here. I was concerned because this whole thing tonight sounded fishy to me. What's this about shooting someone?"

"Lombardo said I could make my bones tonight. Then I could really be somebody in the family. There would be two guys coming down the stairs. I had to take out the first guy. The second guy was OK, one of ours. I had to prove myself."

Ernie tried to process what DePalma was telling him. Only one thing made sense to him.

"They're coming to kill you, Jimmy. It's a setup," Ernie said calmly.

"What? Why?" sputtered a confused and disbelieving DePalma.

"Lombardo wants to get you out of the way so he can have your wife."

Jimmy looked like he'd been hit with a shovel. He couldn't speak and began muttering senseless pieces of his jumbled thoughts. His head and shoulders slumped, and his arms hung at his side, one still holding the gun.

Ernie walked to him and put a hand on the back of his neck, squeezing a little to get his attention.

"Look at me and listen, Jimmy," he said. "Get the fuck out of here. Use the door at the back that I came through. Get the fuck out of here, and go home to your wife. I'll take the heat. I'll tell Lombardo I came by and sent you home."

Before DePalma could respond, there was noise above them. It was the door that led down to the basement from the hallway. DePalma looked at Ernie, his face paralyzed with fear.

"Get down, Jimmy. Get back behind those chairs, and be ready to use that gun." Ernie took out his own Beretta and began looking for a spot where he could set up to get a drop on whoever came down those stairs. He could hear footsteps on the stairs and muffled voices. He found himself in a corner next to the fuse box and had a thought. He began pulling fuses until the basement went almost completely black with just the street lamps outside the front window wells along the sidewalk providing some light. He would know where the killers were, but they wouldn't be able to see him or DePalma. "Aim at the stairs, Jimmy, but don't shoot unless I do," he said in a loud whisper.

Then there were flashlights piercing the darkness from the stairwell. Ernie had decided that he would shout out and tell them who he was, figuring that would give the killers pause and maybe even end the whole thing. But as the first flashlight entered the basement, DePalma suddenly stood up, shouting, "Don't shoot. Don't shoot." There was a second of silence before gunshots came from the stairs in the direction of DePalma. Ernie started shooting at the flashlights and knew he hit one as the other dove for safety. One flashlight rolled across the floor. Then he heard a familiar voice

"Who the fuck is there? You're shooting at police officers you know."

"Flynn, is that you?"

"Lentini? What the fuck are you doing here?"

"I could ask you the same thing."

"Listen, Eel," said Flynn. "I'm following orders from my boss and yours. Let's figure out how to clean up this mess. I'm coming out."

Ernie saw the flashlight come back on, searching for him. "Point that flashlight in the other direction, Flynn. I've got you in my sights if you pull any shit."

"Okay, okay, Eel. Can you see me?" Ernie could make out Flynn's silhouette with both his hands raised, one holding his gun, the other the flashlight pointed toward the ceiling. He kept his gun trained on Flynn as he picked up the other flashlight and headed toward DePalma, whose dead body rested on top of some overturned chairs.

Then he walked over to Flynn, who was looking down at the other cop on the floor. "Looks like you got him," said Flynn.

Ernie shined his flashlight on the man's face and saw that it was Dommy Bassini. He screamed out, "No, no!" Then he dropped to his knees. "Dommy, Dommy." He took Dommy's head in his hands and saw blank eyes, but his mouth was moving as he tried to talk.

Then he was startled by a gunshot. He grabbed his own gun and turned to see Flynn walking back from DePalma's body. "Had to make sure he was gone, Eel," said Flynn calmly.

Ernie turned back to Dommy, "Dommy's still alive, Flynn. Call in for an ambulance. We've got to get him to a hospital."

"No can do, Eel."

"What the fuck you talking about? He's dying," shouted Ernie in a near panic.

"No, he's dead."

Ernie looked up as Flynn pointed his gun at Dommy's head. "What the fuck you doing?" he screeched.

Flynn pulled the trigger, his gun practically touching Ernie's ear as he knelt. Ernie swung his arm and knocked Flynn's gun away. Then he pointed his own gun at Flynn and kept shooting until it was empty.

He knelt over Dommy's body, sobbing, streaking his own face with blood as he wiped away tears. Then he slowly got up and made his way back through the door out into the alley, not knowing where he would go or what he would do.

***

Domenic listened to Ernie's story in silence. He felt a strange sense of calm as he slowly got up from the chair, but he felt his heart racing and his body shaking. Closure. No questions left to ask. Nothing left to wonder about. It did nothing to lessen the pain. That same hot rock in his gut continued to burn. And probably always would. But at least now he felt he knew everything there was to know. He walked over to the desk and looked down at the gun he had just set there as Ernie continued to talk.

"After I left Margaret Street, I started walking. I would stop, step into a doorway or alley, and put my own gun to my head. But then I would start walking again. I puked a few times until there was nothing left to puke but kept walking until I found myself standing at the railing of the new bridge going over the Mystic River. I stood there a long time and finally began to think things through a little."

Ernie went back for his third shot of whiskey, not able to look at Domenic.

"I thought about you, Domenic. Going back to the day we met on the *Cretic* and what you did for me. And how you always warned me about how I was going to turn out someday if I didn't change. Turns out you were right. Now I had not only let you down. I knew I had destroyed your life." Ernie stopped as he fought back tears. "And I had killed the person both of us loved the most in this world.

"But as I stood there, I thought that before I confessed to you, I would take revenge on the people who planned to kill Dommy. And tonight that happened. Walter Anderson and Cologero Dragotto are dead. Colin O'Riley is dead. Joseph Lombardo has been summoned by Raymond Patriarca to answer for what he did." Ernie hesitated. "I am the only one left who had anything to do with Dommy's death, and I'm here to answer to you."

Domenic didn't respond. He slowly picked up the gun from the desk and placed it back in the drawer it came from. Then he turned to look at Ernie. "You are dead too, Ernesto. To me." Then he put on his coat and left Ernie's house without saying another word.

9 PM
NOVEMBER 7, 1951

DOMENIC ENTERED A quiet and mostly deserted Parker House rooftop ballroom later that night. Only a few people still milled about, the bartenders were shutting down the bar, and hotel personnel had already begun cleaning up. Looking for Joe and Martha, he walked by a large blackboard with a lot of numbers on it and stopped to try and decipher it all. Then he felt a hand on his shoulder and heard Joe's voice.

"It says I got my ass handed to me. Even worse than we thought it might be. KO's going to end up with over 150,000 votes, I'll be lucky to get half that."

Domenic turned and looked at his old friend. "Sorry, Joe."

"I guess we still have a ways to go, Dom, but we'll get there. So where have you been? Have a hot date?" Joe flashed the well-practiced Rossario smile, but it hung from a sad face.

"I thought you might know."

"I can't know, Dom. I was hoping this is where you would be all night tonight. That's all. Not for me, but for you and Pete and Martha's sake. I thought that might be the best..." Joe swallowed. "Never mind. You're here now." He gave Domenic a hug. "Let's go find them. I figured if I was going down I'd go down in style, so I booked the Beacon Hill Suite for the night, the best hotel room in Boston. Martha and Pete are down there with Lou. And there's someone else there you might like to see too."

The two men slowly made their way down the circular staircase from the rooftop ballroom to the fifteenth floor of the Parker House and the Beacon Hill Suite.

"Not a bad spot for two old wops to spend an evening, eh Dom?" said Joe, putting one arm around his old friend and gesturing to the ornate furnishings around them. "We've come a long way since we shared that tiny bedroom with Ernie."

"You were never a wop, Joe."

"No, but I've been called one many times. Many, many times."

As they walked down the long corridor leading to the suite that was at the far corner of the hotel overlooking both School and Washington Streets, Domenic asked, "Does my family know anything about all this business? About Ernesto and O'Riley?"

"I don't know what business you're talking about, but the answer is no as far as Lou and Martha go. But there is another person waiting for us who might. Francesca Dragatto."

Domenic stopped in his tracks. "Francesca is here? What is she doing here?"

"She was a strong financial supporter of my campaign, Domenic. Probably the worst investment she's ever made. That would appear to be the reason she's here tonight. But I think the real reason is she wanted to talk to you."

"But Cologero, is he…"

"I think you should talk to Francesca," Joe interrupted before Domenic could finish his question.

They entered the suite, and Joe announced to the group gathered there with great flourish, "Look who finally decided to honor us with his presence."

"Papa," screamed Pete as he ran over to Domenic, who quickly picked him up and gave him a hug and a kiss.

He whispered in the boy's ear, "Papà ti ama così tanto, Pete." Looking over Pete's shoulder, he scanned the room and saw Martha seated on a couch with some people he didn't know while Lou stood near a bar with a group of men. Then he spied Francesca sitting by herself in a great Victorian armchair, looking directly at him with a sad smile. To Domenic, she looked like a queen on her throne, beautiful and dignified. Her hair seemed as full and black as the day he met her, her face as alluring, her eyes as penetrating.

Domenic began to make his away across the room, depositing Pete with Martha along the way. He returned a smile and a wave from Lou and was greeted by some old North End friends before he found himself by Francesca, who stood, took his hand, and gave him a friendly kiss on the cheek. "Let's go for a walk, Dom."

***

Ernie pulled up to a pay phone outside a closed gas station on Route 107 in Saugus after disposing of the remains of Boston Police Captain Colin O'Riley. He had been meticulous in his planning and was confident they would never be found. He called the number he had been given. A voice answered simply, "Yes?"

Ernie replied, "It's done. As long as the money is there, you'll never hear from me again." He hung up and continued on his way home.

***

In the den of his home in South Boston, Mayor Kevin O'Riley hung up his late father's private phone. He would have the phone company disconnect the line in the morning. Right now, he had to hurry to the Park Plaza to celebrate his impending re-election victory. As he and his wife went to the waiting car, he was already looking ahead to everything he wanted to accomplish in his second term.

***

As Ernie drove home, he too was looking ahead. If he stayed in Boston, his future, if he had one, would be decided by Patriaca and Angiulo. He knew his rebellion against Lombardo had destroyed any chance he might have of finding a place in Patriaca's burgeoning New England crime family. Disloyalty was the worst crime any family member could commit, and he would never be trusted again.

By the time he pulled back into his driveway, his thoughts were solely on the plans he had made to return to Italy. The house he had bought years before in Francavilla al Mare was waiting for him. No one else knew about it, and he felt he could adapt to a quiet life on the Adriatic, possibly running some type of small business in the town. He was mentally and emotionally spent and had plenty of money. He had repaid an old debt the best way he could this night. It was not enough, he knew, but it was all he could do. He knew he would carry a burden of guilt to his grave. Domenic would never speak to him again, and he was a liability now to Joe. And those were the only two people in all of America he really cared about.

He stepped out of his car lost in thought. Then it seemed the sudden shadow that blocked the light from the driveway lamppost, the pop of the gun, and the bullet hitting him in the chest all happened at once. He fell to the ground as he thought, *So this is how it ends.* He was conscious and unafraid as two men emerged from the shadows. One he knew only as Pino, a member of the Angiullo Family. The other was Big Quiet.

"I'm sorry, Ernie," said Pino. "If it helps, you should know that Lombardo is done. He's out, retired. But you know you broke the rules by going around him." He turned and walked away, giving a squeeze to the huge shoulder of Big Quiet as he did.

Ernie tried to nod his head as he laid on his back. The stars in Italy shone brighter, he thought, looking up, but he would never see them again. He knew they were going to make Big Quiet kill him to prove his loyalty to the family. He couldn't speak, so he tried to convey to Big Quiet that he understood with his eyes and as much of a nod as he could muster. Big Quiet's face showed no emotion as he looked down at him. Ernie closed his eyes. He would never know if Big Quiet got the message.

✳ ✳ ✳

Neither Domenic nor Francesca said a word as they left the Beacon Hill Suite. They walked in silence to the elevators where Domenic pressed the button for the lobby. Both welcomed the silence and sensed the other did as well. After everything that had transpired at Ernie's home, Domenic was emotionally drained. It had taken a great effort to force himself to go to the Parker House and be around so many people. Surely everyone there could see through him; the secrets he now held were so heavy that the strain of keeping them hidden had to show.

Especially to the people closest to him. He fought every second to suppress the anxiety and sadness he feared would remain with him forever.

Before the elevator doors opened, Francesca reached over and took his hand as they stepped out into the brightly lit lobby together. Somehow, her touch ignited a tiny spark of hope deep within him. As if sensing this, Francesca spoke, "I think, Dom, that today was both an end and a beginning for each of us."

The two walked out of the Parker House lobby onto School Street and instinctively turned right in the direction of the North End, although neither one knew nor cared where they were going.

"Dom, you need to know that Cologero lives," Francesca said quietly. "As much as I hate him for everything he has done to me, and what he did to you, I could not bring myself to…" She hesitated, unable to even say it.

"Kill him?" Domenic said. "I'm not surprised. You are a strong person, Francesca, but it takes a special kind of strength, a special kind of person, to kill someone no matter how much they might deserve it."

"So did you…"

"No, I did not, but a piece of me wishes I had pulled the trigger. For Dommy. But I thought about Pete and how I need to be there for him without blood on my hands I would never be able to wash away. It was something better left to Ernie." Domenic paused. "I probably shouldn't be telling you any of this." But it felt good to talk about it, to give life to what he was feeling. And who better than this woman.

They walked again in silence for a while before Francesca spoke again. "Although he still draws breath, Cologero is dead to me. I have left him and I have made some people aware of many things he was hiding from them, including the Internal Revenue Service. He is finished. I have long owned a house in my own name back in our neighborhood where I belong, and I have plenty of money to support myself. And I have this."

Francesca stopped walking, opened her purse, and took out the marble broach Domenic had given her so many years ago onboard the Cretic. Domenic recognized it immediately.

"You kept it all these years?"

"Yes, and I remember what you said. You said you would love me forever. Do you, Dom? Do you still love me?"

Domenic stood stunned. He was overwhelmed by so many confusing thoughts, so many conflicting emotions that it was impossible to think clearly. But he looked into Francesca's dark eyes and knew he wanted to pull her into his arms and hold on with all his might. To have her draw out of him all the fear, anger, and grief he felt. To start over. But before he could answer, he heard Joe calling his name.

"Domenic, Francesca, so there you are," cried out Joe as he hurried to catch up with them. Lou and Martha followed closely behind with Lou carrying Pete in his arms. "We thought we'd lost you two." He stepped up between them and put an arm around them both. "We're on our way back. Little Pete has had enough."

As the others caught up, Martha took Domenic's arm, and they began walking with Joe still between Domenic and Francesca. As usual, Joe started talking, "Remember the first time I walked with you to the North End, Dom? You were literally right off the boat. You, me, Ernie, and my dad."

"Yes. Yes, I do," said Dom.

"So you do remember?"

"Sorry, Joe, I was talking to Francesca."

THE END

EPILOGUE
JULY 1993
BOSTON CITY HALL

BOSTON CITY COUNCIL President Pete Bassini checked his tie one more time in the mirror in his crowded office. He turned and smiled at his wife, who stood by the door with his two sons. His mother Martha, stepfather Lou, and his half-brother Domenic were also there. They were all getting ready to head into the city council chambers where he would be sworn in as acting mayor of Boston. Former Mayor Raymond Flynn had been appointed ambassador to the Holy See in Rome by President Bill Clinton, making the city council president the acting mayor until the coming November election.

As they prepared to leave, he looked at the portrait of his mentor, Joseph Rossario, hanging on the wall. His mother noticed this and said, "He would be so proud of you, Pete. The first Boston mayor of Italian descent. It was a dream of his."

"I know, Mom, and I wouldn't have gotten here without him."

"And you know what he'd be telling you now?"

"He'd be saying start lining up support for the real election in November."

Then he turned to look at the two photographs he kept on his desk right beside the one of his wife and children. One was of his father, Domenic Bassini in his Boston policeman's uniform, a man he never knew. But the stories he had been told about him – his athletic and academic achievements, recruitment to Harvard, bravery in World War II, dedication to the police force – made him proud to be his son.

The other photograph was of someone he did know very well and who he missed every day, his grandfather Domenic Bassini. He touched the photo of the grandfather who had always been there for him and uttered the words he would always hear him say, "Other things may change us, but we start and end with the family."

AUTHOR'S NOTE

WHAT ONCE WAS PROMISED is a work of fiction. Every effort has been made to keep the many references to real people and events consistent with their actual places in history, but many liberties have been taken in describing them to fit the narrative of the story. For example, Frankie Gustin and "Dodo" Walsh were shot to death in the offices of C&F Imports on December 22, 1931, but certainly not as described. Bartolomeo Vanzetti was a fervent anarchist/Galleanist, but he was radicalized after arriving in America, not before. Several sources were helpful in providing a historical framework for the novel including Stephen Puleo's ***The Boston Italians***, Thomas O'Connor's ***Bibles, Brahmins and Bosses***, Emily Sweeney's ***Gangland Boston*** and Paula Todisco's ***Boston's First Neighborhood: The North End***.

Printed in the USA
CPSIA information can be obtained
at www.ICGtesting.com
JSHW080015160624
64870JS00002B/9